# STAR WARS

# A CRASH OF FATE

## ZORAIDA CÓRDOVA

DISNEY
LUCASFILM PRESS

LOS ANGELES • NEW YORK

For my brother Danilo J. Córdova.

I have nothing left to teach you, young Padawan.

# PROLOGUE

The girl climbed the rock face, higher and higher. She scraped her knee only once, and the cut had already begun to scab over as they neared the top. The frilly dress she wore was covered in sweat and dirt. Her father would be angry with her. He'd sewn in extra panels only the day before because she'd had another growth spurt practically overnight.

"Come on, Jules!" she shouted. "We're almost there!"

"No fair, Izzy," the boy called back. Loose pebbles fell over his head, and though he'd convinced himself that he wasn't afraid of heights, he made the mistake of looking down, only for a moment. His palms were sweating and his belly flip-flopped from the fear of falling. If he wanted to fly, he'd have to get over his fears, and to do that he needed to conquer them. The trouble was, it was easier to *think* rather than *do,* and the doing was proving rather difficult. When the boy looked back up, sunlight beamed in his eyes, but he could still see the girl was already a meter or two ahead. He grunted and pushed himself to climb faster. "Your limbs are longer. That's practically cheating!"

"*Practically* but not *exactly*," she said.

Izzy Garsea held on to the nooks and crannies in the jagged rock. The suns beat overhead, relentless during the dry season. Not a single cloud provided shade, but they'd covered their heads with the scarves Jules's mother had dyed bright blue only the previous week. Jules had helped, and his fingers were still stained from accidentally sticking his hands into the dye buckets. Blue and purple freckles dotted his golden-brown forearms like constellations.

Using a spire like a ladder to get to a cliff shelf, the boy and girl threw themselves on their backs, victorious smiles painted on their faces. So far away from Black Spire Outpost, it felt like the whole world was laid out just for the two of them. They could scream as loud as they wanted and not be reprimanded. They could do *anything*.

"One day I'm going to beat you," Jules said, sitting up.

Izzy giggled and brushed off the pebbles that stuck to her hands. "Keep dreaming, Jules. I'm taller."

His big toothy smile was sweet. "You won't always be."

Despite being one year older than the girl, Julen Rakab was still a head shorter. For a six-year-old on Batuu, it meant he got his allowance stolen quite a bit by bigger kids and transient travelers prowling for an easy mark. But the girl never treated him that way. Left alone during the long stretch of day when their parents had to work, they'd forged a bond. With her, he was safe—well, as safe as two little ones could be while rock climbing. But he borrowed some of her fearlessness and followed as far as she was willing to take him.

They settled beneath the shade of gnarly trees that had somehow managed to retain their leaves. From their vantage point, the lands of Batuu spread beneath them, a swell of green and jutting rock. While their respective parents toiled away on various farms, the girl and the boy made plans of their own.

They unpacked their snacks from their pockets: a bag of popped grains he'd made the night before, dried fruit from the Garsea pantry, caf beans covered in chocolate she'd snuck from her mother's hidden tin of sweets, and a canister of fresh water. They shared everything, but the boy always gave the girl a *slightly* larger bite of fruit, let her have her fill of chocolate and water.

"Da says I can start working on the farm for next year's harvest," he told her, handing over the metal canteen.

The girl gasped. Her already wide green eyes went wider. "But, Jules, who will play with me then?"

"I'll still play with you, I promise."

"Not every day. I hardly ever see my parents at home. They leave at suns-rise, and by the time they

3

come home, it's dark and they're too tired to do anything but eat and sleep."

"Yeah, but they're old." The boy shook his head, hoping to reassure her. "My sister gets home and works on her knitting to sell in the market."

"Why can't you start when you're older?" the girl asked.

"Because Da says if I want my own ship, I have to save for it myself."

"Your own *ship*?" she said with wonder. She tipped her head to look up at the sky. A small luxury vessel was making its way to Black Spire. The Outpost was only a little cluster of buildings from that distance, but she knew how busy it was. Her father had let her go along with him once. She had drunk in the open shops, the bustling streets, the smell of roasted meats and nuts. "Will you take me with you?"

"Of course, Izzy. We can explore new moons and planets." He sat up on his knees and found a disk-shaped rock. He simulated a flight path in the space between them. "I was at Oga's—"

"What were *you* doing there?"

"I like to see the new travelers when they land. There's always someone wearing what my dad calls 'flashy and absurd,' whatever that means. Anyway, I overheard two men talking about a moon that's completely covered in ice and snow."

Izzy scrunched up her face and twirled the tip of her long black braid. "I don't like being cold."

"What about a planet that's all water? Think of all the creatures that could be discovered down there. Or where the sky is all different colors all the time. Or a city with billions of people!"

Izzy finished the last of the water. She wasn't sure what kind of world she wanted to visit, but she was sure she didn't want to spend her days without Jules. "Can I be princess of the ship?"

"I don't think that's how princesses work," he said as he landed the rock-ship at their feet and it became a plain stone among the others.

"How do you know? Have you met many princesses?"

He considered this. "Fine, you can be princess. But I'm the captain."

"Why do *you* get to be the captain?" She tapped her finger on her chin thoughtfully. "I could be both."

"You can't be *both*."

"Who says?"

"It's *my* ship. I have to do something."

"Fine." She held out her hand and repeated words she'd heard her mother utter many times: "You've got yourself a deal."

They shook hands the way they'd seen the grown-ups do, then rested in the shade awhile longer. If there had been clouds in the sky, they would have played a game of giving them shape. Once, she was sure she'd seen a flying bantha in a cluster of rain clouds. Instead, they watched as more ships flew in from the atmosphere and headed straight for the Outpost. Izzy could see the patch of farms where both their parents spent their days toiling, the bright grasslands, and the hills. She loved Batuu from up above, but most of all she loved watching the river snake across the planet's surface, weaving among dense trees and jutting spires that had once been trees themselves.

The boy pointed at a familiar ship. "Isn't that the *Meridian*?"

The *Meridian* was her mother's ship, a light freighter usually stationed in one of the docking bays. Because their home was so small, they used the ship for storage. The girl held the scarf over her eyes and squinted. It was too sunny, and the glare hurt to stare at too long. "That can't be. My mother's at the farm, and Da never flies alone."

A growl erupted from behind them, pulling their attention away from the sky. A four-legged creature crouched behind the crooked trees. It moved too fast for them to get a good look, darting behind a cluster of rocks.

"What is that?" the boy shouted. "It's too big to be a rat."

The girl picked up the largest rock within reach and flung it as hard as she could. It smacked off the boulder and went over the ledge, rattling all the way down. The creature leapt again, black as a shadow. The boy followed her example, and they chased off the creature with pebbles and rocks.

The girl approached the cliff's edge and looked down at the sharp rocks and crags below. "Coast is clear."

"We should go back home," the boy said.

They gathered up their few belongings, but the animal leapt from where it had been hiding. Never in his life had Jules seen anything quite like it before: part feline and part lizard, with a splotchy coat of fur and yellow split-pupil eyes. It bared tiny sharp teeth and snapped hard at the air. The boy tumbled back and fell. His head slammed on a rock, and blood dripped down over his ear. The beast climbed up on a boulder, ready to pounce again.

"No!" The girl's scream echoed off the rock around them. She had no weapon but herself. Throwing her body in front of the creature, she shut her eyes and shielded her face. Jaws closed around her forearm, and pain splintered through her.

The boy scrambled back to his feet and found another stone, small but sharp. He aimed true, and it landed in the beast's eye. It let go with a howl and finally retreated.

"Izzy!" the boy shouted. "You're bleeding!"

He unraveled his scarf and wrapped it around her wound to staunch the blood. He tied the ends into a knot.

"You were brilliant," she said.

He marveled at her. She didn't cry or wince; she simply grinned at him. "You saved me first."

"You're my best friend, Jules. I couldn't stand it if something happened to you."

They sat under the hot suns for a while longer, waiting for the creature to come back. But they were not afraid. They had each other.

"Can you climb down?" he asked her.

"I think so." She looked over the cliffside, and for the first time the steep climb made her nervous. But she couldn't very well live on top of a rock, if only because she knew Jules wouldn't leave her, and then *he'd* be in trouble, too. "I will."

They used each other like chain links, moving down, feet digging for purchase, hands clinging to stone and to each other.

When they were on solid ground, they shared a victorious cheer. The boy did not have many things he could call his own, but he had a family trinket. He twisted the ring from his middle finger. It was smooth black stone with natural flecks of gold along the surface. His father had carved one for each of their family members.

"Here," he offered.

Izzy held it on her palm like it was the most precious thing she'd ever been given. "I shouldn't. I have nothing to give you."

"My father says you shouldn't give a gift if all you want is one in return. You do it as thanks or to show someone you care."

The girl slid the ring onto her pointer finger, where it fit the best. "Thank you, Jules."

On the long walk back home, they retold the story to each other, the creature getting bigger, hairier, and toothier each time. But they kept glancing behind them, silently fearing it would follow.

They went their separate ways for the night.

When the girl walked through the front door of her house, she was surprised to see her father home. That time of day he was supposed to be at the farm. Thank the skies he was there. Her arm had begun throbbing. He took her to get her wound looked at by a medical droid. Fortunately, the beast that had bitten her carried no diseases, but it would leave a mark.

The girl slept long and hard and dreamed of falling off the cliff. She woke when her father scooped her into his arms.

"Where are we going?" she asked.

"Hush now," he whispered. "It'll be an adventure."

The girl loved adventures, and she fell back asleep.

She remembered the sigh of the boarding ramp, then her mother's tense voice asking if they'd left anything behind. They hadn't, but Izzy had.

The girl woke completely when they were flying out of the atmosphere. Strapped into the seat, she thrashed and cried, "No! We have to go back! I didn't say good-bye!"

Didn't they know that she and Jules were going to travel the worlds and be a princess and a captain and—

But her words were drowned out by the rattle of the ship as they sped deep into space. All she saw was the green speck of Batuu, then the rush of stars as they hit lightspeed.

"I'm sorry, my darling girl," her father said when it was safe to stand. "But we'll find a new home and you'll make new friends."

He pulled her into his arms. She stopped her crying and stared over his shoulder at the infinite stars and planets that lay before them.

When she was alone in her bunk, the girl twisted the ring around her finger and whispered, "I'll find you, Jules. I'll come back for you."

That was the first promise Izal Garsea ever broke.

# IZZY

## CHAPTER 1

Izal Garsea spent all day waiting for fireworks to fill the sky.

That anticipation had been the only thing getting her through the mundane tasks of the day. Damar Olin had given her a list of things to do, as per Ana Tolla's orders. Ana wasn't even their *boss*, and Izzy and Damar weren't official members of her crew yet. But somehow Izzy kept getting stuck with what amounted to chores, neglecting her own ship's maintenance.

First she'd helped the crew load Ana Tolla's ship with crates of supplies they'd need for their next mission. Then she'd been sent on a pointless errand to pick up a replacement power converter, when they had a perfectly functional one already. The only thing she felt good about doing was fixing a glitch in the ship's navicomputer. At first, she thought it was all part of Damar's ruse to *truly* surprise her, but as night fell over the rusty skies of Actlyon and they crowded onto the cantina's patio for one last drink, Izzy grew anxious. Why did she ever expect Damar to change?

Located in the crowded lower district of Actlyon City, the cantina was dimmer and rowdier than most, with a cloying scent of stale liquor. Izzy made sure her blaster was in place. It was an older model with surface modifications, but it had been her mother's, and she never went anywhere without it. Ana Tolla led the way to the back doors, her long red whip of a braid swinging from side to side. The outside patio had seating overlooking the mountains on one side and the docking bays packed with transport vessels arriving for the night on the other. There the crowd was drunken but not dangerous, at least not at the moment. Though the burning scent of fuel from the port nearby drifted their way when the wind blew, the blanket of stars made up for it.

They positioned themselves at a sticky table, and because there weren't enough chairs to go around, Izzy stood. Lita didn't sit, either, though as a small reptilian-faced Ketzalian, she could hover beside Izzy on filmy purple wings.

A live band, Sentient 7 and the Clankers, tinkered away on what passed for a stage. Izzy drummed her fingers on the table as they waited for a server but regretted it when her fingers came away sticky. She paused for a moment as the Rodian keyboard player winked a star-speckled eye in her direction. There were dozens of people crammed onto the patio, shimmying to the electric song, but Izzy was positive the musician was looking at her.

*At least someone is,* she thought.

Izzy tugged on Damar's jacket, the deep-blue leather one she'd given him because it was an exact match to his dyed hair. His gray eyes were shadowed in the dimness of the patio, and Izzy didn't miss the lightning strike of irritation that wrinkled his brow.

"Iz," he said, batting lazy eyes at her. He only called her that when he was trying to correct her without picking a fight. Lately, with Ana Tolla's crew around, he only seemed to call her Iz.

"Should we, you know, be going over tomorrow's job?" Izzy asked him.

"We will," Damar said, tucking her hair behind her ear. He looked to the others, flashing a too-bright smile. There had been a time when Izzy would have done anything to see that smile. That night was not one of those times. He flagged a waitress. "Definitely. Let's get some food first. I'm half-starved."

Lita shot him a dark look. "It's a good thing you ate my last java cake or you'd be *fully* starved."

They placed an order for food and drinks with a particularly frazzled Trandoshan waitress, who grunted as she scribbled on her datapad. Izzy was positive the waitress was drawing stick figures, and wouldn't hold her breath that their order would be correct.

Ana Tolla flipped her fire-red braid over her shoulder and surveyed the crowd. Her pale blue eyes had always unnerved Izzy because they looked colder than the top layer of Orto Plutonia. She looked like she didn't hear Izzy or didn't care. Her crew surrounded her, a queen holding court. There was Safwan, a young human-Twi'lek male with light peach skin that phased into multicolored lekku and tattoos modifying his muscular arms. Then, of course, there was Lita, who didn't mind sharing cakes with Izzy after the previous expedition. Last was the beefy, fuzzy-faced Zygerrian, whose name always escaped Izzy because he was surly and quiet in a way only people who'd spent a lifetime hiding tended to be. Izzy couldn't help thinking that her mother had been a similar kind of quiet.

When their order arrived—definitely wrong, but no one was going to complain—the crew drank and ate their fill of the local fried meat doused in fiery brown syrup. Izzy felt more like an uninvited guest than an intricate part of a well-oiled crew. Even Damar chimed in on the reminiscing of missions he wasn't even present at. How about the time Ana Tolla kidnapped a low-ranking senator who owed some Hutts a small moon's worth of gambling debts? The senator was never seen again. How about the time Ana Tolla was hired to eliminate an oil baron's prime competition and accidentally set a city ablaze, and the competition along with it?

Izzy couldn't bring herself to laugh along but managed a pained grin. Wasn't this what she wanted? A crew. Something to be a part of. When Ana Tolla was hired for a job, she got it done. There was an expectation that went with her name. If Izzy was going to get rich *and* survive, she needed to be with someone like Ana. That was what Damar had convinced her was best.

Damar had been the one to find Ana and her crew in a dusty port in Abelor when he and Izzy were out of fuel, food, and contacts. Izzy had grown up believing that the one industry in the galaxy that would never run dry was smuggling. But it proved difficult getting potential customers to trust her and her ship when every corner of the galaxy felt the ripples of the current chaos. Though it'd been months since the destruction of the Hosnian system and the government of the New Republic, the upheaval that followed had no end in sight. Most of her only contacts were either dead or in hiding. Ana Tolla had lost half her crew, and joining forces with her seemed almost fated. Ana was especially pleased that Izzy and Damar came with their own vessel. Izzy hoped that the next mission would be the one that solidified them as a unit.

But as Izzy drained the dregs of her Naboo Cooler, she couldn't shake the feeling that she was in the wrong place, with the wrong people, at the wrong time.

The music played on, the crowd grew louder, and their waitress was nowhere in sight. The collision of nerves and anticipation left Izzy's mouth dry.

"I'm going to get another drink," she said offhandedly.

"Could you get me a refill?" Damar asked.

Ana Tolla shook her empty glass between long, calloused fingers. Her finely drawn eyebrow arched up. In her deep, smoky voice, she asked, "Would you be a dear?"

Then the rest of them piled on.

Izzy's eye twitched, but she told herself this was a way to show she was a team player. She wanted to be more than *"Hey, Damar's girlfriend, fetch me the hydrospanners."* Oddly enough, Damar never had to prove himself. He was simply there, with his beautiful cheekbones and easy manner. He had a talent for making himself *belong* anywhere, or at least convincing people of it. He'd talked the two of them out of enough situations. Though, if Izzy was honest with herself, he was just as good, if not better, at getting them *into* situations.

She cut through the crowd, ordered, and lingered at the bar, fidgeting with the brass zipper of her night-black leather jacket. Her drink practically materialized in front of her. She sipped the melon liquid and found that it smelled sweeter than it tasted, but it cost fifteen credits and she was going to drink it. Izzy glanced up at the dark, starry sky. With each jovial note struck by the band, her mood soured.

Maybe that was all part of Damar's plan—to truly convince her that he'd forgotten. After all, a month earlier, when they'd fought and she'd threatened to leave, he promised that he had something big planned for her. Huge. Fireworks. *Explosions!* "Unforgettable" wasn't *quite* the word he'd used, but then again, when he held her hands and looked at her in that way of his, like she was the only person in the galaxy, she could fill in the blanks of the things he wanted to say. Damar had a way of making her feel special, like the only girl in a single star system. Sometimes she wondered if he was charming her the way he did others. Sometimes she convinced herself that she was too clever to be fooled. It was easy to trust Damar when he uttered the right words. Izzy fought her own instinct that something was wrong because, deep down, she knew that having Damar was better than being alone.

But shouldn't he be more than that?

Then again, Damar had been the one to pull her from the petty errand jobs she'd been reduced to just to keep her ship in working order. Damar was the one who understood her better than anyone else. Damar never did anything without a little flair and a perfect smile that could crack a moon in two.

On the cantina patio, he was hunched over a table

of half-empty drinks with Ana Tolla and the others, speaking more animatedly than he had all night. Ana rubbed her bare arms against the chill of the night, and Damar handed her his jacket. Izzy grimaced but was surprised that it wasn't jealousy that needled her; it was disgust. Neither Safwan nor the Zygerrian had rushed to hand over their outerwear to their captain, but Damar had. He was so eager, so needy for Ana's attention. Anxiety twisted in Izzy's gut. When she glanced at the band, the Rodian keyboard player winked at her again. Maybe a bug flew into his eye. Maybe he was actually looking at the pretty human girl dancing behind her. Izzy decided to ignore it. A group of women were talking to Izzy's right, and something caught her ear.

"Do you think the rumors are true?" one of them asked.

"I think I want to get as far away from both sides as I can," another girl interjected.

"Broadcasts say medical freighters leaving the Mid Rim are being grounded," said a third. "It's like they don't want *anyone* having access to them. What are sick people supposed to do when supplies run out?"

"My cousin says he saw in a holo that the Resistance shot one out of the sky!"

"Tell me you don't believe that!"

They descended into rapid-fire arguing Izzy could

no longer eavesdrop on. Everywhere she went in the galaxy there were whispers about the Resistance. She didn't particularly care. All she wanted was to do her job. Smuggling wasn't what her father had wanted for her future, but neither of her parents was alive to make that decision for her anymore. Besides, as long as she developed a reputation for actually *delivering* her cargo, she'd be golden.

A fish-headed Bivall wedged himself next to her to get the barkeep's attention and shoved her in the process. She sighed hard and looked up at the sky. Maybe there was still time.

The rest of the drinks finally appeared before her, and she realized she didn't have enough hands to carry them all. Somehow she managed to transport the two brown bottles, two Naboo Coolers, one rosewater with fizz, and her melon drink in a tight grip against her chest.

She wove through the dancing crowd, hands and other limbs trying to pull her into the reverie, sticky liquid sloshing over her fingers. Floating orbs of romantic light hung low, and she blew them away. Her eyes flicked back to the door for a moment. The crowd tensed in unison as a fight broke out on the other end of the patio. The first brawl in a cantina only meant it was before midnight.

Izzy reached the table and slammed the drinks in

the center. While the beers and fizz had made it intact, the Naboo Coolers had not. Ana Tolla picked one up and held it at eye level.

"Did you drink both on your way over?" she asked in her scratchy, deep voice.

Izzy stared at the crew captain. Ana Tolla was only five years older than Izzy, but she'd made her living taking jobs others didn't want. She was said to have stolen a diamond choker from a Cuyacan princess while the princess was still wearing it, and razed the crops of a small vegetable farmer who refused to sell a plot to developers building metal skyscrapers across the planet surface. Such a woman wasn't going to be impressed with Izzy's waitressing skills.

"You're welcome," Izzy muttered, and took her drink from the bunch. She ignored the persistent crawling sensation on her skin that told her something was wrong. She told herself to enjoy the night. The weather was on their side, and the music was upbeat.

"Here's to a good run," Izzy said, and held her glass up for a toast. Every night before a job they'd done the same. But this time, there was a pause.

All eyes turned to Damar, who ran his fingers through his artfully styled blue hair. He was so meticulous about his trousers, his polished boots, his sleek and unmoving hair. If he fussed with it, mussed it up with twitchy fingers, it meant he was nervous. He hadn't glanced her way even once since she'd gotten back, which added to the feeling—no, the certainty—that she was missing information. This was not the evening he'd promised her. She would have preferred it if he'd never made a promise to begin with.

Izzy was still holding up the tall glass of overpriced melon water, but no one joined her in celebration. Though the tiny umbrella had stayed in place, the murky orange liquid had gotten on her blouse while she traversed the dancing crowd. She'd *splurged* on that blouse. Izzy didn't have the kind of lifestyle that called for soft fabrics or intricate stitching, but that night was a special occasion. Huge. Unforgettable. Fireworks. All that.

"What's up?" she asked. Her smile was tight, and her cheekbones hurt from the strain.

"Iz—" Damar began, then seemed to swallow his words. A lock of blue hair flopped over his strange gray eyes. "Iz. I am so sorry."

Around him, the rest of the crew averted their eyes. Suddenly, everything about the dodgy cantina was interesting to them—the floating orbs, the Twi'lek bartenders throwing bottles across the bar to each other, the garnishes in their drinks.

"Sorry for what, Olin?" she shouted over the music. "The 'fireworks' you failed to deliver?"

He sucked in a breath, his full lips rubbing together

in that way they did just before he made an explanation. No, not an explanation. An *excuse*. Like the time
he blew all their money at the races, or the time he
bought an astromech unit with all the guts missing
from inside it, or the time he got them arrested for
forgetting to clear their location history on their first
real job after the destruction of the Hosnian. Why did
she keep believing his promises anyway? Why hadn't
she walked away when she'd told him her doubts about
Ana and the others. About him. Maybe because this
time, the promise was *for* her.

"I swear, Izzy," he'd said. "It'll get better. Besides,
I have something special planned. I'll light up the sky.
Boom! You'll love it."

The Clankers played louder still, the tempo of the
bass matching her rapid heartbeat as she waited for
Damar to speak.

But then the music turned into screaming. The sky
was finally alight, only instead of fireworks, it was the
hazy red of blaster fire.

Izzy grabbed her weapon and aimed. A group with
their faces covered in black masks flooded the patio.
*Who in their right mind would rob a cantina full of smugglers and
bounty hunters?*

The answer was simple—other bounty hunters who
were there to collect.

"We have to go, *now!*" Ana Tolla shouted at them.

Her long red braid whipped in the air. She grabbed the edge of the patio's railing and hopped over. The others followed. It was a brilliant escape route that led directly to the docking bays where both their ships were stationed. Damar went over the railing. Izzy grabbed hold of the metal. She was ready to jump when something yanked her back.

Izzy rolled over and kicked. It was the Trandoshan waitress. She was trying to get away. Izzy looked to Damar for help, but he just stood there, dumbstruck. Izzy grabbed her blaster when a member of the black-masked gang grabbed the waitress by the back of her neck, muttering something about a debt owed. *Everyone owes everyone in this galaxy*, she thought darkly.

Behind them the other men in masks were raiding the place, turning over tables and smashing drinks. For a flash of a moment, Izzy wanted to stay and help. Then she remembered Damar. He didn't even move to help *her*.

Her eyes found him. He hadn't moved a millimeter. Ana Tolla lingered a few meters behind him, still wearing the blue leather jacket. Izzy had bought it on his birthday months before. They'd been in a market on Chandrila and she'd used the credits she'd been saving to repair the rear cannons on the *Meridian*.

"Now, Olin!" the captain shouted once more, and ran.

"Izzy," he said. "I'm sorry. The job—Ana—What I mean is—You're not coming. Don't hate me, please."

She blinked slowly, as if time were dragging the planet's orbit to a standstill and she was caught, unable to move a single limb. He turned and left her alone in the middle of a brawl.

A hand seized her shoulder and spun her around. "Give me your—"

Izzy's hand was still around her blaster. She pulled the trigger and the masked man's last words died with him.

As the rest of the gang retreated, their prize caught, the band crawled back to their instruments. The waitresses carried their drinks. The cleaner droids swept debris into neat piles and dragged bodies away. It must have been just after midnight.

She wasn't *new* to death and violence, but as she sat on the patio inhaling the stench of smoke and acrid flesh, she considered that she was new to heartbreak.

"Hey," said someone in a soft voice.

"Go away," Izzy said, and set her blaster on the table and finished the rest of her drink. As fate would have it, Ana Tolla's table was one of the few left unturned. The sweetness of the drink soon turned bitter. *Don't hate me, please.*

A green hand set a fresh drink in front of her. The liquid was pale green, like the Rodian's skin.

Her brows knit together. "What?"

"Izal Garsea?"

"That's a pretty great name."

The Rodian chuckled, and it had a strange resemblance to bubbles. "I know. You were named for your grandparents."

Izzy stilled but kept sipping, kept pretending that her world hadn't been rattled moments before.

"Says who?" she asked.

"Says someone who has a job for you, if you care to listen."

She didn't want to listen. She wanted to take the drink and go. But where? Her supposed crew had just abandoned her. The boy she'd traveled with for ten months had broken up with her and given her gift to someone else. Izzy found it disconcerting that she cared an equal amount for Damar and the leather jacket. But before she could dive into a hate spiral, Izzy took the drink and brought it to her lips. It was fizzy and fragrant and didn't make her want to retch, so she decided she'd stay. "I'm listening. How do you know my name?"

"I make it my business to know many things," he said. Glass crunched beneath his boot as he took a seat. The music picked up again, and the dance floor was repopulated. "Oh, and by the way, happy birthday."

# JULES

## CHAPTER 2

The day after Julen Rakab quit his job as a grain farmer, his body betrayed him and still woke him moments before suns-rise. He could sense that his sister and brother-in-law had left recently, because their small apartment carried an early morning draft. He rolled to his back on the cot, tucked away in his makeshift bedroom behind a cloth divider and the back of the couch.

Normally, he'd get up and make a pot of caf and get ready for the day, but that morning of all mornings, Jules kept staring at the ceiling, willing himself to sleep just a little bit longer. For thirteen years his body had been trained to be up at first light. He'd done everything he set out to do. He'd kept his word to his parents to stay close to family. He'd saved every credit he could spare, even if it meant taking side jobs on his days off.

All of it was put toward the grand, epic future he'd been planning since he was a boy. There were times when that future was clear—buy a ship and see the galaxy like the travelers he'd spent his whole life admiring.

He could invest in a business. He was sure Dok-Ondar or even Oga would point him in the right direction.

In the moments that future dimmed, Jules was bombarded with more practical questions. Sure, he could buy a ship and fly it. But where was he going to go? What would he do once he got there? If he invested in one of the wild ventures one of his friends always seemed to be cooking up, what would he do if he lost everything? The passersby and strangers that walked the Outpost for a day or a year made it look so easy. Jules didn't look for *easy*. He'd never been afraid of hard work. But he needed a direction. How could he find adventure if he didn't know where to start?

And yet, despite vacillating between fear and certainty, he'd gone through with quitting his reliable job at Kat Saka's farm. It was the right thing to do. He was sure of it. He was mostly sure of it. By the time he heard his neighbors calling out greetings from the halls, he was 50 percent sure of his decision.

"Too late now," Jules muttered to himself. Kat had only grown in business and hired a bunch of new hands for the harvest yield. Depending on whom you talked to, the Outpost either had jobs to spare or none at all.

Jules's big feet dangled off the end of the cot. Even though he was nineteen and was pretty sure he'd stopped growing the previous year, he thought he had another couple of centimeters on himself that morning. Either that or the bed was somehow getting smaller.

Jules threw off the soft wool blanket and gave himself a sniff, the previous night's revelry coming to him in flashes. After spending his last day harvesting Surabat grain on Kat's farm, a couple of the older guys had convinced Jules to celebrate the end of an era. His friend Volt was convinced that thirteen years didn't constitute an era, but Jules hadn't lived as many lives as Volt claimed himself.

Jules couldn't say no to his friends, though *friends* was a loose term after the pounding headache he'd been left with. He poured himself some water and tried to piece together the events after he got off his shift. He'd driven his speeder to a popular clearing in the grasslands. Volt was there with the whiskey he'd started brewing in the hollowed-out remnants of an astromech droid salvaged from Savi's junkyard a few months back. Volt—a tall, bald human with an unnatural rage toward droids—used his downtime trying to innovate different spirits he could sell to Oga Garra. Jules didn't have a palate for the stuff, but he liked to support local industry.

Jules had even helped Volt get started, making sure every part of the droid was sealed and the thing could resist the heat. Jules knew that nothing was ever too broken to fix or too old to be repurposed. Like many things, and even people, on Batuu, there was always another life to live. The drink, however—which Volt was advised not to call Volt's Special Juice—didn't deserve a second life. Not only did it taste like gargling with rusted screws, it burned something awful going down. The night before, Jules had considered it a good investment, but his stomach said otherwise that morning.

A knock on the door made him wince. Jules shuffled over, combing his calloused fingers through tangles of dark brown hair. Whoever was on the other side of that door at that hour would have to put up with his appearance.

His four-year-old Nautolan neighbor was at the door. Her pond-green skin was smeared with what smelled like baby food. At least he hoped it was baby food. She gaped at him with beetle-black eyes and waved her hand in front of her pert little nose.

"Peee-*yew*, Jules," she said in her bright voice. "You smell like Volt."

Jules shut his eyes and gave a tired sigh, but he couldn't help laughing at the small girl. "Do you want me to tell your mom about the secret stash of candy under your bed, Ksana?"

She sucked in a breath and righted herself. "You wouldn't."

"I could."

"Don't be mean, Jules!"

He crouched down to her eye level, suddenly worried that he'd make a child cry before breakfast. "I'm not a rat, Kay. Do you need something? Where's your gran?"

"Sleeping. We're out of milk. Do you have some?"

He left the door open to clear out his smell and let her in. They strolled lazily to the kitchen. There was exactly enough green milk left for his breakfast, but he handed the glass bottle over to Ksana's eager little hands.

Finally, he had purpose for the day. He'd resupply milk! The thought was as disheartening as it was *a thought*. Maybe he could invest in Bubo Wamba's milk stand. Though he quickly talked himself out of it as he thought of the way banthas smelled. Surely no better than he did at the moment.

"Remind me why your gran can't get you milk, Kay?" he asked her.

"She's sleeping and won't get up."

"Maybe I should check and see if she's alive," Jules mused.

"She is very much alive," came a shrill voice from the open door. The elder Nautolan waltzed in, her long purple tentacles speckled with sun spots from a lifetime on Batuu. Jules was certain she'd bash him with her cane the way she had all the neighboring kids when they were younger. He rubbed the ghost of a bruise on his shoulder from a time he'd kicked a ball through her window.

"Bright suns, Mother Katlock," Jules said without his usual warmth.

"Don't *bright suns* me," she said. "Waking a body up at all hours of the night with your caterwauling. Who do you think you are, Gaya herself?"

"Who's Gaya?" Jules and Ksana asked at the same time.

"One of the biggest stars in the galaxy!" The matriarch grumbled on about how "this generation" wouldn't know music if it docked in their ear canals. Jules watched them leave, Ksana chirping her final thanks.

It was already a longer morning than he'd ever had. After a hot shower, Jules felt alive again. On the small kitchen table was a bowl of fruit Belen had left for him as she'd always done after their parents had passed. As he ate, replacing his milk with water, Jules considered that things had never been easy or simple in their lives. Their father always said an easy life was earned by those with the will to make something out of nothing. Jules often wondered if he'd ever measure up to his da's philosophy. He loved his home planet, mostly because he'd never been anywhere else. But there were days when he was so restless and full of want for the unknown that he scared himself. When Jules had first spoken of quitting, hadn't Haal, his brother-in-law, laughed and reminded Jules that he wasn't going anywhere?

Maybe Jules didn't know what he actually wanted, but he knew what he needed. And that was not to spend the day cooped up in the house. He had the sudden craving for some fried tip-yip from Cookie's. How was he supposed to think on an empty stomach?

He tugged on his boots and tucked his arms into the deep red coat Belen had sewn for him the previous season as a gift for a good harvest. He was about to step outside when he noticed a small human boy waiting for him in the courtyard. The boy had dark brown skin and was about ten, with a shrewd stare and a floppy hat that always covered his buzzed head. Tap was one of Dok-Ondar's many runners in town. Jules knew his first day of freedom was over before it started.

"Bright suns, Tap!" Jules said, locking the door behind him. "I was just on my way to—"

Tap cut him off. "Boss has a job for you."

"How could Dok have a job for me? The suns aren't even up! Did he forget I don't work for him anymore?"

"He asked for you specifically. Can't see why." Tap lifted his shoulder and dropped it dramatically. "Only ones sleeping in today are you and the puffer pigs."

"Watch your mouth, kid."

Tap barked a laugh, but didn't appear sorry for the insult. "It's impossible to watch my own mouth when I don't have a mirror, Jules."

"Very funny. What's Dok want?"

"A couple of the runners didn't show up this morning, and he lost another apprentice to the white masks."

Jules didn't think anything of it, as Dok's runners came and went, sometimes leaving Batuu in the middle of the night without a word. He was used to familiar faces disappearing. A few years back, when jobs were scarce, Jules had started delivering packages for the old Ithorian. That's how he'd bought his first swoop bike when he was just a little older than Tap. Hearing about the apprentices was troubling, however. They stuck around longer than most, practically worshiping the treasures in Dok's shop.

Jules's lingering headache protested. If someone didn't want to show up to work, why was it his problem? He knew the answer almost as soon as he conjured the question.

He was good, dependable Jules Rakab.

Jules swore under his breath when he remembered he'd left his speeder in the middle of the clearing the night before. That was the last time he was humoring Volt's Gut Rot. Jules shuddered, then felt a sense of shame as he asked the ten-year-old for a lift.

Jules got on the back of Tap's beat-up 74-Z speeder bike, barely holding on to the back, which was better fashioned to carry small crates than another person. The fresh dawn breeze beat against his cheeks, and for a few moments, all he could do was watch the rocky terrain dotted with green alight as the suns rose. When he was a little boy, his father would sit and drink hot black tea with his mother on mornings like this. It was an insignificant ritual, but they never seemed to skip it. Sometimes he'd listen to the murmur of their voices before he fell back to sleep.

Tap came to a hard halt, and Jules hopped off the speeder bike in an ungraceful dive. The clearing was a popular place for bonfires and celebrations when the cantina was overflowing with travelers or when Oga raised the drink prices if she knew wealthy convoys had just made port.

"What *happened* here?" Tap asked, half amazed and wholly terrified.

The memory of the rest of the night was a barrage on Jules's senses.

He'd drunk his farewell drinks and practiced his aim on the targets they'd lined up. The rows consisted of old Imperial helmets, bottles, and droid heads that must have been in the salvage yard for more years than Jules had been alive. He hated blasters, but after drinking Volt's Gut Rot, he cleared the targets, then hitched a ride home on the back of a landspeeder.

He didn't actually remember getting home, but a flash of his sister's angry face was imprinted in his mind's eye. Belen wasn't always so cranky, and she didn't much care what Jules did with his time as long as he didn't bring any trouble inside their new apartment. Something had been upsetting her all week, but he didn't want to pry, especially if it had to do with her marriage.

More than ever, Jules was convinced it was time he set off on his own. He had the spira saved up, but there was something keeping him in the same rut. Most Batuuans his age—those who hadn't taken off years before and those who hadn't enlisted in the New Republic Defense Fleet or followed whispers of a new Resistance—were already set in the work they'd be doing for the rest of their lives. They were pairing up and getting married and talking about having kids. He couldn't imagine doing all that before he'd had a chance to see the galaxy.

Belen's voice rang in his memory: *"Don't throw a good thing away, Jules!"*

She was so worried about her little brother falling in with the wrong crowd or taking off with a bunch of pirates. Sometimes he wondered if the quarters of a smuggler's ship would be roomier than the cot in his sister's living room.

Granted, it was a very nice living room with rugs and the knitted throw blankets Belen had been making and selling on the side for years.

"Adult things, Tap," Jules finally answered, coming back to the present.

"So why were *you* invited?" Tap countered.

On another morning, Jules would have flicked the kid's ears, but he let it go. Though the scorched remnants of blasted metal had been cleared out, probably by Volt himself, the smell of wet earth and stale whiskey made Jules's stomach turn. Blaster bolts left bald patches in the ground and burn marks on boulders. Jules's speeder, along with two others, was haphazardly leaning on a slab of rock surrounded by wild grass.

Tap waved his hand over his delicate nose. "You couldn't wait till I was gone to cut one, Jules?"

Jules grumbled but didn't want to further explain the night's debauchery. Tap was a good kid, and Jules hoped he'd stay that way.

"Tell Dok I'm on my way, all right?"

Tap gave him a tiny salute, then sped off. Somehow, the kid's hat always stayed in place.

Jules powered up the speeder. The sooner he was done with Dok's business, the sooner he could get back to contemplating his daunting, amorphous future.

# IZZY

## CHAPTER 3

*It seems simple enough*, she told herself as she tossed and turned on the bed of her ship. To think she'd nearly let Damar Olin convince her to sell the *Meridian*. To think she'd let him kiss her and whisper promises about a future that was now erased. She wished she could scrub the thoughts the way she could wipe a droid's memory systems.

She forced herself to, instead, replay the instructions from Pall Gopal, the Rodian she'd met the night before. This one seemed to be a simple drop-off. Half the payment from Pall and the other half from his contact once she'd made port. It was the easiest money she'd ever been offered, and that meant it was too good to be true.

"Why me?" she'd asked him, sipping the fizzy juice he'd bought her to soothe the desertion and betrayal she'd experienced moments before. He might as well have said, *Happy birthday. Your boyfriend is a filthy, lying womp rat.*

"The *Meridian*," Pall Gopal said. "The original owner, Ixel Garsea, to be exact." Even hearing her mother's name stung like a fresh wound. "Your mother did a couple of jobs for me before she settled down. I keep track of my investments."

"Investments?"

"Sold her the ship you now call home."

She frowned at that. Her mom did say she bought the ship on Rodia. Or was it *from* a Rodian?

"My mother never mentioned you."

"Did she tell you why she named it the *Meridian*?" Pall waited for Izzy to nod, and she did. "When she saw it fly, it looked like an arrow sailing clean—"

"Across the meridian," she finished. Her mother didn't usually tell her stories, but that one was an exception. "So, what, I'm indebted to you because you sold my parents a ship?"

"On the contrary. Your parents and I were square, as far as I remember. May they rest in the Force."

She wanted to roll her eyes but contorted her features into a stoic calm. Her parents had believed in the ancient cult, much good it did anyone. But she couldn't insult her only prospect and job offer. If she wanted to be taken seriously, then what choice did she have but to accept it? It wasn't like she was going to go chasing after Ana Tolla's crew. They hadn't truly taken anything from her except her pride and, well, her dignity. Not to mention a day's worth of work.

Izzy would recover. It wasn't like she'd ever told Damar that she loved him back when he'd said it months before. She told herself that she didn't care. Lying to herself made everything hurt a little less, but not by much.

"Thank you," Izzy said, trying to keep her words even. "How did you know I'd be here?"

"Sad when a generation loses belief, isn't it?" The Rodian gave a wistful smile as he traced the rim of the cocktail glass. She said nothing. "But to answer your question, I recognized the ship. I'd heard about what happened—years ago. Then I saw your name on the ship manifest."

Izzy knocked on the table, trying to keep her calm. She narrowed her eyes at him, like she could see through any lies he was telling. She was quite good at telling lies when it suited her, and she'd thought she was good at detecting them. Clearly, when it came to Damar she'd failed.

What was wrong with her? She couldn't doubt skills she'd taken time to hone, because of that loser. *You didn't think he was a loser when you wished he'd kiss you,* she thought, and cringed.

She felt very young when she asked, "What kind of job did my mother do for you?"

"Ixel once did a run for me that no one else would. Too dangerous."

She knew that was all he would say. Izzy thought of her mother's fierce green stare, her full lips, beautiful but somehow always set in disapproval at her daughter. She'd spent more time teaching Izzy how to clean a blaster than how to brush her hair, how to fly through an asteroid belt without tearing the ship apart than how to talk to kids her own age. Nothing was too dangerous for Ixel Garsea, even dying. Sometimes she hated her mother for all those things.

She decided the Rodian was telling the truth.

"Sounds like her." Izzy bobbed her head to the strange music track that had replaced the live band, and managed a grin that didn't quite reach her eyes. This deal could change her luck after a rotten day. She had to make sure it was worth it. "Is that what this is? Dangerous?"

"Depends on how many questions you can stand to ask without getting an answer. I need someone to deliver a parcel to the Outer Rim."

"We are in the Outer Rim," she said.

"Further out. The edge of Wild Space." Pall touched his chin with Rodian suction-cup fingers, which had always reminded Izzy of flower bells. "It's straightforward enough. Deliver the parcel, collect your payment, and don't ask questions."

She raised a brow. The last time she'd delivered something no questions asked, a dozen varactyl eggs had hatched in her cargo hold. "I like to be prepared in case something I'm carrying is going to eat me."

"Very well. The contents of the parcel cannot harm you or your ship. It's locked and you will not be provided with the key."

"Let me get this straight," Izzy said, leaning forward. She wanted to believe she had her mother's ability to steel her facial features, to narrow her eyes into the kind of stare that had been capable of silencing even a Trandoshan thrice her size. But Izzy didn't feel as menacing as her mother had once looked. "If something goes wrong I won't be able to open it?"

"If a simple delivery is too much for you, Izal Garsea, then perhaps you are not your mother's daughter, and I'll find someone else."

She was overcome with the urge to put a hole through his chest. Instead, she took a deep breath and sat back. "If you *could* find someone else, then why are you wasting my time?"

It was a bluff if she'd ever uttered one. There were hundreds of smugglers and pirates he could hire, especially on Actlyon. "Seems to me like you need me for a more specific reason. So, what is it?"

"My dear girl, no one in the galaxy knows your name, which allows for fewer complications. Like I said. It's a simple delivery transaction. All of the information is here. I won't offer again." He placed a datacard on the table between them.

She should have dumped her drink over his head

41

for that "no one in the galaxy knows your name" comment. He might as well have told her how insignificant she was, how she didn't matter enough for the people she loved to stick around. No one knew her name? Well, she would change that. With or without Ana Tolla and Damar.

Izzy snatched the datacard off the table and raised her glass. "To new investments."

He echoed her words. That's when she realized he hadn't told her where *exactly* she was going.

"You can reach me on this and this alone," Pall said, handing her a holocomm. "I'll be by your ship later to give you the parcel." Then he left her at the table.

When she returned to the *Meridian* to wait for Pall's delivery, she keyed up the datacard to read about her mission.

After thirteen years, Izal Garsea was returning to Batuu.

# JULES

## CHAPTER 4

On his way to Dok-Ondar's shop, Jules felt his speeder shudder.

He smoothed his hand across the dashboard and whispered lovingly, "Come on, I just gave you a new turbine engine."

Jules rode between the rocky pillars surrounded by dark green shrubbery, careful to avoid Kat's farmland in case Belen spotted him and asked him too many questions later. On the way, there was an outcropping of abandoned homes. Though it had been about twelve years since the fires, traces of bitter smoke from scorched debris clung to the area. He shook off the memories of that day and sped up.

As he approached Black Spire Outpost, Jules's mood improved. Long gone were his aches and the doubt that crept into his mind at the thought of what might lie ahead. It was a good thing that someone like Dok-Ondar found him dependable. Around the Outpost, Dok's word was worth its weight in the rare golden lichen that grew on the spires.

He sped through the still-empty roads. The Market was just waking, with vendors setting up stalls and unloading crates. Stragglers, probably from Oga's Cantina, were stumbling down the alley, singing in a language Jules had tried to learn but could never get his tongue to cooperate with.

When he got to Merchant Row, he parked next to Tap's speeder bike. Jules unwrapped the scarf around his neck and tasted a faint trace of dust on his tongue from the ride. Dok-Ondar's Den of Antiquities was still covered in shadow. The strange statues leaning against the side of the building had bothered Jules ever since he was a little kid. He couldn't quite put a finger on why until Dok let it slip that one was a grave marker, though he wouldn't say whose. A tarp that had been tied over a stack of crates nearly two meters high had come undone, and it flapped in the morning breeze. As Jules tied it back down, an eerie chill seeped into his bones.

He realized why when the morning patrol of storm-troopers turned a corner, and he quickly let himself into the shop. It was brighter than usual inside, which meant Dok wasn't around. He'd never understood how Dok could work in the dark, but maybe the Ithorian had excellent vision.

Jules heard a muffled groan as he entered, but when he listened close, he was sure he'd imagined it. Dok's had a way of playing tricks on your mind. The first time Jules had snuck out of his house and spent the day at the Outpost by himself, he'd gone into Dok's shop. For a child, it was like a cavern filled with treasure and wondrous things from every reach of the galaxy. Everything from metal reliquaries to the supposed bones of Jedi to crown jewels of destroyed worlds to a dianoga in a tank. But the thing that had sent Jules running was the taxidermic wampa. Back then he'd been *positive* the beast was alive. Even as an adult setting off into the world, he could have sworn the creature's eyes followed him as he strode farther into the shop.

Jules found Tap at a corner desk, unloading trinkets from a small box for sorting.

"Where's the boss?" Jules asked.

Tap shrugged and didn't look up from his task. He pulled out an old metal tube with the head of a Zillo Beast on either end. "He was here when I went to get you. Must've stepped out, but he left you a list of things to do." Tap lifted his chin to a piece of paper—Dok still used paper, of all things—with a list of errands.

"Me?" Jules asked. He snatched the paper. "Don't you mean *us*?"

"The way I see it, Jules, someone has got to stay here and watch the shop until Dok gets back."

Jules sounded his frustration but wasn't going to argue with a kid. He leaned against the wall of the raised mezzanine. There was something strange about not seeing the Ithorian behind that railing, long fingers tugging at the long wisps of his white beard. As he scanned the list in Dok's barely legible scrawl, Jules knew he could get all this done and be free in time for lunch at Ronto Roasters. Clean out storage vault, payment for Hondo, payment *from* Oga, find a fancy glass container for Bubo's milk stand display, sort and log new acquisitions. Since Tap had picked the very last, and easiest, thing on the list, and since everyone else seemed to have vanished, Jules thought this favor might get him on the old man's good side. Dok wasn't a bad boss, but he wasn't the kind anyone wanted to cross.

Tap had already prepped the carton of glass and the case of spira for Hondo. Jules was about to haul the goods to his speeder, but he doubled back before reaching the door. "I need something to carry Oga's payment. Last time I almost got jumped by some Snivvian pirates."

"Check behind the sarlacc tank," Tap said. He was still toying with the metal tube. "Hey, Jules, what do you reckon this is?"

"It's a fingernail cleaner," Jules said, trying his best to keep a straight face. He was positive Dok kept that finger trap as a prank for his assistants. Who knew the ancient Ithorian had a sense of humor?

Jules sorted through a bin of standard-issue military uniforms from the Republic days and a pair of macrobinoculars with one lens missing. He wished he understood the way Dok's mind worked when it came to storing stuff, but Jules didn't see that happening in his lifetime. At the bottom of the bin was a large leather backpack that looked like it had spent time in a war zone. Jules wouldn't have been surprised if it had, though he hoped the dark stains were oil and not blood. He packed the spira and slung his arms into the straps.

"Don't miss me too much while I'm gone," Jules said as he rushed to the front door.

"I won't have to try too hard," Tap said, then gasped when he realized his fingers were stuck in the metal trap. "Hey, Jules! Wait, come back!"

Jules's mother had always warned that every deed carried out was returned in kind. So he shouldn't have been surprised when he swung the door open to find a green-eyed girl at the threshold and her fist collided with his face.

# IZZY

## CHAPTER 5

Izzy managed to get a couple of hours of sleep before she was jolted awake by restless nerves and dreams in which faces from long before coalesced with the previous night's music.

She sat up and got the *Meridian* prepped. As a little girl she'd trailed behind her parents making sure everything was in place and cargo was secure. The ship's exterior needed light maintenance she'd neglected during their days on Actlyon. During that time, she'd been working on Ana Tolla's ship instead of the *Meridian*. The memory made her grimace as she took inventory. She had enough fuel to get to Batuu, nutrient rations, and a bag of chocolate-covered caf beans she'd splurged on for the occasion of her eighteenth birthday. She didn't have the appetite for them yet.

Izzy fired up the thrusters and took off, sparing a single glance at the empty seat beside her. When she was a little girl, she would strap in behind the copilot seat, where her father had left the imprint of his strong body in the leather. Right before they leapt to hyperspace, her father would pause to look at her mother—every single time. Izzy knew what adoration looked like because she'd seen it often on his face. When she missed her family most, she thought of those moments. Times like this, when she felt like she was starting all over again, Izzy wondered what her mother would say to her. Correct her shooting stance. Admonish the company she kept. Then she realized: *Nothing. She'd say nothing.*

All she could do now was put everything her parents had ever taught her to good use and keep going.

Izzy soared out of Actlyon's polluted atmosphere and into the darkness of space. She relished the first seconds of that transition during every flight. She wasn't sure what about it captured her awe—the endless stars blinking in front of her, the promise of new worlds she'd yet to explore, the solitude of space that could never quite be simulated. Or perhaps it was the ability to look at a world from above and then put it behind her as she moved on to the next place. For a girl without a planet to call home anymore, a ship flying through space was as close as she was going to get. Wasn't that what she wanted? The freedom of being untethered.

It took her longer than usual to set a course for Batuu, then punch the hyperdrive. Pinpricks of stars gave way to the marbled blue of a hyperspace lane.

Fortunately, Actlyon was close enough to Batuu that she didn't need to take more than one route and she would save herself a refuel.

Izzy feared being alone with her thoughts. The night before, she'd broadcast a stream of news and music to have something to lull her to sleep. Out there all she could do was wait, clean her blaster, and retrace her entire relationship with Damar. His abandonment bruised her. What could she have done differently? Be a different person? More like Ana Tolla? She didn't want that. The rational part of her mind told her it was for the best. But the rest of her was indignant. *Angry.* So much so that if she cleaned her blaster any harder, she'd wear off the grooves on the handle. Izzy knew she deserved better. She had a job and a destination, and that was a start.

When her dashboard beeped hours later, signaling she'd arrived, Izzy buckled in and braced herself to come out of lightspeed. When the stretch of stars faded out of view and took the shape of a planet, her first thought was that it looked like so many other worlds—an expanse of green cut by patches of brown and some blue, swirling storms gathering at the poles. She was born on the *Meridian*, while her parents were in the middle of their travels, and Batuu just happened to be the nearest planet. "One rock is as good as the

next," her mom used to say. But as the *Meridian* broke
through the coverage of clouds, Izzy took in the jutting rock spurs of petrified trees and jagged cliffs that
made Black Spire Outpost so unique. *Home*, a part of
her thought. Another part contradicted her. *Home is
where this ship is.*

Thirteen years before, her parents had picked up in
the middle of the night and left Batuu without so much
as a word to their neighbors or coworkers on the vegetable farm where she'd believed both her parents were
employed. Soon Izzy discovered her mother had never
been a farmer, only her father. Her parents were not
the best at explaining things, like why they moved so
often or why her mother always needed to scan a room
before she entered it, and Izzy had learned quickly not
to ask questions her mother would never answer.

She scoured the sprawling land beyond the Outpost
and couldn't even remember where their house had
once been. Could it have been in the cluster of settle-
ments to the north? The grasslands? Faced with her
return to Batuu, Izzy felt bothered that some of the
best memories of her life had grown blurry after so
many years. That planet on the edge of Wild Space was
where the Garsea family had settled down for the longest uninterrupted stretch of their lives together. Her
parents might have found it easy to abandon, but Izzy

had left a part of herself on those cliffs on the horizon, and she had the scars to prove it. Her time there belonged to a different girl in a different era.

Izzy made for the Outpost and set the *Meridian* down at a filling station. Clouds of dust obstructed her view of the landing pad. The ship made a strange sound, like metal warping.

"That can't be good," she muttered, and powered down.

As the suns rose, a bronze light illuminated the rock spires surrounding the domed station. She realized she hadn't been honest with herself moments before. There were some memories from Batuu that *were* clear. One person. She reached into her blouse and pulled out the smooth black stone ring flecked with bits of gold. It only fit her pinky finger, so she kept it strung on a leather cord. The boy who'd given it to her as a token of friendship had been her only friend on the planet—perhaps her only real friend ever. It was difficult to build lasting relationships when her family wasn't in any one place for more than a couple of days, and on the off chance that they lived somewhere for as long as six months . . . Well, Izzy remembered how hard she'd cried when they left Batuu. As the years went by, she figured out that it was easier to leave a place when there was no one there who might miss you.

For a while, she'd had Damar. As she slipped the ring back under her shirt, she wondered if she had put up with him for so long because she truly cared for him or because she had gotten tired of being alone.

Izzy had always been used to noise—her parents laughing; cantinas; markets; her aging, beautiful ship; even Damar running through the list of things that could go wrong with a job, or his constant commentary about the state of the galaxy, which was usually uninformed. Was she really so terrified of silence that she couldn't be alone for a few hours? She should know better.

"You have to learn to love your own company. That way you're never alone," her mother had once told her. Like so much of Ixel Garsea's advice, it came as part command and part truth, and with zero explanation.

If her mother could see her, Ixel would set those crystalline green eyes on Izzy and drip disappointment with the barest frown.

Izzy shook her head. She needed to focus. The job was easy and paid well. Pall Gopal had been the lucky break she'd been searching for, even if his words had bruised her ego. All she had to do was deliver the mysterious parcel to the legendary Ithorian, Dok-Ondar. She'd caught a glimpse of him once on the rare occasion her father took her to the Outpost. After that she was free to do whatever she pleased. The *Meridian* needed work and fuel. For the first time in months she wouldn't have to scrape the credits together. If she remembered correctly, Batuu was known for its copious market stalls, offering all kinds of wonders from around the galaxy. Maybe she'd even shop for her birthday. Her boots were beginning to fray and thin out at the soles. The next day, she'd be somewhere else. It had been a while since she'd been to the other side of the galaxy. Maybe she'd travel to Canto Bight to search for new job prospects or visit one of its spas.

Things were looking up for Izal Garsea, and her mood brightened. She made sure her heavy black boots were tightly laced, double knotting them and tucking in the ends. The package the Rodian had given her was safely in the cargo hold. When he'd brought the medium-size briefcase to the *Meridian*, it had made her nervous enough that she'd hidden it beneath a panel in the floor. She dug her finger under the divot in the floor and lifted the panel. When she was little, the crawl space had served as a hiding spot. It had been days after they'd left Batuu and she had still been angry with her parents. It was hard to imagine that she was ever small enough to tuck herself in the same space that she used for bottles of stolen wine or the purebred cat of a senator's wife that Izzy had smuggled out of the couple's home during a divorce settlement.

Izzy grabbed the briefcase by the handle and hoisted it out. The surface was a smooth silver metal with scuffs and scrapes on it. She traced her thumb over the front, where the square keypad was nestled at the center. Her curiosity piqued, she shook the case, but it did not rattle. Perhaps the contents were locked in place. Perhaps Pall Gopal had simply felt sorry for her because he'd witnessed her humiliation, and was sending her on a personal errand as a former friend of her mother. Though she had to admit that would be extremely elaborate, and in Izzy's experience, no one anywhere did anyone favors out of sheer kindness.

Damar had left her because she wasn't cut out for their job. The Rodian had chosen her because no one knew her name. She'd been gone from Batuu long enough that it was probably true. But she'd prove them both wrong.

She snatched a large tattered backpack from the closet and stuffed the briefcase inside. There was no way she could walk around a port city with anything that screamed *mug me*. This way, she was a tourist buying Batuu's local and imported offerings.

She shoved in the bag of chocolate-covered caf beans, along with part of the payment Pall Gopal had given her and a nutrient packet. It tasted like watery clay, but she had to be prepared.

She dug in the closet for a leather jacket that didn't

smell like Naboo Cooler. Sometimes wearing her mother's collection of outerwear made Izzy feel like she was playing dress-up, but she had to admit, the forest green with black stripes down the arms looked good on her. Maybe her mom wouldn't approve of the sentiment, but sometimes Izzy wanted to feel closer to her. Securing her blaster at her hip, she lowered the boarding ramp.

She could taste the dust in the air still settling from her arrival. The morning chill seeped into her bones despite her jacket.

"First customer of the day!" a sweet high-pitched voice greeted her from the shadow of the filling station.

Izzy stepped on the hard earth and strode to meet the approaching human woman. She appeared to be in her early twenties, with medium brown skin and black hair tied back in a perfunctory way. As Izzy got closer, she could better see the blue markings on the woman's smiling face. It was too early for anyone to appear so cheerful, but this woman managed it. She wore a deep-blue tunic belted around the waist, loose brown pants, and heavy boots. On her right hand she wore a fingerless glove.

"Do I win something?" Izzy asked.

"You win the pleasure of my company," the woman said, and extended her arm to the side. She folded herself in a dramatic bow, and even Izzy couldn't stop her lips from quirking into a grin. "Bright suns . . ." The girl hung on the last word.

"Izzy."

"Bright suns, Izzy. I'm Salju, and I run this here operation. What brings you to our corner of the galaxy?"

Izzy had met people who asked that question expecting to get something out of it, whether information on a shipment or on a possible bounty. Most of the worlds she went to avoided asking at all. But there was something genuine about Salju that made Izzy believe the woman truly wanted to know, not out of malice or greed but out of politeness. Friendliness, even.

Damar had liked weaving elaborate fictions, where it felt more like they were playing than doing a job. Before that she'd kept her lies simple, less to remember and even less of a possibility she'd trip herself up. Her mother liked to say that the best lies flew close to the truth. But now that she'd actually set foot on Batuu, part of her didn't want to be just another stranger. Not in the one place she'd once called home. It was an irrational, sentimental thing that her mother wouldn't have understood.

"I used to live here as a girl," Izzy said, shoving her hands in her jacket pockets. "I remember there was plenty of work to go around."

Salju glanced at the small ship behind Izzy and made a face that was a cross between curiosity and pity. The ship needed work—more work than Izzy could afford or manage herself until that day.

"Well, clearly you can fly if you made it all the way out here in that thing," Salju said with a chuckle. "I take it you need repairs on the fuel drive pressure stabilizer and the left laser cannon?"

*Among other things, yes.* Izzy glanced back at her ship, her indignation catching in her throat. Salju was already walking past her to the *Meridian*. Izzy followed and said, "You can tell from just looking at it?"

"It's one of the many languages I'm fluent in," Salju said, cracking her knuckles. "I'll take half now and half when you pick up. Should be ready by midday if I get started now."

Izzy sighed. She didn't want to be there long, but no matter where she went next she'd need repairs. She began to pull some credits out of the inside of her jacket when Salju put her hand up. "Sorry, my dear. I can only take Batuuan spira, I'm afraid. You can get Dok-Ondar to exchange them for you, I'd wager."

Izzy could hardly contain her smile when she recognized the name. That was precisely whom she needed to see. She knew Black Spire Outpost was small, but was she so lucky? Her father had never believed in luck. For a man who'd once been a scholar, he spent a lot of time reminding her of the way the universe worked, moved and shaped by the Force itself. For the moment, she'd call it luck and count her riches when the job was done. Perhaps Dok-Ondar would see how quickly she'd brought his parcel and keep her in mind for future work.

"I'll head on over there, thanks."

"Oh, and if you're looking for work," Salju continued, "Dok's been short on couriers the last few weeks. Both of his apprentices up and left, too."

Izzy arched her brow. "Is that normal?"

Salju glanced around, pressing her hand to the side of the ship like she was waiting for the metal beast to literally speak to her. "There's nothing like normal in BSO, but you'd know that, since you were from here and all. Work has slowed, what with—the new arrivals."

The last bit she said in a careful, hushed tone. She shook her head, and Izzy knew not to pry.

"Right," Izzy said. "Do you mind pointing me in Dok's direction?"

"Course," Salju said, and pointed down a well-trekked road that led away from the station. "Take this road to the left and it'll lead you straight to Merchant Row. Once you see the big statue of a Jedi priestess, you'll know you're there."

Salju's energy was contagious. Izzy gripped the straps of her backpack and set off with a new smile on her face.

"May your deals go well, Izzy!"

— ◇ —

Izzy hurried down the path. Fresh footprints marked the way. Already the vendors were setting up stalls, beating dust and errant dried leaves from canvas tarps with large sticks. The whirring and beeping of droids fought for her attention with the howling chirps coming from a tent. Dozens of cages in the tent were covered up tightly, though at least some of the critters inside were clearly awake. For a moment, Izzy considered lifting an edge of the fabric to get a look at what kind of creature might be beneath it, but a crash behind her made her jump. It seemed two vendors had collided. One of them was a heavily robed, white-bearded human who'd been wheeling a cart full of bright green fruit. A hooded Gran, with floppy ears and three eyes, had interrupted by laying out a rug in the very middle of the road to unload some wares. Both were waving their hands animatedly, snapping back and forth in Basic and guttural Huttese.

Not wanting to stick around in case they got violent,

Izzy kept walking. The previous night's fight had been enough for her.

When they'd lived on Batuu, her parents had rarely ventured into the Outpost. They were never recluses, but her mother wasn't the kind of neighbor who was going to trade ronto stew recipes, either. She could count on one hand the number of times her father had taken her to the market with him—usually to buy spices and repair his beat-up datapad.

Izzy touched the ring beneath her shirt and struggled to find more memories of the cobblestone streets and cylindrical structures built right into the ancient spires and stones. She wondered what it would be like to live inside one of those apartments. Somehow the metal domes and the petrified trees made sense together, marrying the world's ancient past and present. Izzy drank in the colorful banners that hung overhead to shield market-goers from the suns. As she neared an obelisk in a courtyard, she stopped to listen to the chirping sounds of languages she'd never be well-versed in. Standing in the middle of the market just before it filled with bodies made her feel like the road was open just for her.

Perhaps that was why she took a wrong turn at one of the courtyard archways. She kept an eye out for the big statue Salju had mentioned, but she second-guessed herself and doubled back. She took a right at a dark alley that smelled of puddle water and char. It looked like there had been a fire in one of the bins.

That's when a figure stepped out of the shadows. Izzy had seen First Order stormtroopers on the holonet feeds after what had happened to the Hosnian system. But she'd never seen one in person. The armor glistened white, with black seams marking joints, like a skeleton made of plastic. There was a high-powered blaster rifle strapped to his back. Why would he need that on a planet where there was no military presence?

"What's your business here?" he asked in a voice that sounded wrong, like it had come through a faulty holomessage.

Izzy's body betrayed her and froze. Why would the First Order be there of all places? There were busier ports that moved valuable exports elsewhere. Why Batuu? Her mouth dried up at the thought of the parcel in her pack—a parcel the contents of which she wasn't supposed to ask about. Could there be something inside that might get her in trouble? When she took too long to answer, the trooper leaned forward.

"Well?" His voice was hard and impatient.

"It's my first day at Dok-Ondar's and I got a bit lost," Izzy said, softening the edges of her voice.

"What's in the pack?"

She was stupid for thinking that a display of innocence would have any effect on this kind of soldier. Staring at her own warped reflection in his helmet made her queasy and she felt even worse when she realized she might get sick on his boots. She hadn't hesitated to pull the trigger on the gang member in the cantina the night before, but there was something purposely faceless about these particular helmets that unnerved her enough that it made her want to prove she'd done nothing wrong.

Then the stormtrooper straightened, raising his hand to both silence her and let her know not to move.

"On my way. Copy," the trooper answered, then lowered his helmet toward Izzy. "Isn't it your lucky day?"

Then he turned and left her alone in the alley with a pounding heart. She ran back out onto the main road. There were more people crowding around stalls, and the sound of shuttles zooming overhead gave her small comfort. As if the stars had aligned for her, there was the statue Salju had mentioned. The Jedi looked severe, reverent in ways Izzy had never learned to be. Cargo crates were stacked against the cylindrical structure. She darted around the perimeter until she reached the domed entrance of Dok-Ondar's Den of Antiquities. She pressed the doorbell a couple of times, but nothing happened. She tugged on the straps of her backpack, shoulder blades aching, and tried to calm her frantic pulse. Why had that trooper bothered her so much?

Perhaps it was a deep-seated memory; perhaps it was that she hadn't recovered from the night before.

She realized the doorbell was either broken or simply decorative. She raised her fist and banged. Behind her a silver-and-black protocol droid ambled along, herding what looked to be mud-covered piglets. At least she wouldn't be bored on Batuu, she thought, then raised her fist to bang again.

Only instead of hitting the door, her fist collided with a person.

# JULES

## CHAPTER 6

"Ow!" Jules exclaimed as his head snapped back. He cradled his nose with his hand, blood flowing down his lips and filling his mouth with a metallic tang. Despite the sharp pain blooming across his eyes, he reached blindly for a rag. His hand closed around the nearest piece of cloth on a counter and used it to stop the gushing. He was vaguely aware of Tap laughing in the background and a voice repeating an apology.

Jules was positive he'd used the same rag to clean the baby sarlacc terrarium a couple of nights before, but there was nothing else within reach.

"I am so, *so* sorry," said the girl who'd sucker punched him. She followed him inside the parlor.

At once, Jules registered something: he knew this girl. His mind raced through memories, trying to place her high cheekbones and pointed chin. The delicate arch of her full upper lip. Her dark brows knit together over green eyes that stared at him as if he'd grown three heads. Looking at her made the pain around his tender, most likely broken septum hurt just a bit less. The door slid shut behind her, and the morning breeze rustled her black hair, which reminded Jules of the silk ribbons Dok imported from the tropical moon of Linasals.

Where had she come from with her hit-first-apologize-later attitude? Jules was convinced he *knew* her. Not from Kat Saka's farm, that was certain. The dark-green leather jacket, black leggings, and scuffed boots marked her as an off-worlder. There were hundreds, thousands of people who came and went in the Outpost—refueling, hawking wares from the back of clunky freighters, hiding from deals gone wrong, or going on sabacc benders at Oga's Cantina. Those faces blurred together after a time, but the sight of this girl slammed into him with the strangest familiarity.

"Are you okay?"

Jules realized that she was asking him a question and had been attempting to talk to him the entire time he'd been trying to place her in his memory.

"He'll be fine," Tap said in his high-pitched, know-it-all voice. "He gets hit on the head a lot."

The kid wasn't wrong. Jules had taken quite a few hits over his lifetime, mostly from roughhousing with local friends, rock climbing in the Surabat River Valley, or tangling with off-worlders looking for an easy mark. But he thought he'd grown out of the latter.

"Neither of you look okay," Tap said, standing between them, bewildered eyes darting back and forth.

The girl tilted her head to the side and narrowed her stare. He was sure she was trying to remember him, too—or assessing the damage. When she brushed her hair back, her jacket sleeve slid up and he noted the scars above her wrist. They stood out quartz white on her golden skin.

Jules could see her then, a faded memory from so long before, he'd nearly buried it: a girl with fearless eyes, in a dirty dress at the top of a cliff. He vacillated between convincing himself that it *couldn't* be her and being certain that it was. As a little boy, he'd stared at the sky in hopes of seeing the arc of her family's ship, but it had never come back.

He worked his lips and mind into forming words, and settled for a single one. "Izzy?"

She gasped and took a step back. Her hand flew to the collar of her simple black shirt. He could practically hear the gears in her mind turning.

Fortunately, blood had stopped spewing out of his face, so he lowered the rag. He bunched it in his hands because a part of him wanted to throw his arms around her and—say what? He'd been a farmer for so long, he almost reflexively wanted to ask how her crop yield was doing. What exactly did one say in that situation? *How's the weather in whatever world you came from? So, why are you back? Are you thirsty? Because I'm thirsty.* He was practically short-circuiting. There was once a time when his days began and ended with the company of his best friend. Until they didn't. Now she was standing there dressed in leather that looked like armor, with a blaster strapped to her thigh.

She went rigid, straightening her shoulders against the heavy weight she carried, and the silence wound between them. Perhaps he'd imagined it. He could blame it on Volt's Gut Rot—his mind playing tricks on him, dredging up memories from the past. It had been twelve years. No, thirteen. The Garseas had left before the fires.

He had begun to talk himself out of the certainty that the girl before him was Izal Garsea when she said his name in a swift exhale. "Julen Rakab."

Then she lunged at him, wrapping her arms around his neck. He was too aware of his clumsy limbs as he embraced her, of his heart struggling to beat at a normal rate. The bridge of his nose throbbed, but when they stepped back and stared at each other, he didn't care anymore.

"I can't—" they started to say at the same time.

"You go first," they said, once more in sync.

Jules motioned for her to speak.

"You're—taller—than I remember," she said, and he warmed at the surprise in her voice.

Jules held out his arms and presented himself to her the way he'd seen some of Dok's assistants greet wealthy potential buyers. Not that he was selling himself. Not that he was trying to sell her anything. He was overcome with a knot of frayed nerves like never before and was nearly thankful when Tap inserted himself directly between them.

"Those deliveries aren't going to carry themselves," Tap muttered, turning to Izzy with small fists squared on his hips. He'd finally managed to free himself from the finger trap. "What do you want, then?"

"I got this, Tap," Jules said, and pulled the kid's hat over his eyes, then gave him a shove back to his corner of the dimly lit shop.

"My parents never let me come here when I was little," Izzy said, eyes roaming the display cases. She wove around stacks of open crates, an Ewok headdress covered in feathers and teeth overflowing out of one of them.

"All things considered, this is one of the safest places in the Outpost." Jules shrugged. Then his eyes darted to the reinforced tank that housed a juvenile dianoga near the metal railing. He wasn't sure if it was growing too big for its confinement or if it just liked to press its ferocious fanged underside against the glass. "But now I understand why some might object."

Izzy peered up at the taxidermic body of the wampa on the raised mezzanine, the creature's last growl frozen for all eternity.

"Is that real?" she asked.

Jules felt his body answer before the rest of him. He went to her side in two long strides, and for the first time in a long time, he didn't curse his too-long legs. "As real as you or me. Dok prides himself on rare and authentic."

She flicked her gaze to him, then back to the beast. "You work here?"

He didn't want to get into the circumstances that had brought him to Dok's that day. "For today. Usual staff seems to have taken off. Almost feel sorry for the ones who cross Dok-Ondar."

Izzy quirked her brows skeptically. "What happens when someone gets on his bad side? Slow torture by droids?"

"You get fed to Toothy!" Tap piped up.

"Ignore him," Jules said. "The dianoga is only fed ronto meat. But if you plan to stick around the Outpost, you don't want to get on the Doklist."

"The Doklist?" she asked, weighing a crystal ball in her hands. "Is that like being blacklisted?"

"Around these parts you're better off packing up and finding work on a distant moon and never coming back. My parents made that clear practically at the time we could walk."

"Mine failed to mention it." She made a thoughtful sound and picked up one of the many glass jars filled with shimmering golden lichen. Despite her abrupt greeting, he got the feeling she was doing everything in her power to look at anything but him.

"What are you doing here, Izzy?" he asked, voice lower than he'd intended.

What did he want her to say? That she'd come back to the edge of the galaxy for him? Belen always reminded him he was a foolish dreamer, but he wasn't foolish enough to believe that Izzy Garsea had returned just to see him after thirteen years.

She took a deep breath and scanned the metal chandelier above. The Ithorian wind chimes had gone perfectly still. It was difficult for him to read her. How could he? She was practically as unknown to him as anyone who passed through the Outpost. Contrary to his current inability to think straight, usually he was quite good at striking up conversations with strangers. It was the closest he'd get to knowing about the greater galaxy. For now.

Izzy adjusted the strap of her pack and said, "I'm here to see Dok. I have a parcel he requested."

Tap lifted his head and joined the conversation

again. "Dok's not here, but you can leave it with us."

Izzy's hand went to the bottom of her rucksack, much like the one Jules was wearing.

"My instructions were to deliver to Dok and Dok only."

"Suit yourself." Tap shrugged. "He stepped out, but he doesn't stay gone for long."

Right then, Jules was overcome with the need to do anything to make her happy. For a fraction of a second, he even wanted to turn into a two-centuries-old Ithorian to make her day better and take away the lightning-bolt frown that marred her otherwise smooth brow.

She muttered a curse under her breath, but then gave him a small smile. "I don't suppose you could help me with changing credits to Batuuan spikes?"

Tap snorted behind his hand.

"Spira," Jules gently corrected.

"That, I can do." Tap slid off the stool he'd been using and sauntered over. He hopped over the metal railing that encased the raised platform where Dok was usually stationed. Jules could hardly remember another time when the Ithorian hadn't been there mulling over his illegible ledgers.

"Thanks, kid," Izzy said.

Jules had his own work to get done, but he was grounded to the stone floor. He couldn't rationalize his need to be seen by Izzy, truly seen. He wasn't entitled to her attention, or time, or anything she didn't want to give. They were virtually strangers. But the part of him that had searched the skies hoping to see her again longed for the friendship they'd once had. No one, not even Belen, had understood him the way Izzy had.

*That was long ago,* he reminded himself.

Julen Rakab believed in fate. It was a notion he'd learned from his mother. Between his parents, she was the dreamer, the one who found a bit of hope and goodness in any situation. She believed that there were things brewing in the wide galaxy that couldn't always be explained. Whether it was the movement of the planets, ancient deities, or the Force—something was at work. Haal, his brother-in-law, liked to make fun of Jules for trying to string together mundane events and call them "fate."

Jules had once bent down to pick up a coin, some sort of currency that must have fallen from an off-worlder's pocket. Because he'd moved out of the way at that precise moment, he'd narrowly missed getting hit by a runaway hover-raft full of scrap metal. He'd traded the coin to Dok for a used hologame. Another time, Jules had taken a wrong turn into Smuggler's Alley and came up on a Togruta kid getting mugged. They'd *both* gotten pummeled by a couple of wannabe gangsters, but he'd made a lifelong friend. Haal didn't believe that anything had a greater meaning or purpose. For Haal, days and nights blended together because that was the order of the world and nothing more than a string of coincidences. But wasn't coincidence just a version of fate for those who didn't believe in anything?

Izzy Garsea herself was standing right in front of him. If he'd left the shop a minute sooner, if he had swung by the fields to wave to his sister or grabbed some grub at Cookie's like he had wanted to do from the moment he woke up—if he'd done anything different— he might have missed Izzy entirely. Granted, perhaps it was just the Force's way of telling him he needed to be punched in the face, but Jules was nothing if not optimistic.

Tap exchanged Izzy's credits and handed her a sizable pouch of spira, which she then divided between the inside pockets of her jacket.

"Thanks," she said. "I have to go pay the lady at the filling station so I don't get stuck here tonight."

That stung. He wondered what their home planet might look like to her. Most people didn't see past the craggy exterior of the spires, an outpost built among dusty old ruins, and market stalls patched with canvas that never quite matched the original. But Jules loved where he came from. Was that love why he'd never left as he'd planned? He pushed the thoughts away.

"Would that be so bad?" he asked.

"It's been a rough couple of days. My plan was to keep moving."

"I could give you a ride back to your ship," Jules blurted out.

"I thought you were working."

He shrugged like it was no big deal. Truthfully, he couldn't watch her walk away without at least talking to her. Where had she gone? What had her life been like off Batuu? Why had she had a rough couple of days?

"You'll find everything is on the way around these parts," Jules said, and winked. He never winked. Why had he winked? He cleared his throat and kept going. "Lucky for you I'm the best tour guide the Outpost has to offer. Come with me on my runs."

She considered him with those bright green eyes, the yellow flecks like the golden lichen that only grew on the black spires of Batuu. "All right." He didn't miss the way she took in the rest of him, a smirk playing on her lips as she lifted a finger and motioned around her face. "But you might want to—uh—clean up the blood on your chin."

Tap chortled in his corner, and Jules climbed up to the mezzanine of the den and found a fresh rag. He poured water from one of the canteens and checked his reflection in the foggy glass case that housed blue Oshiran sapphires. Ithorians weren't exactly vain creatures, so there weren't mirrors to go around. When he was sure he wasn't a bloodied mess, he dumped the rag in a waste bin that would need to be emptied.

Dok's work area was the kind of organized chaos that only made sense to the Ithorian, but it felt like something was missing. Though it did strike Jules as strange that Dok had left his comlink behind. It rested at an angle beside the giant magnifying glass and stacks of orders. Jules felt the urge to push the gold and silver beads of the abacus but knew better than to touch anything on the desk without permission. Rumor had it that Dok had a collection of fingers and digits of those who'd angered him. It was then that Jules noticed something he hadn't when he'd rushed up there. Under the workstation was an overturned metal figurine of a goddess. Jules doubled back a few steps and found the empty shelf where she belonged.

The carved walking stick the Ithorian carried around was gone, and the door that led to Dok's offices was closed, which meant Dok had definitely stepped out. Though it had been a while since his last job, Jules knew Dok was particular about the way everything was placed in his shop. Perhaps he'd knocked the statue over or it had fallen and he was in too much of a rush to right it. Jules made sure the dancing goddess, which was said to give great fortune to its owner, was propped up and facing the entrance of the office again as she was supposed to.

Jules hopped off the mezzanine and waved at Tap once before following Izzy outside. Dozens of people walked in opposite streams, filling the streets with early-morning chatter. Even there he could smell the simmering food from the market.

He led her to where he'd parked his speeder beside Tap's bike and the dozens of crates that were always coming and going with Dok's shipments. He stowed his pack in the cockpit, and Izzy did the same.

"It's not much," he told her, "but it rides like a dream. I bought it for three hundred credits off a farmer who'd come here from Tatooine. You should have seen it. It was missing the windscreen and the side panels. But I spent weeks digging through the salvage yard. Retrofitted it with new deluxe turbine engines."

"It's great, Jules," she said. "Do you remember when we were little and would look for rocks shaped like speeders to pretend to race?"

He was surprised that she remembered that. "Unlucky for you, the year after you left, my sister and I got a used flight simulator."

"I remember you always wanted to fly." She tied her hair back and jumped in the speeder.

Jules followed suit and took off, still feeling like he was holding his breath. As he navigated through the traffic lanes that would take them to Salju's, he stole a glance at Izzy.

She turned her head to the side as if caught watching him first. Warmth spread across his cheeks, though it could also be the rising heat of the day.

"I thought you'd have left the first chance you got," she said. "You always said you would."

He gripped the wheel tighter. Haal's words reverberated through his mind, growing the seeds of doubt that had always been there. But he didn't want that to ruin this moment with Izzy. It didn't matter why he'd never left Batuu.

"It never felt like the right time," he said. "For a while I kept saying I'd leave next season, and then the one after that. I've been saving credits since day one. Just this morning I was thinking about what my next move would be."

She nodded. Did she understand, or was she being polite? The Izzy he remembered hadn't been as tense or quiet. But then, how much had *he* changed in those years? He still felt like the same Jules.

"I hear you. I was at the academy on Eroudac. Small Mid Rim world. But it didn't take," Izzy said. "What's your next move going to be, Jules?"

Next move? Before he could answer, his heart sank. A whirring noise erupted from his speeder as it came to a crawling halt, sputtering in the middle of the dirt road not halfway to Salju's. The console flashed green and red, but at least the repulsorlift kept the speeder hovering.

"Right now?" He let out a slow breath, turned to her, and smiled. "Our only next move is to haul it."

She jutted a thumb against her chest. "Our? Maybe you should put those muscles to good use."

He quirked an eyebrow at her. "It's good to know you've noticed my muscles, Izzy." Before she was able to process what he'd said, Jules continued, "You owe me one."

"How do you figure?"

"For breaking my very delicate nose this morning." He hopped out, took off his jacket, and threw it on the seat, daring her with his grin.

And because there was still a fraction of the girl he knew buried under that dark exterior, she rose up to meet his challenge.

# IZZY

## CHAPTER 7

As Izzy peeled off her green leather jacket, she was grateful for something physical to keep her busy. She couldn't very well *stare* at him the entire time they were together.

Her mind had reeled at the sight of him. She thought of Jules back then—a small wiry boy as thin as a reed, with too-big teeth and a high-pitched voice. He was nearly two heads taller than she was and broad-shouldered. Strong in a way that came with hard, physical work. Hadn't he promised one day he'd catch up to her? Despite his appearance, the boy she'd known was still there. She was sure of it. Saw it in his kind smile, his flop of brown curls, and his brown eyes so dark that looking into them was like falling into a deep sea.

What she hadn't expected was her reaction. The way she'd hugged him after bloodying his nose was a bit mortifying. She didn't go around *flinging* herself at anyone. Fortunately, he'd been glad to see her. He'd remembered her, even after all those years.

Jules was the kind of handsome that made it hard for her to look at him for long. She'd tried to avert her gaze while in the shop, busying herself in a way that made her feel childish. She was eighteen. Besides, it was *Jules*. Julen Rakab. She repeated his name over and over in her thoughts as if to assert to herself that she hadn't conjured a mirage. How many times had she wished she could run away to find him, angry at her parents for separating her from her best friend? Of course, those feelings had faded over time. But Batuu was a place where the past lived right alongside the present. Jules was a huge part of her past, and now he was beside her—and she had no idea how to act.

Then she realized that taking him up on his offer to see the Outpost while she waited for Dok might not be the best idea. She wanted to. But being with him would come with questions. How could she even start to fill in the blanks of their lives apart? Could she look into her old friend's eyes and tell him everything she'd done since her parents had died? What would he think of her? Did she care? She shouldn't, but she couldn't help it. Still, when else would she return to Batuu?

Despite the rotten luck of his speeder malfunctioning, he didn't seem worried. And she'd been surprised when he removed his deep red canvas jacket and practically dared her to help. She wanted to ask about the scar on his left forearm, pearly and white against tawny brown skin. What she needed to do was push harder and stop staring at him.

So she pushed the speeder with all her strength and did her best to stare at the uneven road ahead of them, lined with sheets of rock covered in patches of moss and pale grass.

"I swear, it's like my speeder was waiting for this to happen. At least we're halfway to the person who can get it fixed," he said, his tone light despite the circumstance. If this had happened to her alone, she'd be furious. If she'd been with Damar, she'd have been better off just leaving the speeder and walking to her destination.

"Are there no tows in the Outpost?"

He considered this. "We could get a line from Savi and Son Salvage, but this early in the morning they're out combing through mountains of scrap metal. And if Salju is working on your ship, she'll be plugged in listening to that skies-awful music she broadcasts from Coruscant DJs. Tired already, Princess?"

Izzy glowered at the nickname. She snapped her head up to look at him, and he was positively grinning like a fool. "Don't call me that."

"If I recall," he grunted, "you used to demand that we address you as princess."

"That was before . . . I mean, only you and my father called me that." She cringed at the little girl she'd been—demanding and kind of rude. Her mother, when she'd been around, had not humored her. Somehow, her father and Jules had let her be who she was. Most people didn't get that luxury.

Though she missed her parents pretty much all the time, she didn't expect that a small detail from her past would make her miss them even more. She had no extended family she knew of, no friends who'd called to send their condolences. She'd mourned them alone. But Jules remembered them.

Jules began to speak, but a pedestrian caught up beside them.

"Bright suns, young Jules!" The old Quarren male dressed in a brightly colored tunic waved as they pushed the speeder along. "Do you need assistance?"

"Not today, Mako," Jules said, somehow flashing a genuine smile despite the sweat running down his temples. "We're nearly there."

Mako walked only a fraction faster than their sluggish pace. The tentacles that made up his chin had a fine layer of what looked like shimmering dust, and he carried some sort of pickax over his shoulder.

Two more beings walked by and offered help: one human woman with a heavy bundle over her shoulder and a bulbous-eyed Utai male. Jules declined on both accounts. A Dug on a low-riding speeder only stopped to mock them before taking off.

"Now there's that Batuuan hospitality I've heard so much about," Izzy said. Her arms were tired, so she turned around and pushed with her back, digging her boots into the ground. "I don't remember this many people ever talking to my family when we lived here."

Jules, still facing forward, glanced over at her. She could feel his eyes on her and blamed the suns for the heat on the tops of her cheeks. "Batuuans help each other. The ones who stay for years, at least. My dad used to say that it was the only way to survive. Together."

*Used to.* Perhaps it was because of her own past, but she latched on to the phrase. She looked up at Jules and straightened. She forced herself to look into his eyes and say, "I'm sorry."

He squinted against the clear skies and dusted off his hands. The speeder stalled ahead of them once again. "I'm sorry, too, Izzy."

"How did you know?"

"I didn't." He raked a hand through his soft mess of curls. "I had a feeling when I called you princess and you had this *look* about you. I figured you'd say something if you wanted to."

A moment of understanding passed between them, like dust settling, fog rolling back to reveal the road ahead. She never talked about what happened to her parents—not to Damar, not in the short-lived friendships she'd had before that. It didn't make sense that Jules could *guess* anything about her. By what? A feeling? Even she didn't feel like she knew herself or what she wanted half the time. She wanted to both revel in that and reject the idea that someone might know her so well.

Izzy settled for avoiding it altogether. They pushed the speeder the rest of the way to Salju, whose booted feet were sticking out from under the *Meridian*. Izzy blinked twice, panting as she tried to make sense of what she was seeing: a blue feline creature prowling toward the girl with something metallic in its mouth.

"Look out!" Izzy shouted, and abandoned Jules and his speeder to chase off the critter.

"Izzy, wait!" Jules sprinted after her, running ahead to block her path. "He won't hurt her."

Salju rolled out from beneath the underside of the *Meridian* and shoved her goggles up. A music player slipped from her pocket and rattled to the ground. "Oy, Kuma, where's that wrench?"

It was then that Izzy realized the creature was some sort of assistant or pet, or combination of both. It dropped the metal tool in Salju's outstretched hand, then slinked closer to Izzy. It had blue and green stripes, talons better suited for a bird, and stark gray eyes. With its back arched and teeth bared, it hissed at her.

"Kuma does not seem to like you very much," Salju noted, scratching her head with the wrench. She tucked it into her ponytail, then surveyed the two people standing before her. "I see you found your way easy enough, Izzy. Now *you* I haven't seen in a while." She saluted Jules with two fingers tapping on the side of her forehead.

"It finally happened, Sal." Jules wiped his brow with the back of his hand.

Salju winced when she saw the speeder behind them. "No! You just changed the left turbine engine."

"That's not it." Jules grimaced and patted the side of the speeder. "Can you take a look at it?"

Salju turned to Izzy, who already had a feeling what the mechanic was going to ask. "If Izzy here doesn't mind?"

"It's all right," she found herself saying. It surprised her. There was a disconnect between her reason and her instinct. Perhaps she'd spend time with him and the spell of nostalgia would show her that they had nothing in common and their memories were nothing but days gone by, and they'd go their separate ways. Or she'd have her friend back, if only for a day. When faced with the decision, she was willing to take that chance. Besides, she wasn't going anywhere until Dok-Ondar returned. "Jules needs the speeder for work. Can you fix it?"

Salju cracked her knuckles and said, "I've been known to work a mechanical miracle or two. Unless you two want to be pestered by my tooka here, I suggest you come back in an hour."

Izzy looked at Jules, who had somehow subdued the furry creature. It nuzzled into his arms and purred, wagging its fat, short tail.

"He likes Jules enough," Izzy said.

Salju rested her elbow on Izzy's shoulder and winked suggestively. "Jules is easy to like."

Izzy wanted to be offended by that, but had to reluctantly agree. She handed Salju her deposit.

"Sal's animals have always been drawn to me," Jules said. "I think it's my hair. It reminds them of a nest. Now, how about that breakfast?"

Izzy's gut squeezed when he smiled at her. Maybe she was hungry. Definitely hungry. Jules stood, and the tooka wove around his ankles. She formulated a new plan: devour much-needed food, see the Outpost with her long-lost friend, return to Dok's, collect her money, and leave the past where it belonged.

# JULES

They folded into the foot traffic leading to docking bay seven, carrying their heavy packs. As much as he wanted to trust Salju, he knew better than to leave a parcel anywhere it could be snatched. He'd learned to spot pickpockets after the first time he'd been robbed while buying thread for Belen. The day's crowd was quiet, and he sensed the dwindling clientele all over the Outpost by how much louder the vendors became, trying to lure passersby into spilling their credits.

Normally, Jules liked gawking—discreetly of course—at the new arrivals in the Outpost. He could usually tell them apart because they craned their necks at the spires and stalls as they walked, their attention bouncing from sound to sight. It filled him with a sense of pride when off-worlders found something about Batuu to love. He hoped Izzy would feel that way.

She kept an easy pace beside him, though he found himself slowing down to let her eyes roam the eroded sides of buildings laced with green vines, the couples sitting on stone steps sharing mugs of spiced tea.

He stopped in front of a tall tree. He'd taken

a slightly longer route, but the look on her face was worth it.

"What is this?" Izzy asked, reaching for the closest branch. Around the slender wood were dozens of ribbons and scraps of cloth. They ornamented the tree, tied any place there was available bark. The loose ends moved in the wind like leaves.

"It's the wishing tree," he said. "You take a piece of string or cloth or whatever you want and tie it up here. When it breaks off by itself, your wish has been granted."

As soon as he said it, he could imagine what he must sound like—a boy from a small outpost who'd never left home and believed in magic.

"Has it ever worked?" she asked him.

He'd come to the wishing tree once and tied a blue strip of Belen's yarn around a branch. There was no way he could tell if it was still there, because there was yarn tied in every color. Besides, the tree had grown right along with him. But his wish had been simple. He couldn't even meet her gaze as he said, "Yes, but it took a long time."

The look on her face was skeptical, but that didn't stop her from digging into her pockets for a string. She came up empty. She touched the cord around her neck but seemed to decide against it. There was a string coming loose from the side of his tunic, and he pulled it, snapped it off, and handed it to her.

She pushed up onto her toes, as high as she could reach, and added her wish to the tree.

"What did you wish for?" he asked.

She bit her bottom lip and shrugged. He could already see the lie forming on her lips before she said, "Food."

"We're close to Cookie's," Jules said. "He's new to these parts. Downright mean, always angry. You might understand."

"I'm not always angry!" she shouted indignantly.

But she was. It clung to her in small moments, like stubborn clouds drifting slowly across the suns. Anger was the hardest thing to let go of, other than love. He'd seen his mother go through it. After his father died, she'd succumbed to a deep sorrow. The same woman who'd taught him to dream became someone who cursed the sky. Jules had hoped he and Belen could love their mother enough to make up for the loss they all felt, but it never quite worked. He didn't want the same for Izzy. She wasn't his to fix. He didn't wish that on Izzy. But maybe he could help if she let him.

He began walking away from the wishing tree and back into the road, giving the right of way to a skittish eopie loaded with luggage, a little girl riding atop while her mother led the creature.

"I have a deviated septum that says otherwise. But you're certainly not the same giddy little girl who used to chase me around."

"If anyone chased anyone, it was you chasing me," she corrected him.

They entered the hangar at docking bay seven, where a ship converted to serve as a traveling restaurant was stationed. Jules waved at those he was acquainted with, like the Xexto mechanic who'd fixed Belen's cleaner droid and off-duty human bartenders from Oga's. He made straight for the grill counter. That early, there was no one to help Cookie serve the tables, and in the short time he'd known the Artiodac, Jules had learned that the easier he made Cookie's life, the better service he'd get.

"You should have seen how packed this place was when he first arrived," Jules told Izzy. "I might have snuck off work early just to get an order of fried Endorian tip-yip or seven."

"Beats the nutrient packs I've been living off." She took a seat beside him and swiveled until they were face to face. He noticed four black freckles clustered on her cheek.

Something about being so close to her all of a sudden made him feel like a vise was around his insides. He had to look away, turning to the lively tables in the hangar below them. Two humans and a masked Kel

Dor were minutes from a food fight over a game of dice. Beside them a group of purple-skinned aliens with large eyes shoveled food into their wide mouths like it was a last meal. They were probably going to the market soon to open a stall. He tried to see if Volt was in the order queue, his bald head easy to spot. Jules wondered if he'd be too hungover to show up to his shift at the creature stall. Hell, maybe even Dok had snuck away to go to Cookie's.

"What's moof juice?" Izzy asked.

Jules smiled widely and shrugged. "Sometimes I don't ask. I just order and hope for the best."

"This coming from the boy who could survive on popped grain for days." Izzy watched him in a way that made him fidget.

"Well, I'm not afraid of heights anymore, either," he said. "Especially after our last scramble down that cliff." He wanted to ask what happened after that night when her family had taken off, but there was something so guarded about her. He didn't want to scare her away by saying the wrong thing.

"How'd you end up at Dok's?" she asked. "Last I was here you were starting at one of the vegetable farms."

"For a year. Then there was the fire."

"Fire?"

He picked at the frayed menu and leaned on the countertop. "The year after you left there was a drought. The brush caught fire and spread through the forest and our homes. We got out. Da, being Da, ran back and made sure everyone was safe, but he inhaled too much smoke."

"You don't have to talk about it," she said softly.

"It's all right, Izzy," Jules assured her. He felt good remembering them whenever he could. "My parents never talked about where their people came from before settling on Batuu, but one of their rituals was remembering the dead to keep them alive. Ma went two years ago from a virus that swept the Outpost."

Izzy listened, once again toying with the pendant she kept under her shirt, like a secret. "Then tell me."

"After Da passed, I got a job with Dok. Belen and Ma never liked it. I got beat up a lot. You would have done great here if you'd stayed."

She wrapped her hand around his bicep and playfully shoved. "I'm sorry I punched you. Will I ever live it down?"

That feeling around his insides tightened when she touched him, but he forced himself to focus. "Belen got me a job at Kat Saka's farm, but I was restless. I almost enlisted in the New Republic Academy when practically all the kids my age left."

"What stopped you?"

Nothing had stopped him. Or perhaps everything had. He'd wanted to leave for so long, but when the opportunity lay in front of him, he simply returned to his routine. Every time. At first it had been his mother getting sick. Then he couldn't leave Belen. Then Kat Saka had implored him to stay on for another season because business was booming. Then? Haal's words cycled through his mind once again. There was nothing anchoring him to that world anymore. Was there?

"It never felt right." He wanted to impress her. He wanted to let her know that there was possibility in his future. "What about you?"

"There's not much to tell." Izzy busied herself with the single-sided menu frayed at the corners. She tucked her hair behind her ear, exposing a metal cuff.

"Oh, come on. When we were kids you wanted to be a senator of a planet you called Ata Walpa and give the citizens all-you-can-eat puffed candies and no bedtimes."

When Izzy laughed, really laughed, her eyes crinkled at the corners and she clutched her stomach. It was only for a moment, but the pride he felt eliciting that kind of joyful reaction from her—well, it was something he was not supposed to feel so quickly, and he wanted to do it again all the same.

As some of the only children running around their community all those years before, they'd been bonded by sheer default. They cared for each other while their families were at work. They made up entire worlds to discover. Part of him missed how easy it was to make plans when there were no ramifications or expectations or possibilities of failure. He wondered if that was why it had been so difficult for him to decide what his life would be after quitting Kat's farm. Izzy, by the force of her presence, reminded him of the kids they used to be, the kids who used to climb up spires, run across fields, laugh until it hurt.

"I'm a long way from politics," she said, worrying at her bottom lip.

"What trouble are you getting yourself into?"

"Why do you assume I'm involved in something bad?"

"I'm born and raised here, remember? I can spot a potentially bad deal from a mile away."

"Is that so?" She pursed her mouth into a challenge he would have given anything to meet. "Let's have a look around, shall we? That group over there. What do you suppose his deal is?"

Jules leaned in closer to her, and a stray lock of her hair tickled his cheek. "See, I have an unfair advantage here because I happen to know Schelhorn's crew. They carry wood shipments for the Wooden Wookiee."

"Fine, who *don't* you know then, if you're so good at reading people?"

Jules spun in his seat and surveyed the tables dotting the hangar like a mess hall. A severe-looking group clad in black lingered at the hangar entrance. Izzy seemed to notice them just when Jules did.

"They're here to recruit," Jules said, careful not to point at them. "But anyone could tell that."

"That explains it," Izzy murmured.

"Explains what?"

"I got lost and ran into a stormtrooper earlier."

Jules's eyes widened, and it dawned on him that was why she was nearly beating down Dok's door.

"I've got nothing to hide," she said quickly, almost too defensively. "I've never seen one in person before. Do they have to look so—"

"Creepy?" they said together.

They were drawing closer, as if their whispers could only carry as far as the bubble around them.

"When they first arrived they stayed put, but they've taken—liberties—with their presence."

"Can they do that?" Izzy asked.

"Doesn't matter if they can, they still do," Jules said. "My sister's been pulling extra hours on Kat's farm because half her crew picked up and enlisted. I'm surprised any of the First Order would even want to eat here out of fear of being poisoned."

When Izzy frowned, that tiny worry mark between her brows was accentuated. "Why's that?"

Cookie still had his back turned to them, smooshing some kind of meat patties with a large spatula. Juices sizzled on the hot grill, and voices rose around them with lively conversations about fuel prices and the chaos on Toledian after a mining accident destroyed its main city. Normally, Jules would have eavesdropped on every bit of information he could about the galaxy, but for the moment Izal Garsea was a thousand worlds in a single person.

Jules cleared his throat. "Cookie doesn't like to talk about them."

Hearing his name, the great Artiodac chef stomped around to face them. Cookie's arms were two sizes—one meaty and long, the other thinner and shorter. How he fit behind that grill comfortably was a mystery to all, but it was where he looked the calmest. He wielded his spatula on his shorter side.

"Cookie doesn't like to talk about *who*?" he asked in heavily accented Basic.

"Cook!" Jules said, not allowing room for explanation. "I brought you a new customer. This is Izzy Garsea—an old friend."

Cookie peered at the girl, who stuck out her hand. Jules was half certain Cookie was going to slap it away with his spatula, so he was as surprised as anyone around them when the large, gray-skinned hand closed around hers. He muttered a greeting.

"Old friend, huh?" he said. Then his bulbous eyes went to the black-clad group at the door. The officers seemed to stand straighter out of sheer discomfort, their noses tilted to the sky as if trying to get as far from the ground as possible. They did not enter the hangar. "First Order *scum*. The nerve to show up here. How far in the galaxy do I have to go to get away from them?"

Izzy leaned forward with deceptively doe-like eyes. Jules had seen her use that look when she wanted something from her father. "I might regret asking this, Cookie, but what did they do to you?"

Cookie turned, stomping heavy feet as if he was locked in a box. Jules was briefly worried the chef would destroy his own grill counter in a fit and then fry up steaks on the embers that remained.

"They blew up the last place I worked. Maz Kanata's castle." He growled in the back of his throat, a forlorn look in his eyes. "Shame. Such a shame. That's why I took my show on the road. Lucky for you lot."

Jules had heard the story so many times from Cookie, he could nearly recite it. The First Order had come to his world, chasing the Resistance that people whispered more and more about these days. Instead of listening to Cookie, Jules watched Izzy's facial expressions. Her eyes widened and she gasped at the right moments.

"That's awful," she told him.

"I make do," Cookie said, his voice dialing back to conversational. "Business is good. What'll you be having?"

Izzy didn't even glance down at the menu again. "Surprise me. I'm sure it'll be great."

Cookie seemed to like that. His wide mouth made a strange movement. Jules thought Cookie looked as though he was in pain, but then he realized that was what must pass for a smile.

As their chef milled back to his grill, Jules couldn't help staring at Izzy.

"What?" she asked.

"I'm just imagining you charming your way around the galaxy." He'd meant it to be a compliment, and yet there was a flash of sadness on her face. He wanted to take it back. It had only been a matter of time before he said something wrong. But a moment later she shook it off, then turned back to the hangar and pointed at a young Togruta and a human boy with brown skin and hair buzzed close to the scalp.

"What about them?" she said, resuming their game. "Do you know their story?"

"Oh, I don't know," he said thoughtfully. "Those two are a very dangerous sort."

Izzy tilted her head to the side and made an incredulous face. "Really?"

Jules could hardly keep his laughter back as he said, "Pirates. Will rob old women of their spectacles if they can. I'd wager they're on the Doklist and everything."

As if sensing he was being stared at, the Togruta lifted his head and his face broke into a lazy smile that was anything but dangerous. The pair shouted his name.

"You're trying to trick me, Julen Rakab."

He grinned. "Is it working?"

"Not one bit."

"Jules!" The Togruta ran over to him. "Good to see you, mate."

"Izzy, this is Neelo and Fawn. They're playing at Oga's tonight."

The Togruta, Neelo, wore a black tunic and had modified markings on his arms. He grabbed Jules by his shoulders and squeezed. "You're coming, right? We need you to be there and bring people. Have to show Oga we've got the goods."

"We go on after Rex," the human boy named Fawn said, his voice deep and naturally monotone. "Bring your friend."

"Me?" Izzy said, pointing at herself. "I can't."

Jules felt a hard pang of disappointment. Of course, he knew she wasn't going to be there for long. She was going to deliver whatever Dok had ordered, and then she'd be gone. He wondered if he'd miss her more or less the second time around.

"Bummer," Neelo said, but held out his fist to Jules.

Voices soared like a gathering of bees moving through the crowd as a new crowd entered the hangar from the courtyard. Dishes were doled out faster and faster, and Cookie slid two glasses of cold moof juice in front of them on the house on top of their order. Jules never got free things.

"I'll be right back," Izzy said, standing so abruptly she almost tripped. He caught her by the arm, and she turned around.

"What's wrong?" he asked.

"Nothing," she said, her voice climbing in pitch. He detected the lie, but who was he to press? An old friend? She didn't owe him anything, not even an explanation. Still, he worried. "I have to call my boss. I should have done it before but—I'll be *right* back."

She gave him a strained smile, and Neelo and Fawn stepped aside to let her pass. Keeping her head down, she folded into the crowd. Could she be on the run from someone? There were no stormtroopers, and she hadn't reacted that way to seeing the First Order officers at the door. The dice players were gone, but there were new arrivals—a crew Jules had never seen before. One was a tall human boy with blue hair combed back with glossy product. He whispered something to his companion, a young woman around the same age as Jules, perhaps older, with a bright red braid that hung over her shoulder like rope.

"I smell trouble," Neelo said, taking Izzy's empty seat. He snatched Jules's moof juice and drank.

"Trouble can be fun," Fawn said, shrugging in that easy way of his.

Jules realized his friends were talking about him. And Izzy. "It's not what you think."

"I don't think you know what we think," Neelo said, wiping his lips with the back of his sleeve. "Are you going to eat these?"

"Yes," Jules said, but knew Neelo was going to help himself to his friend's tip-yip anyway. The only reason he didn't complain was because he knew they'd had a hard time booking gigs after the Outpost crowds had dwindled. And because he was, in part, watching and waiting for Izzy to return.

"Spit it out," Jules said. Before Neelo took him literally, he explained, "Say what you're thinking."

"I can already see your heartbreak coming from ten klicks away," Fawn said, nodding his head to a beat only he seemed to be able to hear.

Neelo washed the tip-yip down with the rest of Jules's drink. "You always do this, mate. You trip over off-worlders who leave you in the dust."

Jules didn't have to listen to that, but he sat there anyway. "Name one ex—"

"Fawn's cousin visiting from Coruscant three years ago," Neelo said, starting to count on his fingers.

"I genuinely liked her music," Jules shrugged.

"The smuggler from Onderon," Fawn said, cocking an eyebrow. "Jali—"

Jules rubbed his hands across his face, then winced when he pressed too hard on his nose. "Anjali. And I was just giving her directions."

"Yeah, to your safe," Neelo snorted.

"That's enough," Jules said. It was difficult to relive his own bad decisions, but his friends were mirrors he could not escape.

"Don't forget that senator's daughter from Naboo."

How could he forget? If he recalled correctly, they'd run out of fuel and stopped on Batuu for what amounted to hours. Jules had been working the stall for Kat, and the senator's daughter wanted to buy the colorful popped grains. He'd been so taken by her beauty, the glamour of her bronze dress and the way her ropes of dark hair were braided. He had been sure that it was love at first sight—so sure, in fact, that he'd forgotten to charge her. He'd needed to work extra hours to repay Kat for the sale. He never got her name.

"You're all making me sound like a lovesick idiot," Jules said.

ZORAIDA CÓRDOVA

Neelo and Fawn traded looks that said it was exactly what they thought of him.

"It's not like that," he explained. Putting the words together meant admitting things he wasn't ready to. Instead, he said, "Izzy was my first friend. She used to live next door to me. Yeah, it was a long time ago, but you don't forget someone you used to spend every day with."

"I don't remember her," Fawn said.

"Her family left before you two came here. It doesn't matter. I haven't seen her since and I'm showing her around the Outpost. That's it."

Neelo nodded along to his words. "You say that, but you haven't stopped looking at the entrance since she left."

"You didn't take her to the wishing tree, did you?" Fawn winced.

Jules wanted to ask Cookie to beat him senseless with that tip-yip-covered spatula. "I won't say that I did."

"He totally did!" Neelo laughed.

"Look, you're going to do the *Jules* thing," Fawn said.

"What does that even mean?" he asked incredulously.

"You know. The gestures and honesty. That's who you are. Just look after yourself once in a while."

Jules knew, deep down, that they were right. As

they prepared to leave, he met their extended hands for a quick good-bye.

"Good runs, mate. And don't forget about the show," Neelo reminded him.

"I'll be there," Jules shouted to them across the hangar.

He picked up a piece of fried tip-yip and dipped it into the fiery sauce that came with it. He glanced at Izzy's empty seat, then the entrance once again. He couldn't shake the feeling that something had scared her. She'd taken her pack. What if she needed help?

He got up, ready to go look for her, but then thought about what his friends had said and forced himself back into his seat. He had to trust that the Force itself had brought them together that day. And he had to trust that if she wanted to return on her own, she would.

But then minutes had crawled by and he'd finished his entire plate, and there was still no sign of Izzy Garsea.

# IZZY

She muttered a string of curses as she walked away from Jules and his friends. Her entire body flashed hot with rage, then sadness, then back to anger. Out of all the planets in the galaxy, Ana Tolla and her crew had to be on Batuu. Izzy wanted to find a plot to bury her own body in. She couldn't see them again. She crept along the greasy walls of the hangar, keeping her head down. She'd always wanted a cloak, and in that moment it would have been useful for hiding herself as she stepped out into the courtyard.

She wasn't going to leave Jules, but she needed to breathe. What were they doing there? She thought of the job they'd left to do the night before. Had they been on Batuu all along, or stopped somewhere else on the way?

"It doesn't matter," she muttered to herself. "They're here and they can't know *you're* here."

The last thing she wanted was for Damar to think she had been *following* him. She felt queasy at the thought of him, the way she'd let him whisper stupid promises in her ear. She hated what her morning with Jules was turning into because she was a coward and decided to hide.

She climbed into a bricked-in courtyard and pressed her body against a tree when she noticed Neelo and Fawn leaving the hangar.

Then a hand clapped over her mouth and pulled her into the dark shadow between the wall and the tree trunk. Izzy threw her elbow back and reached for her blaster.

"Easy," came a familiar voice, and the hand released her.

Izzy whirled around to face Ana Tolla, whose red rope of hair rested over her shoulder like a serpent. Izzy kept her hands at her sides, where she could best grab her blaster. Though Ana Tolla kept her arms raised showing she meant no harm, Izzy wasn't ready to let her guard down.

"What do you want?"

"I'd wondered if you'd seen us," Ana Tolla said. She leaned casually against the wall and smirked. "You didn't have to hide."

"I'm not hiding," Izzy said, hating how petulant she sounded. Of course she was hiding. "You just happen to be the last faces in the galaxy I want to see."

Ana Tolla glanced down at her nails. "That's not how Damar tells it."

"What do you want?" Izzy asked again, indignant.

"About a million credits and a small moon where I can work on my tan," she said, then chuckled darkly. "But for now, I want to know why you followed us here. No one knew my instructions, unless of course you want to tell me if someone in my crew felt sympathetic enough to give you their location."

"You mean Damar? Please." Izzy scoffed. "I'm here on my own business."

Ana raised a thin red brow. "I'm sorry about how things went down. You were—well, you had your uses, but you don't have what it takes for this line of work."

"You went out of your way to come and insult me," Izzy said. She walked her fingers through the air. "Feel free to keep moving as far away from me as possible."

"I went out of my way to ask for a truce."

"Rest assured, I didn't come here looking for you."

"I know that at least. Your self-preservation skills rival my own."

Izzy wanted to scream. "I'm nothing like you."

"You'd be better off if you were," Ana Tolla purred. "Do we have an agreement? Stay out of my way and I'll stay out of yours."

Izzy glanced at the people walking past them. It was so easy to go unseen around that place. No one seemed to spare a second glance for the two young women in the shadows.

"I don't care what you do or why you're here," Izzy said, steel in her words.

"That farm boy you were with. What's his story?"

Izzy's body flashed hot. "Why?"

Ana's sharp eyebrows arched. She crossed her arms and had the nerve to look bored. "Curiosity."

She'd been around the crew leader long enough to know that Ana Tolla never took interest in someone lightly. She had a motive behind everything. Ana could keep Damar. But Jules—he was off the table. It took all Izzy's strength to swallow the anger that burned through her. She knew she couldn't stop Ana Tolla and the others from doing their job, but she could make Jules sound less appealing to them.

"He's just a stupid farm boy who's never going to get off this rock," Izzy said, hating the words even as she spoke them. "He's no one."

"You came all this way to tumble a farm boy?" Ana Tolla said, needling her. "Damar really isn't worth all that."

This time, Izzy flashed a smile she'd seen her mother give—one that dared someone to fight her. "Stay out of my way and I'll stay out of yours."

"Maybe I was wrong about you, Izzy." Ana Tolla

pushed herself off the wall and shouldered past. "Though I hope our paths never cross again, for your sake."

Izzy pressed her hands on the trunk of the tree until she stopped shaking. If Ana Tolla was on Batuu, it couldn't mean anything good. *You don't have what it takes for this line of work.* The happy reunion with Jules had to be cut short. Her own disappointment shouldn't have surprised her. But her fear of running into Ana Tolla again was stronger. Izzy had to get off-world and as far away as possible. She'd have to make up an excuse to Jules and hope he'd understand. After a few moments, she returned to Cookie's. Ana Tolla and the others were gone. *Good,* she thought.

She spotted Jules chatting with the chef. Slowly, she made her way back to him, going over how she'd say good-bye this time. Her heart gave a painful squeeze at every idea. But she knew it was for the best.

*The best for who?* She thought. *Jules or you?* He wouldn't care. He had a good life. Izzy was just another straggler passing through. He'd forget her in a few days' time.

*It's been thirteen years, and he still remembered you,* her restless mind answered.

"Hey," she said, and when he turned to face her, she could swear he looked relieved. It felt good to know that he cared about what happened to her.

"How goes, Izzy?"

His smile shouldn't wreck her so badly. A part of her wanted to reach out and twirl a finger in an errant curl that flopped over his forehead. She wanted to rest a hand on his broad shoulder and—what? Congratulate him?

*You came all this way to tumble a farm boy?* Curse Ana Tolla for putting that thought in her head. Though she'd be lying if she said it hadn't crossed her mind already, if just for a flash.

Before she could blurt out her string of excuses, Cookie came up to the counter in front of them.

"You haven't eaten your tip-yip," he said in a low grumble.

She picked up a piece of the flaky fried meat and dipped it in the red sauce. It was delicious, even cold. She realized she'd hardly eaten since the day before. Satisfied with her reaction, Cookie moved on to another customer trying to grab his attention. She owed Jules an explanation. Something.

He watched her patiently. Maybe it was the food or the warmth radiating from the grill, but she felt settled once again. No, when she finished consuming her meal and looked up at him, she knew it was being with Jules that calmed her. She dragged out the moment and let herself sink into the easy comfort of his presence. He evoked soft, beautiful lines. She felt like blaster fire and chaos, even if the chaos was all in her head.

That made it all the more difficult to say, "I have to go."

He stuck out a thumb toward the entrance of the hangar. "The restrooms are past the courtyard."

"I meant leave," she said, biting back the laugh. "I have to go to Dok's and drop this off."

He leaned on the counter and moved closer to her. She was suddenly very thirsty and grabbed for the moof juice. It was pleasantly sweet and creamy.

"What are you running from, Izzy?" he asked.

She wasn't prepared for his dark eyes to be so intense. But she squared her shoulders and shoved her doubt deep down where it couldn't resurface. "My boss needs me. This parcel isn't going to deliver itself."

"Lie." He wagged a finger at her, his grin a bit smug. "I'm glad I can still tell when you're lying."

Izzy was affronted, mostly because she didn't think she was so transparent. She'd cultivated her lies throughout the years, learned how to calm the pitch of her voice when she was in trouble. She was a solid pilot and an average shot, but until that moment she'd considered herself a *great* liar.

"I'm insulted," she said.

"*I'm* insulted that you think I wouldn't know." He leaned on his elbow. Though he wasn't angry, a fraction of hurt crossed his eyes. She didn't want to put that there. "You don't have to tell me, but I'm not here to judge you, Izzy."

Why was he so infuriatingly patient? It would be easier to walk away from him if he was—more like Damar.

Izzy inhaled deeply, then relented. "I saw someone I recognized."

"Bad breakup? Wait, no. A bookie. Your old professor who gave you demerits. Don't tell me, I'm great at this game."

None of it was funny, and yet she couldn't help laughing.

"I can keep going."

"You can stop because you already guessed it."

His brown eyes searched her face. "Professor?"

"Bad breakup. Pretty much the worst one of my life." Not that she had much experience in that department. She'd had a boyfriend in her Galactic Politics course when she'd been at the academy, before she'd dropped out. But that had ended when she'd met his parents, who didn't care for an orphan girl with no social standing or any aspirations of become a politician's wife.

"Huh," Jules said. He crossed and uncrossed his arms, avoiding direct eye contact. It was endearing watching him try to keep his calm. It was the most reserved and quiet he'd been all morning, which meant that he was teeming with questions. "I guess I really am great at this game."

"It caught me off guard."

His knee bounced in place as he scanned the hangar's late breakfast crowd. "Is he trying to win you back?"

"He's definitely not here to win me back."

"Then he's an idiot." He finally smiled again.

If she didn't know any better, she'd think he was jealous. She wanted to reach out to him just then but kept her hands firmly on her own knees.

"I'm curious, Izzy," he said. "Why else would you both have ended up in the same outpost if he wasn't looking for you?"

"He's with my old crew. I wasn't privy to the job they're working, though."

"Wait," he said. "Is that why you came here? Running away?"

"No! I'm doing exactly what I came here to do. Deliver a package, get paid, and get out."

There was that hurt look again. She regretted it the instant she said it, but it was too late to take back. She cut her gaze to a small boy at the other end of the hangar chasing a feathered creature and shouting, "Here, tip-yip!" At least Cookie's food was fresh, she thought, before turning back to Jules. As much as she hated to be the cause of that wounded look that had flashed across his face, she didn't want to stick around and run into Ana Tolla's crew again. Then she had a thought. . . . No, he'd never do it. Would he?

"Come with me," she said.

It was worth it to see his lips part from utter surprise. "What?"

"You said you wanted to leave. I can take you anywhere," she said, her skin growing hot as she spoke. She quickly remembered that her ship had only one cabin, because the other was full of junk to keep the cargo bay clear. *Tumble. Farm boy.* She needed to stop those thoughts. How had they gone from talking about their childhood to this?

"I can't," he said.

Her relief rivaled her disillusionment. Of course, she didn't think he would actually do it. She thought of the little boy he'd been, playing with rocks and calling them ships. The boy who never left. There was something keeping Jules on Batuu, and she wished to know what. Would he tell her?

"It was just a silly thought. Forget I said it." She gulped the rest of her drink.

"It's forgotten. Come. I'll walk you back."

They paid and bid Cookie good-bye. As they stepped into the sunny morning, she shielded her eyes with her palm. Jules pulled the white-and-blue scarf from his neck and offered it to her. It felt like a peace offering, and she draped it over her head, then threw one end over her shoulder.

The scarf itself had a sweet scent, like sharp grass and nectar and something uniquely Jules. She had never given a second thought to what anyone smelled like, except "pleasant" or "unbearable." She couldn't even think of what Damar smelled like. The chemicals of his hair product, perhaps. Why was Jules different?

*You know why, stupid,* she thought as they walked the uneven path back to the filling station.

Jules had turned down her offer. The crew that had abandoned her not a full day before was too close for her to relax. Part of her wanted to crawl into her quarters on the *Meridian* and hide. But why should she be the one to hide? She hadn't done anything except trust the wrong person. She was stronger than this. She had to be.

"You know, I could send someone to take care of him," Jules said. "Just say the word. Oga's is always filled with guns for hire, or we could take a stroll through Smuggler's Alley."

She barked a laugh. "I know we haven't seen each other in a long time, but I highly doubt that you're capable of having someone murdered."

He grinned and somehow managed to look innocent despite the subject matter. "I never said anything about murder. I'm saying one of Bina's shipments of juniper bugs could wind up in his bed. They're not carnivorous, but they itch like crazy."

She shook her head but brushed her shoulder against his. "That's what I get for not listening to my mother."

"What did your mother say?" Jules asked.

She could feel the heat of his stare, but she wasn't ready to look into his eyes just yet. Izzy ran her fingers along the soft edge of the scarf. "She told me the only person you can trust is yourself."

He frowned. "That's a lonely way to live, Izzy."

"What would you know about it?"

"I know that one scoundrel isn't worth rejecting the trust of the entire galaxy. Trust is a skill, and if you only have it in yourself then you aren't even trying."

"You don't know what happened," she snapped.

"You could tell me," Jules said softly, moving a wooden ornament that hung from a canopy so he wouldn't hit his head. Why couldn't he snap back at her? Why did she think the answer to everything was yelling?

She was turned around again. Every pathway in Black Spire Outpost seemed to bleed into the next, and she couldn't quite get her bearings. Every petrified tree looked like the last. She was thankful that Jules was by her side, or she'd end up in another dead end facing down a trooper. *You trust Jules,* she tried to reason with herself. But her mother had taught her a terrible thing—how to be stubborn.

"So, if you got food poisoning from Cookie's, you would just go back for seconds because you trusted it wouldn't happen again?"

He gasped, feigning a wound. "You take that back."

"See?" She began turning toward an archway.

"I see no such thing, Izzy Garsea." He tugged on her sleeve and sent her in the right direction, down an alley that smelled of dye and soap. "Those two situations have nothing to do with each other. One is food and the other is love, though I would argue that they are one and the same."

"You're just avoiding saying that I'm right."

"Wrong," Jules said, mussing his soft brown curls with frustration. "If I got food poisoning at Cookie's— may the spires forbid it—I wouldn't starve myself because I was afraid of getting sick again. Everyone's got to eat."

Izzy wanted to deny that she had ever loved Damar. But wasn't that why she was so furious at his abandonment? She found that the heaviness in her chest had everything to do with what she wasn't saying.

So, she told Jules about the day before and how Damar had left her in the middle of a brawl. She left out the part about it being her birthday because it made her feel childish.

He was silent, his hands balled into fists. His strong jaw was set hard, the muscles there tense.

*I've done it*, she thought as she watched his anger spark. *I've upset Jules Rakab*.

"My original offer still stands," he finally said.

"I don't need anyone to fight my battles for me, Jules. Besides, I'm fine. Tell me about Belen."

She reached for his hand, and his fist softened at her touch. His fingers were calloused and warm. He had strong hands that came from a lifetime of hard work. She forced herself to let go, even though she only wanted to hold on tighter.

He spoke of his sister and brother-in-law and their small shared flat. He seemed so grounded, like he belonged there. Passersby and vendors called out his name. They brightened at the sight of him. If her parents had never taken her from Batuu, how would their friendship have changed? Would they have survived the fire? The virus? Would she and Jules be closer, or would they have grown apart the way some friends were fated to do? She wanted to believe that the need to be among the stars was so embedded in her bones that she would have left eventually. Maybe he would have left with her.

When they got to the filling station, Salju had finished with his speeder and was back to working on the *Meridian*. She wiped her hands on a rag, and by the peculiar look on her face, Izzy imagined it was bad news.

"You won't believe this, Jules," Salju said, "but it's running just fine. I reset the dash, tinkered with the engines, and took a spin around the Outpost. Whatever happened must have been a glitch."

"A glitch?" Izzy repeated it as a question. Her arm muscles were starting to feel the entire hour they'd pushed the speeder.

Worse was Jules laughing as he pulled a tip-yip morsel from his pocket and bent down to offer it to the feral tooka cat that was yowling at her feet.

"I'll have my comlink close if you break down again," Salju said, taking off her goggles. They left an outline of grime on her forehead. "But like I said, it's in working order. Now if you'll excuse me, I have to get back to our lovely guest's ship."

"I'll give you a lift back to Dok's," Jules said. "It's on my way."

Izzy had walked a lot of the Outpost, and she suspected that he was exaggerating how "on the way" it was. She accepted anyway and threw her backpack into the cockpit. Jules brushed his hand across the dashboard and tuned in to a broadcast. A droid's voice came through: "This is Deejay Ar-three-ex spinning the galaxy's latest hits. Here is 'Black Spire Harvest' by Mus Kat & Nalpak, playing at Oga's Cantina tonight only."

"Is this where Neelo and Fawn are playing?" she asked, and Jules flashed a smile as he turned up the volume. She wanted to memorize his smile before she left.

When he dropped her off behind Dok's, he hopped out to say good-bye.

"It was good to see you, Jules." She offered his scarf back, but he shook his head.

"Borrow it," he said. "Maybe you'll have a reason to come back."

She didn't want to make another promise she wouldn't be able to keep. Instead she hugged him. Everything about him was solid, like an anchor—grounded as the rock formations around them. She closed her eyes and told herself that she was doing the right thing. She'd have to leave sooner or later. Jules belonged there; he just didn't know it yet. Where would she belong?

As always, she'd figure it out. But first she had to get out of their embrace.

"May the spires keep you, Izzy," he whispered in her ear, then let go.

She didn't know what that meant, but she was certain it was some sort of good-bye. She reached into the cockpit and grabbed her rucksack, then watched Jules drive away.

# JULES

## CHAPTER 9

Jules glanced over his shoulder only once. Izzy wasn't looking back at him as she entered Dok's den. When he was far enough down the road, he let the past couple of hours with Izzy sink in, and let out a frustrated scream. She'd asked him to leave with her. Izal Garsea had virtually asked him to run away with her. *Come with me*. There was a moment when he was going to say yes. When would he get another opportunity like that? But the fear came out of nowhere. What if they hated each other after that day? If there were any doubts, he couldn't take the risk. So like the ever-loving fool he was, he'd said no.

He was right to say no. She hadn't meant it. She was upset after seeing her old crew, her old . . . He wasn't sure he'd ever felt so irrationally, ridiculously jealous. Jules had known terrible people in the Outpost—criminals and gang members who might sell their own families for a payday—but he couldn't fathom the idea of leaving someone behind. Someone you were supposed to care about.

And yet, wasn't that what Izzy and Jules had just done—leave each other behind?

He punched his steering wheel and nearly swerved

into a woman herding a horned ikopi. Shouting an apology, Jules focused on the road.

He was right to say no. Wasn't he? If he'd left with her, he would have been taking advantage of her while she was lonely. What would he have told Belen? Not to mention everything he would be leaving behind. He hadn't figured out what he wanted to do yet. Words popped into his mind—*investments, family, the future.*

Then, a terrifying thought: After all those years, they'd found each other again. What if Izzy had offered him a future and he'd just turned it down. Not a future *with* her but a start at the adventure he'd always dreamed of. Say he had taken her up—on an offer he was sure she didn't mean—then where would he go? He had only ever lived on Batuu. What if he couldn't cut it off-world? Maybe Haal had been right about Jules never leaving the Outpost.

One consolation was that his speeder was gliding like new. Though Salju could fix anything in a way he'd never seen from anyone before, Jules marveled at the idea that there had been nothing wrong with it. How could that be a coincidence? He returned to his theory of fate. Had it simply stopped working to get Izzy and Jules into Cookie's at the exact moment that her old crew would be there? If his mind kept spinning, it would glitch like his speeder.

Izzy had made a decision to leave, and he couldn't

follow. He decided to take the long way to Hondo's to clear his head. It was a rare day when the sky was clear enough to see all three suns. Without his scarf he enjoyed the heat on his back. Black Spire Outpost looked different when the suns illuminated the spires and wild trees around them. Ruins of days long gone hugged the newer edifices. Jules had always liked that about his homeworld. Unlike people in other places he'd heard of in the galaxy who destroyed all remnants of their past, the people of BSO lived alongside their history, on top of it, within it. It was the best way to know where you came from. His father used to tell him stories about the ancients. Everyone had their own ideas of what they'd looked like, who they were, to the point that they were nothing but bedtime stories anymore.

As he zoomed past the road, Jules noticed three figures fighting up ahead. He slowed down to see a humanoid with scarlet skin and a young human attacking someone. Jules powered down his speeder. The trio didn't seem to hear him. If Belen could see him she'd tell him to keep going, that he had work to do and this wasn't his business. But a hard feeling in his gut told him he had to stop and help. Sometimes if felt as though his father was calling out to him from beyond the veil and guiding him. Hopefully not when Jules was drinking and shooting droid heads in the plains, but definitely now.

"Hey!" Jules shouted, and leapt from his speeder.

The scarlet-skinned humanoid froze and whirled around, his single black eye glowering at Jules. His partner, a human girl just younger than himself, but equally muscular, spit at the ground.

"Walk away, moof-milker," she said, her pale ruddy cheeks sunburned.

Jules rested his hands on his waist and shook his head. "Can't do that."

*Yes, you can,* Belen's voice said in his mind. It would be so easy to keep going, to pretend that he'd never seen someone getting robbed on the side of a dirty road. He'd survived his life in the Outpost by learning how to fight back only when he needed to. Not everyone could say the same.

"At least we'll even the odds," the young guy behind them said. His eye was bruising like passion plum, and he used a staff to push himself to his feet.

The attackers glared at each other, then took off.

"I suppose they decided my trinkets are not worth the risk," the boy said.

Jules shook his head, his heart still racing from the anticipation of a brawl. "You all right?"

"I've seen better days." Covered in dusty scarves and a long brown robe, the boy grabbed his side and winced. Jules offered his forearm to help him climb back up the slope and onto the dirty road littered with round white stones.

"I'm Nate Grattonius," he said, extending his hand to Jules. "I'm in your debt—"

"Jules. And you aren't. Will you be all right?"

Nate tugged the hood of his cape up and lowered himself to the ground. Jules realized that there were things scattered on the dirt, not only pebbles. It looked like a bunch of junk, but Jules knew that a bit of junk was treasure to anyone who scavenged. The boy had bright blue eyes and hair that looked recently shorn. The tops of his cheeks and bridge of his nose were shadowed with blooming bruises. When he reached for the metal trinkets on the ground, he hissed.

"Easy, friend," Jules said. "They did a number on you, didn't they?"

Nate chuckled despite the pain but didn't stand. "It's no matter, thanks to you."

Jules had been mugged by off-worlders twice when he was nothing but a skinny runt, before he'd gotten so tall and bulky that people thought twice about picking a fight with him. The first time it happened, he was eight and he'd spent all day rummaging in the salvage yard, one of his first jobs working for Savi and Son Salvage. He'd found a fighter pilot's helmet from the Clone Wars. How it'd ended up in that wreck was something he'd fantasized about while playing with the other boys. He'd been walking down by the docking bays, wearing the helmet, when two bigger kids yanked it off his head. Jules had put up a fight. Being small was no excuse for not being brave. One split lip and a bruised cheek later, he'd run home and told his mother all about it. She warned him to stay away from strangers, not to walk alone on the outskirts of the Outpost. Mother Rakab had never liked venturing into the market or the spaceport. She preferred the solitude of the inner lands, where her family had settled when she was a little girl, and wished Jules felt the same.

Another time was five years back, when he'd been with some of his friends at Oga's Cantina. He was careless and had wanted to splurge on one of the extravagant drinks they mixed, though he knew he wasn't supposed to. The minute he'd stepped outside and started back home, three guys jumped him and took the last of his spira. He'd promised himself then and there, as he threw blind punches, that he'd never be picked on again. He learned every street of the Outpost, who lurked in the alleys, who did jobs for whom. He wouldn't lose himself in the bitterness of those humiliations, but would use the experiences to drive himself forward. And he knew that when he saw it happen to someone else, he would intervene. Especially now that he was big enough to fight back properly.

"I seem to be in the right place at the right time today," Jules said. "Or the wrong place at the wrong time. I'm not exactly sure."

"Both things can be true, Jules." Nate's face split into a bright smile. "For my assailants it was the wrong time, for me it was the right one."

The boy adjusted the cluster of necklaces around his neck. It reminded Jules of the scores of trinkets Dok always wore. Nate wore a peculiar little crystal strung around one of the necklaces. He started collecting small metallic pieces and circuit wire from the ground.

"Here, let me help," Jules said, and toed the stray bits of grass with his boot. It was easy to spot metal glinting in the rising suns.

"You're very kind," Nate said. "I hope I'm not keeping you from somewhere you have to be?"

Jules chuckled lightly, picking up something that looked like a metal finger. Maybe this man knew where Jules was supposed to be, because as the day progressed Jules had no clue, other than his job for Dok. "Believe me, I've been where you are. What are you working on? Customizing some sort of droid?"

"Sort of," Nate said, wiping his brow. A shuttle raced past above them, and two kids on a speeder bike were a blur on the open road. "Everything can be made new again. Now, I believe that's all of it, friend. I must get on my way." With his pouch filled with bits and bolts, Nate steadied himself on his staff and held out a hand to Jules.

"Are you going anywhere near Hondo's?" Jules asked. "I can drop you off."

Nate squinted against the suns and tugged his hood farther down. He appeared even younger when he smiled at Jules, the dust on his face like a smattering of freckles. It made Jules think of the freckles on Izzy's cheeks even though they didn't remotely resemble each other. "I need to be elsewhere, but I thank you. Should our paths cross again, I hope to return the favor. May the Force be with you, Jules."

Jules nodded but said nothing. He hadn't heard that phrase since he was a child, when a group of Force believers had made themselves known on Batuu. He was raised with the idea that there was something out there guiding him, but while his parents had referenced the Force a handful of times throughout his life, only the very old people he knew still believed in that religion. Jules considered that all his talk about fate and the universe might be the same thing.

Nate turned onto the road and continued his journey in the opposite direction. Jules jumped into the driver's seat of his speeder. He wasn't done thinking about Izal Garsea and what it meant that she'd blown back into his life, even if just for a moment.

# IZZY

## CHAPTER 10

Back inside Dok-Ondar's Den of Antiquities, Izzy settled into the dim, cool shop. Jules's absence was palpable to her. She unraveled the scarf from around her neck because it smelled like him. It wasn't that she wanted to forget him. Not again. Being with Jules, even for a few hours, had sped up the healing of something she hadn't even realized was broken. Why couldn't she do that on her own?

With the arrival of Ana Tolla, she'd officially been pulled in too many directions. All she wanted to do then was crawl into her bed and sleep. She reset the course in her mind to what she'd originally gone there to do, before Jules.

Tap looked up from an ancient holovid game. His eyes narrowed with skepticism until he recognized her.

"Hey, kid," she said.

"Dok's not back yet. I'm powering down until he gets back."

A feeling that something was wrong needled at her. Why would Dok leave his shop unattended, except for a small child, for so long? Besides, he was expecting her. This was her opportunity to deliver the parcel and then get going. She'd already said good-bye to Jules; she couldn't do it twice. What if he came back before she left? Would they have to do the same farewell again? One for the day was enough.

She muttered a curse and stalked over to the metal railing that barred off the mezzanine of the shop. She slumped down to the ground and took off the pack. It was heavier than when she'd put it on that morning, but she blamed the strain of pushing Jules's speeder.

"You can wait here if you'd like," he said, and when she looked at him, she saw just how young he was. What had she been doing at ten? Learning how to clean a blaster in the cargo bay of her mother's ship, she realized.

She fished inside the pack for her caf beans and the holocomm Pall Gopal had given her to contact him. Perhaps if the Rodian told her she could give the parcel to Tap, she could be on her way off this world.

"No," she muttered as she pulled out a dented silver briefcase. It was roughly the same size as hers, but there was no keypad on it. "Nononono."

"No, what?" Tap asked, the beeping of rapid explosions from his game matching the speed of her heart.

Even as she examined the pack, brown and worn, she knew where she'd gone wrong. If she closed her eyes she could see herself reach into the cockpit, her mind so full of emotion she couldn't think straight. She'd grabbed Jules's pack.

That meant Jules was about to hand hers to someone else.

"Where's Jules?" she shouted at the kid.

"You were just with him."

"Please, Tap," she said, shoving the contents back where they belonged. "I need to find him, or all of us are getting on Dok's blacklist."

"The *Doklist*?" Tap set his game down long enough to see her panic. "He'd go to Hondo's and then work his way back to Oga's."

"Where is Hondo's?"

With Tap's quick directions, Izzy took off as fast as she could manage. She wove through the throng of bodies clogging the arteries of the market's heart. Her rapid feet moved to the pharynx flute music coming from one of the stalls. Why hadn't she borrowed a speeder from Salju so she'd never need to accept a ride from Jules? Why hadn't she stayed with him in the first place? She wanted to blame it all on seeing Damar and Ana Tolla, on their presence on Batuu rattling her nerves, but she knew it was more than that. Being around Jules had made her start to feel things she wasn't used to feeling, and she wanted to put as much distance as she could between herself and that planet. Her own carelessness was why she'd switched their backpacks. She couldn't let something like that happen again. She stopped in front of the stall with the pharynx flute and realized she'd been going in circles.

"Stop, think," she said, but her own panic was getting the best of her. She picked a direction and went with it. She was practically *born* there for sky's sake. It shouldn't feel so *strange*.

"Izzy!" A hooded figure a few meters ahead shouted her name. Her first reaction was to turn back around. Only Jules and Ana Tolla's crew knew her there. But when the figure called her name again and waved, she could see the blue and white of the Togruta's montrals under the hood of his tunic. It was Neelo and Fawn, and they were in a speeder.

"Hey!" She caught up to the stalled speeder. She didn't think she could be so happy to see people she'd only met in passing. Their speeder was weighted down with encased instruments strapped down by ropes.

"Where are you off to so quickly?" Neelo asked.

"I need to find Jules. Can you give me a lift to Hondo's?"

"We're on our way to practice over there," Fawn said, sliding to the middle of the speeder's seat, next to Neelo.

"Where do you practice?" Izzy asked, hopping in.

Fawn, the human boy, ran a hand over the tight

curls in the center of his head, the sides buzzed short. Two black earrings had stretched out his earlobes. "Since tourism is down the last few weeks, Oga rents us docking bay four to practice."

"Oga *hates* that, but she'll take the spira where she can."

"Besides, my mom hates it when we play in the house."

Izzy white-knuckled the side of the seat, her hair whipping behind her as they flew. The dry air felt good on her sweaty skin, and the faint smell of smoke and exhaust let her know they were near their destination. "I appreciate it."

"No doubt," Neelo said. "Any friend of Jules is a friend of ours."

She grinned despite the rest of her body flashing with panic. "Jules has a lot of friends here."

Fawn turned to Izzy, a twinkle in his brown eyes. "No girlfriend, though, in case you were wondering."

"I was not wondering," Izzy said, but she had definitely been wondering. "I'm only here for a few more hours."

Neelo tapped the dash like it was his drums. She'd known enough musicians to know that they always had a rhythm waiting to be tapped out by their fingers, their toes, and whatever other limbs were free. Even the Rodian musician/spy/whatever he was, Pall, hadn't been able to stop fiddling with the rim of his glass, trying to coax sound out of it, while they talked.

"What's so urgent that you can't stick around for a little longer? You're young! Live a little or a lot but you've got to live."

*Musicians*, she thought.

"The last time I checked I had a pulse, so by all definitions I'm living."

"You know what I mean!" Neelo said, and Fawn laughed. "What's the point of racing around the galaxy if you aren't going to have fun?"

"I know how to have fun!" she said defensively.

Was that why Damar had left her? Because she'd stopped being fun? He'd mesmerized her at first with his strange gray eyes and pretty words. They'd taken on jobs, many of which had failed. For a time, it didn't feel like failure. It felt like adventure. But she'd grown tired of always being responsible for getting them out of trouble with officials. The less work they could find, the angrier she'd become. And yet, she had been afraid to ask him to leave.

She shook her head. No, that was not the reason he'd left. He had left her because he had chosen someone else, someone who could give him things Izzy couldn't—a crew, adventure, danger. Izzy did not *want* to be Ana Tolla, not even remotely. But hadn't she said she'd prove Pall Gopal and her old crew wrong? If they could see her, hitching a ride with two musicians to chase after a boy she hated saying good-bye to, they'd laugh at her.

"Remember what I said about living." Neelo flashed his white teeth. He stopped and powered down the speeder on a busy pad where a shiny hexagonal Avent100-series light freighter was parked.

She kissed both of her drivers on the cheek. If not for them, she'd still be running over there and most likely turning down another wrong alley. If only cities were as easy for her to maneuver as infinite space. "Thank you, both. Have a good practice!"

Izzy was overwhelmed by the number of people on the maintenance pad. There were hundreds of crates, packages of all sizes, and barrels and buckets of shipments waiting to be loaded into different ships. The hangars appeared to have been built into a curved wall of connected spires. She searched for Jules on the main level. He was so tall he should have stuck out among everyone else, but she was once again going in circles.

A Karkarodon was shouting orders. Izzy froze for a moment at the sight of the jagged teeth lining the arch of its mouth. Its long webbed feet slapped the landing pad. Waving pointy webbed fingers, the Karkarodon was a musical conductor, if the symphony was all mismatched instruments playing in different keys. It clutched a datapad against its broad chest, though it did slap the datapad on the rough blue skin of its head twice in so many seconds. Izzy watched as the Karkarodon pressed a button on what looked like a habitat-regulating bodysuit. It released vapor that the sharklike alien inhaled through the slits of its nose. Though Izzy found Batuu humid, she couldn't imagine what an aquatic being felt like on land. The shark-headed being pulled a silver key card from a hip pocket, and the large metal door slid open.

But her attention refocused when she caught sight of Jules. The feeling that slammed into her gut as he stepped off the loading ramp of the hexagonal red-striped freighter was unexpected. He was smiling, his—*her*—backpack slung by one strap over his shoulder. His hand gestures were animated as he spoke to a middle-aged brown-skinned woman with hair styled in hundreds of individual twists and then piled high in two layers of buns. They disembarked together, shook hands, and she took off, her silver cape billowing as she headed away from the spaceport.

Izzy bit down on the swell of *feelings* that came with seeing Jules Rakab and fought the urge to shout his name. He looked up then, as if he could sense her walking hurriedly over to him. Jules didn't move, didn't do anything but gape at her.

"Izzy—" He appeared both surprised and relieved to see her. "What are you still doing here? I mean, I'm glad you're still here. You won't believe what—" His smile faltered when he took in the sight of her. "What's wrong?"

She shut her eyes, a dull pain building behind her lids. "Please, please tell me you haven't delivered that parcel."

"Why?" he asked cautiously.

Dread pooled in the pit of her stomach. Of all the things that could have happened, this was not supposed to be one of them. Her vision blurred and she was quite sure that she needed to throw up. Jules was saying her name, asking her what was wrong. She went over the things she could do to fix this.

*No one in the galaxy knows your name.* Pall Gopal's words echoed through her mind. Perhaps that was her one advantage. She could leave Batuu and hide where no one would find her. She could evade the Rodian if she had to, change the ship's manifest. She should have done that long before, but she couldn't bear the idea of erasing her parents' names. How long could anyone go looking for her? If the parcel was life or death, why would he send a girl like her? *No one in the galaxy knows your name.*

But Jules did. Dok, wherever on the Outpost he was, knew to expect her. Izzy could run. Hide. And what? Blame Jules for the job gone wrong? Plenty of smugglers had shipments that mysteriously failed to show up. That's why when you hired a smuggler you split the payments to guarantee delivery. She'd accomplished the getting *to* Batuu part. Why not stop there? Her backpack was stuffed with the credits she'd exchanged. There were ways to make that stretch while she looked for another job on the opposite end of the galaxy.

Izzy was beginning to feel as though no matter which way she turned she hit a wall. She'd learn from her mother's mistake. All it had taken was one bad job, a small, insignificant one that she hadn't finished, and she'd ended up dead right along with Izzy's father. Izzy swore that wouldn't happen to her or Jules. Whether she'd intended on it or not, they were in this together the minute they swapped parcels.

Izzy Garsea was not going anywhere. Not until she got that parcel back. She rested her hands on Jules's chest and gripped the edges of his jacket, pulling him close.

"I've made a huge mistake," she said. "You have to help me."

# JULES

Jules hadn't been sure if it was the morning spent with Izzy or the traces of adrenaline from his drive over, but after delivering Dok's payment for Hondo, he'd made the most impulsive decision of his life. After years of talking about getting off-world, he was actually going to do it. He had Izzy to thank for that. He'd been missing her, wondering if she'd left yet, turning over the events that led to their encounter to see their purpose. That was when he bumped into a spice trader named Trix Sternus. She'd given him a tour of the compact light freighter and listened to him talk about his day with Izzy. The next thing he knew, he was taking her up on an offer. Those were the kinds of singular moments he found at the Outpost, connecting with strangers from worlds away. He'd even found a bag of chocolate-covered caf beans in his pack, which Tap liked to hoard from one of the sweets stalls. He ate half the bag before he felt his heart racing and decided it was time to finish his errands.

He was sure he'd conjured Izzy the moment he stepped off the ramp. He'd heard about mirages from travelers who came from desert planets but had never experienced one himself. Somewhere to the right, Lee Skillen, the Karkarodon who supervised Ohnaka Transport Solutions while Hondo was off-world, was screaming in her terrifying knife-sharp voice.

But Izzy was not a mirage, and she was very much pulling him close, telling him that she'd messed up.

"I'll fix this," he said. "Just stay right here."

The stubborn frown on her forehead was set. "I'm coming with you."

He lowered his voice and lowered his head to whisper in her ear. "Hondo's gone legit, but a pirate will always be a pirate. Trust me, when you ask to take back a payment, there will be trouble. Plus, Lee doesn't know you. She'll think you're trying to steal from them. It'll be best if I go to her and explain. She knows I wouldn't do anything to upset Hondo's relationship with Dok." He considered this. "Any more than it usually is."

"I don't like this," Izzy said, letting go of him. He realized he'd somehow ended up holding her hands. "It's my parcel."

"And I'm the nerf herder who handed it away. Please, Izzy. Trust me."

He could see how difficult it was for her to relinquish that bit of control. Now that he knew what her day before had been like, he wanted to do everything in his power to give her some semblance of order. He wanted to think that he'd earned a bit of grace around the spaceport, especially with how often Hondo's people were late with Dok's shipments.

"All right," she said.

"All right." He left her where his speeder was parked, then caught up to the Karkarodon. She always smelled like salt water, which was not unpleasant considering the other smells that sometimes wafted through Black Spire Outpost.

"Hey, Lee, wait up!" Jules shouted after the supervisor. Like Hondo, Lee had traveled the galaxy far and wide, but unlike Hondo, she was cracking under the pressure felt across the Outpost as vendors demanded their goods and merchandise so they could make their payments to Oga Garra. If they kept falling behind schedule, then there would be hell to pay.

"Rakab!" Lee said, though she didn't look up from the datapad she was tapping. Jules craned his neck to see it, because he was sure it was turned off and she just wanted to look busy so people would leave her alone. A green-and-white interpreter droid ambled over and began tapping Lee's shoulder at the same time as one of the many pilots in the hangar joined Jules. Between the droid's distressed metallic voice and distress over a ship that had never arrived, Jules wasn't liking his odds at getting Lee's attention.

"Hey, Lee, I *really* need to talk to you," Jules said.

The human pilot—an old man with frizzy red

eyebrows and a scar on his cheek—held a hand up to block Jules. "No way, me first. I've been waiting for my chair to be fixed. How am I supposed to fly a ship standing up? And where are you signing up these copilots from? The backward farms on this dump?"

Something hot sparked in Jules's core. "I'll have you know these *backward* farmers are the reason you have any work."

The redheaded man jabbed a finger into Jules's chest, but Lee slapped the hand away with her datapad. "Hey, now. If you can't handle the environment, then get off my launchpad. I'm sure Hondo can find another flyboy who can navigate standing up in a pinch."

Jules watched the man attempt to stare Lee down. Lee was bluffing, but he enjoyed watching the redheaded moof-brain sweat.

Lee grinned, the sight of her jagged sharp teeth even made Jules and the protocol droid step back. "Glad we could settle that. Follow Gee-One-Emdee. She'll find you an astromech."

"But, madam," the droid began to say.

"Come back to me later," Lee told GI-MD in a voice that could almost be mistaken for patient—as patient as Lee got.

"Rough day?" Jules asked, reminding Lee that he was still there.

Lee ran a webbed hand down her face. Her eye slips

blinked rapidly as she released more vapor to wet them. "Rakab! What are you still doing here? Don't tell me your deal's gone wrong, because we have nothing to do with third-party transactions."

Jules glanced over his shoulder. Izzy was pacing, biting her thumb.

"That's not it. I've got another problem."

Lee threw her hands in the air. "Everyone's got a problem! My girlfriend's got a problem with the hours I'm putting in! My mother's got a problem with me dating a Twi'lek! But I love her, you know? The droids have a problem! Kat Saka's got a problem with Hondo importing grain for her competition! Don't get me started on Hondo. He never learned how to read a flight chart and just throws deliveries on my tablet and expects me to make sense of it! So tell me, Rakab, what is *your* problem?"

"Wow, okay, that was a lot," Jules said.

Lee shook her head. "I apologize, my friend. You're a good kid. I've never had a problem with you before. In fact, if you ever want to make some real money and a change of scenery, say the word. I tell you, I could use a hand here. Especially now that you can—"

"Thank you, Lee," Jules cut her off. The only downside to having Lee's attention was that she unloaded. On any other day, he might have listened. But Izzy was waiting for him, and he did *not* want to explain the mix-up to Dok. "I know you've had a long day."

The Karkarodon sighed, the shape of her jaw giving her a permanent frown. "I have."

"You understand what it's like. Everyone needs something from you, and sometimes you slip up."

Lee arched her brow. "Slip up how?"

"The parcel I gave you."

"Yeah?"

"That was never meant to go to you. It was meant to go to Dok. And don't ask me what's in it because I have no idea, and I really need to get it back or—"

Lee clapped her palm on Jules's back. It would have been a great thing had Jules been choking, but it was startling. When she laughed he could see the inside rows of her teeth. Jules couldn't figure out what part of what he'd said was funny. But he laughed along with her.

"Look here, Rakab, my first week on the job I sent a crate of worms to the wrong planet and I couldn't get them back. Not like a little box. I mean a *crate*. Now the jungles of Urajab have been reduced to weeds because of an invasive species."

Jules was stunned by Lee's understanding. He'd had other plans. Though he wasn't as good as other kids he'd come up with in the Outpost, his sleight of hand was decent. Just when he thought she might let him into the office and he'd be able to avoid stealing from her, she slung her arm around him, and that much closer she didn't smell pleasantly of salt water. She smelled like the daily catch at the fish stalls. She was walking him away from the center of the landing pad and toward the shut door where he knew the main office was.

"Do you see that door, Rakab?" she asked, her voice low in his ear. She was two meters tall and had to lower her head to level her black-stone eyes with his.

"I do," he said, surprised at how even his voice sounded.

"Nothing leaves that office once it's in there unless Hondo's counting his credits or a delivery is being made." She squeezed her muscular arm tighter around his neck.

"But I have the payment right here," he tried to explain.

"I like you, Rakab," she told him. "Which is why I'm only going to tell you one more time. That, and human blood gets everywhere. Fragile things you are. Nothing leaves that office once it's in there. But I can take the other parcel off your hands if you like. Understood?"

He forced himself to meet her eye, not to blink as she left her jaws open and breathed in his face. He slapped her arm and flashed a smile.

"Understood."

Just then someone bumped into them, muttering a gruff apology. The figure in gray hurried past.

"Great," Lee said, massaging her temples, the data-pad wedged under her armpit. "If anyone asks, I'm in the office."

Lee turned to go in the opposite direction.

"But the office is that way," Jules said.

The Karkarodon pressed the vapor dispenser on her bodysuit and walked away. He couldn't relax yet, and turned to the row of speeders and bikes. Izzy wasn't there. Worry filled his senses at the thought that something might have happened to her.

"Well?" The gray-clad figure appeared beside him, and he jolted straight.

It took him a moment to recognize Izzy under the cloak. *She* had bumped into him.

"What were you *thinking*?" he asked, walking her around a stack of metal crates. He could hear Neelo and Fawn's song "Desert Skiff Sunset" playing from somewhere. "I had things under control."

She lowered her hood. "Not from where I was standing. I thought she was going to bite your head off."

He pressed his palm to his chest. "It was a close one."

"I thought I could snatch her access card from her pocket, but it was empty."

The green-and-white protocol droid, G1-MD, tried

to catch up to the angry redheaded pilot, who'd just quit. Though Jules knew his face around the spaceport wouldn't raise any questions, he wanted to protect Izzy. He leaned one arm against the metal crates behind her, shielding her from view. For a brief moment, her green eyes flicked to his mouth before she turned her face away.

"How are we going to get into that room now?" She touched that necklace under her shirt again.

"I told you. I had it under control." From his pocket, he pulled the access card he'd nicked. Staring into the jaws of the Karkarodon was worth it for the way her eyes lit up and her full lips parted in surprise. "We're really going to have to work on your trust skills, Izzy."

# IZZY

Izzy followed Jules onto the boarding ramp of the hexagonal Avent100 light freighter she'd seen him exiting before.

"Are you sure we're allowed to be here?" she asked, following him into the lounge area.

"I, uh, know the owner," he told her, making sure they weren't followed.

"Lie," she said.

"Fine, former owner," he said. "It doesn't matter. Right now, we have to get in that office and out of here before anyone notices. There's a shift switch during the first lunch hour."

"How many lunch hours are there?"

He shrugged and sat beside her. "We like food and the days are long this time of year."

She was too tense to sit still, drumming her hands on the tops of her thighs. Perspiration ran down her back, and her cheeks were warm. His hair was delightfully rumpled after he got put in that headlock. She thought about how unruly his hair had always been when they were children, while her father did his best to keep hers in tight and even braids. As sweaty and disheveled as he was, she found herself edging closer to him. He did slightly smell like the Karkarodon's salt-water vapor, but she didn't mind.

"What happened at Dok's?" he asked, pressing buttons on the table that he definitely should not be pressing. One of them opened a tray and revealed bottled drinks. Her mouth was dry, so she took a bottle when he offered. It tasted like bubbly flower petals, and she drank half of it before answering.

"He wasn't there."

"On one hand, we have some time to fix this. On the other, I'm worried. Dok doesn't leave the shop unattended. Especially when he's sent most of his staff on errands."

"Tap was worried, too."

He settled into the plush black leather of the couch, one arm outstretched behind her. If she leaned in, she'd be resting her head on his shoulder. She knew she shouldn't let her guard down. She didn't give in to her impulse, though every part of her ached and she longed to rest. How was he able to be comfortable at a time like this? She'd forgotten about his ability to fall asleep anywhere. Under a tree even when there were bugs crawling around. Inside the hollow of a petrified tree. On the ground behind their homes when they'd stare at the sky and try to make sense of the moons and stars. He would tell her stories he'd heard from his parents about the ancient ruins that surrounded them. Then he'd fall asleep while she complained about the cold and worried about grass snakes. The memory seemed to unfold itself from the recesses of her mind, where she thought she'd locked it away. Why hadn't she tried to come back sooner?

"Do I have something on my face?" Jules asked.

She was staring at him. She *knew* she was staring at him, but it wasn't for the reason he thought. Though, how could he know the reasons at all? Heat crept up her neck and settled on her cheekbones, something she blamed on all the running around she'd been doing. Otherwise, Izzy would have been forced to admit to herself that she was staring at Julen Rakab not because of his confounding kindness and optimism but because he was, in so many words, beautiful.

"Dust," she said, and folded her arms across her chest.

"I don't know, Izzy," Jules said. "Do you have any idea what's in the parcel? Maybe we can—"

"If it was something we could replace, Dok wouldn't have had someone deliver it from another planet."

He scrutinized her with a stare that was becoming all too familiar. "You don't know what's in it, do you?"

"No," she said. "Part of the job is to not ask questions. Besides, he's your boss. Do *you* have any idea?"

Jules sighed. "I don't know why Dok does anything."

"Good. That's settled." She held her palm out. "Give me the access card. I'll swap the parcels."

At that he sat forward. "If you get caught—"

"I won't."

"Izzy, it's dangerous."

She shrugged a shoulder and kept drinking her sparkly flower drink. She couldn't read the label, except the words "Flora Wow" in Basic. "You did your part. Besides, I'm smaller. You're a meter and a half tall."

"I'm one point eighty-five meters tall and it comes in handy. Sometimes," he amended with a rueful grin that kick-started her rapid pulse again. She had to get herself under control. All those emotions had screwed her up in the first place. Whatever she was feeling for Jules needed to be shoved in a compartment and sealed shut.

"More of a reason for it to be me. Bring the speeder closer and pray to the spires that it doesn't stall again."

"You only get that one shot at my baby, Izzy," he warned her.

She raised her hands in mock defeat. They didn't have to wait long for the siren announcing shift change to blare. She left behind the cloak she'd swiped from an open cargo box because they agreed it was conspicuous. Instead, she stripped off her leather jacket and Jules removed his tunic, remaining in a threadbare white T-shirt he'd clearly outgrown seasons before.

She used the bathroom in the ship to splash water on her face and tug on the tunic. It was far too big on her, but when she cinched it with her own belt, it was closer to what the local human workers on the launch-pad wore. After tying her hair in a knot, she slipped the card in her pocket and walked off the boarding ramp.

Sometimes, when Izzy was unsure of what to do on a job, she wondered what her mother might do. Ixel Garsea always walked into a room with her head held high. Izzy hadn't quite managed the same pride that had made her mother appear unapproachable, but as she headed for the office with the pack strapped to her back, walking against the chaos of the shift change, she thought she was getting close.

When she palmed the card against the sensor and the doors slid open, she could finally breathe. The air smelled cold, a mix of chemicals and earthy notes she wasn't familiar with. Crates and boxes of shipments were stacked in heaps that were less organized than Dok-Ondar's den. Dok's at least felt like it had a method to the chaos. Jules had mentioned Ohnaka Transport Solutions was losing business. It was a wonder anything could be found let alone delivered.

She crept through the place, eyes darting from wooden crate to metallic crate. She cursed herself for not marking her parcel somehow, but she was certain she could identify it among the others. First she needed to find it. She lifted a stack of furry pelts that shimmered like an oil slick in the rain. With the back of her hand she caressed one, and it was the softest thing she'd ever touched. She knew of no creature it could be from, but her curiosity was piqued. Perhaps when she got out of there she could go in search of one.

Barrels of brew took up a corner. The items there didn't look like they were meant to be shipped at all. Most of the boxes were open. She looked in one and found some sort of round gold coins. Her eyes followed the boxes up. Far out of her reach, there it was: the briefcase with the square keypad at the center. Far too high for her to reach. She grumbled. Jules wouldn't even have had to stretch for it. She decided she would not tell him about this part. All she needed was something to stand on. The crate she was able to move got her within centimeters of the briefcase handle. She jumped and her hand folded around it. Then she repeated the motion to place the correct briefcase. Sweat poured between her shoulder blades and down her breast, but she had it. With her heart racing, she shoved the crate back and turned to go.

Noise came from the other side of the door. She could hear Lee's rough voice. The memory of her sharp teeth flashed into Izzy's mind. If she'd been able to practically put Jules in a headlock, what would she do to Izzy?

There was nowhere to hide. Besides, what if Lee could *smell* Izzy? Did that heightened sense translate on land or only underwater? She didn't have time to debate that, and knew there was only one place safe enough to hide. Lifting half the shimmering pelts, she burrowed between them, staying as flat as she could. She felt a little smug knowing Jules would have been too long to hide in the same spot. But as she tugged the briefcase in with her, her sweaty hand slipped. The case fell to the floor just as the doors whooshed open.

"Blast!" Lee shouted, only a fraction of her slapping webbed feet visible from where Izzy was. "I'm losing my mind. Where is my access card? Thank Karkari I remembered the override codes."

A pair of heavy brown boots and a flatbed cart followed closely behind Lee. "Where am I going?" said a woman with a smooth alto voice.

Lee's growl made Izzy's body clench. She was glad she'd relieved herself in the Avent100's restroom. "Do you smell that?"

"I dunno. Did someone clean?"

Izzy would have snorted if she hadn't been holding her breath. She squeezed her eyes shut, as if that would make her invisible. The pelts were bulky enough, she reminded herself. There was not a single part of her sticking out. Her lungs burned, and despite all the liquid she'd drunk, her mouth felt like she'd been chewing on sand. The slap of feet approached, and she felt the weight above her lighten.

Only just.

She could hear Lee inhale deeply. "Urusida skin reminds me of home. It's all the fish they eat."

"You can smell that?" the other woman asked incredulously.

"Delicate humans," Lee muttered.

"Where am I going, again?"

"Shipments to Corellia on the right, Clak'dor on the left," Lee said.

"But I'm supposed to—"

"I know, you're supposed to have the week off. Orin quitting was . . . unexpected," Lee said. "I'll talk to Hondo about giving you a bonus, how's that?"

There was a moment's pause. Izzy would have jumped at the chance, but she understood not wanting to seem too eager. Then the woman replied, "Clak'dor, you said?"

"Thank you for being a team player, Delta Jeet," the Karkarodon said, like she was reciting from a script. "Ohnaka Transport Solutions is fortunate to have you."

The slap of feet departed. Izzy breathed slowly, desperately wanting to sneeze. She wiggled her arm toward her face and rubbed her nose. All she had to do was wait for this Delta woman to leave and she'd be free. She hoped Jules would stay put. She wouldn't put it past him to come and find her. But they had a plan.

Delta loaded the crates and parcels for her delivery. Izzy slowly pushed up the barest edge of the pelt. Her parcel was still there on the ground.

Then a set of brown hands grabbed it and added it to the stack going off-world. *Corellia and Clak'dor.* Izzy wished she could scream the number of obscenities she'd learned across the galaxy. She had only one shot at the element of surprise. Summoning every bit of courage, every bit of strength she could, she wrapped her hand around her blaster pistol and sat up. The furs tumbled to the ground.

Izzy took aim, and as Delta spun around, Izzy pulled the trigger.

# JULES

Jules knew something had gone wrong when Izzy stepped out of the office with her blaster in hand. He'd been keeping the protocol droid from going into the room to look for Lee.

"Master Jules," G1-MD said, "I have repeated that everything is in order. I must be going to find Madam Lee at once. The cargo freighter to Corellia has not been loaded yet."

"There she is," Jules pointed to the other end of the landing pad, where Lee was surrounded by angry pilots. Was there something in the water making everyone irate?

His eyes widened at Izzy as she holstered her weapon and climbed into the speeder.

"What happened?" He jumped into the cockpit behind the wheel, and she cradled the rucksack against her chest. He powered up the speeder. It jostled and shook for an agonizing moment. He smoothed his fingers along the dash and whispered, "No, no, no, baby, don't do this to me, please."

"Do you know a Delta Jeet?" Izzy asked.

"I've seen her pop arms out of their sockets when

she finds someone's cheated at the sabacc tables."

*Great. Good,* she thought. "I shot her."

"You *what*?"

"She's alive. It was set to stun."

He wondered if that had been a happy accident or if Izzy always kept her blaster on that setting.

"If I don't get us out of here, we're dead," he said.

"Not yet we aren't," Izzy said, and slammed her fist on the dash.

"Easy, will you?" But whether it was his gentle words or Izzy's punch, his speeder charged out of the hangar, leaving a trail of dust in its wake.

They didn't speak for a few moments. He gripped the wheel and let his heart rate come down to a pace that allowed him to breathe. She had her arms around the bag but was staring at him. There were bits of shimmering hair on her face. What exactly had happened in there?

He took a sharp turn down a pedestrian road. He never would have done it if they weren't in a hurry. "We have to get to Dok's. Something—"

They were engulfed by a swell of people spilling from the market. Many were shouting at each other. He caught curses in Huttese and Twi'leki.

"What's happening?" Izzy said. She shoved the pack under her seat and out of sight.

He pushed himself up on the top of his speeder,

leaning on the glass. He'd heard about riots in the Outpost before, when rival gangs and crews would spill from the Galma vicinity into the ports. The crowd was divided into groups. One was the stream of traffic trying to get out of the way, carrying baskets of fruit and the day's supplies in netted bags over their shoulders. The eopie he'd seen earlier in the day was even more skittish, and the mother had chosen to hold the child instead of risk having her thrown from the saddle.

Then there were two groups shouting at each other. He wasn't sure why until he heard the words clearly. *"Give yourself to the First Order! Restore the rule of law across the galaxy!"*

The group shouting that was small—men and some women dressed in simple farmer garb. Jules was shocked to recognize two of them: Dok's assistant and runner who had vanished. The reason Jules had been called in that morning. He'd never truly known them. Both were orphans who'd wound up on the streets of the Outpost searching for work where they could find it. He watched their lips pull back in snarls, their eyes narrowed with certainty. It was like they'd been searching for a purpose and someone had given it to them.

"Jules, don't," Izzy said, tugging on his sleeve.

He could sense the anger thick in the air. Those who were trying to mill through the crowd kept their heads down. Many of the vendors gathered around though. Some threw pebbles—nothing large enough that it would hurt anyone, but so many that it was like being surrounded by summer spire flies.

"Get off the street, you!" a slender blue-skinned Twi'lek shouted.

"You're chasing away our customers!" a round baker woman screamed, making herself hoarse.

"Batuu is a wasteland of criminals and misrule! Gangsters rob your streets and—" one of the young boys shouted, but the back and forth increased, morphing into a dense buzz that drowned him out.

It was the sound of marching that silenced everyone. They came from the shadows of the spires, moving in perfect rows, white armor gleaming under shining suns and long shadows cutting stripes across them as they moved. They said nothing. There weren't even any officers with them. But they stood their ground, forming a protective barrier around the small group of fanatics.

Slowly, the opposing crowds dispersed and all Jules could hear was "Batuu is a wasteland—" But he recognized some of the few who didn't leave, who stared back into the dark eyes of those terrifying helmets.

He didn't even notice at first when Izzy hopped out of the speeder to stand in front of him. "Jules," she said, and repeated it until he focused on her eyes, flecked with lichen gold.

They couldn't stay there, but the way forward was blocked by the stormtroopers. He quickly backed up, but that way was barred by the overflow of traffic. There was only one way out.

He drove straight for the shadows of Smuggler's Alley.

# IZZY

Izzy had never been to that part of the Outpost when she lived on Batuu. There were no welcoming shops or stoop conversations over tea. It was the sort of place where people knew where they were going and whom they were looking for, with none of the curious browsing of the Outpost market stalls.

Jules powered down the speeder in front of a shop that advertised body modifications. He still gripped the wheel. Never before had she seen him so visibly upset. She bit the inside of her lip trying to find the right things to ask. She'd seen his face when the young boy shouted those things about their planet. Though she'd been away for so long, it *had* been her home once. She rested her hand on his, and a static surge shot up her finger. He glanced up, conflict warring in his dark brown eyes. He accepted her touch and threaded her fingers with his.

"I should have stayed with them," he said, leaning back in his seat.

"Has this happened before?"

He shook his head. "Things have been strange all around. Not just people taking off but something else.

I don't even think Oga knows why the First Order is here. Because if she did, she would have handed over whatever it was they wanted and sent them packing."

Izzy scoffed. "One time my mother said that revolution and war was good for business."

She hated that she'd said it, but Jules didn't let go of her hand.

"Do you know what the worst part is?" he asked.

She could guess. She felt his tension beside her. The night before, when she'd been at that cantina in Actlyon, hadn't she wanted to stay and help but forced herself to go? She'd seen the same look in Jules's eyes moments before. Only he was already so much braver than she was because he *always* wanted to do good, not just when things got violent.

"The helplessness?" she offered.

"He wasn't even wrong," Jules said. "Batuu is run by criminals. Everything I've ever done is touched by that. Everyone on this planet."

"You're a farmer, Jules." She squeezed his hand in both of hers. "You're a friend, a brother. No matter where you go in the galaxy there's always good and bad. There are imbalances of power. Batuu is no better or worse. They destroyed an *entire* system. Nothing can make that right."

He kissed the knuckles of her hand, like it was something he had done before that moment. Natural, sweet. She wanted to blame the kiss on the events of the day again. Being with Jules felt like jumping to lightspeed without having charted a course. She wasn't sure if she'd come out of it close to a planet or collide headfirst with an asteroid. But she wanted to see what would happen.

"When I was a boy," Jules said, "my father said that Batuu was once full of those running from evil as much as it was full of those running because they'd done evil."

"What about the people caught in between?"

He chuckled then. "Oh, they're here, too. I think it burned me up when he called Batuu a wasteland because it isn't. For those who choose to stay, it's a second chance."

In all the time she'd spent trying to reinvent herself, to find where exactly she belonged, why hadn't she considered that she could get a second chance, too? What would that look like? Staying on Batuu?

The words never made it to her lips, because she saw someone familiar. It was Ana Tolla. Her head was covered by a scarf, and she'd tucked her recognizable red hair away. But she wore the blue jacket Izzy had given to Damar. She considered that perhaps the crew leader had sold it for fuel, but when the woman raised her hand to knock on a door, Izzy caught a glimpse of her face. It was *definitely* her.

Jules squeezed Izzy's hand hard enough to jolt her. He whispered, "Don't move. Let me talk."

Izzy was confused. Jules hadn't seen Ana Tolla. When she looked around, she saw that it wasn't her old crew leader he'd been referring to. They were surrounded by scruffy-looking pirates.

A human male in his mid-twenties with a twisted brown beard and greasy hair stepped forward. "Oga Garra wants to see you."

Jules hesitated for the briefest moment before he turned on the engines. He grabbed the wheel with one hand but didn't let go of hers as he said, "Tell her we're coming."

# JULES

## CHAPTER 12

Jules could count with two fingers the number of times he'd seen Oga Garra.

The first was by sheer accident. He'd had no idea what she looked like, only heard what the farmers, some who rarely even ventured to the Outpost, whispered on their breaks. Then one day he'd been at the spaceport watching off-worlders file out of emissary vessels in glittering robes, accompanied by dozens of handmaidens. He'd followed them right to the cantina to get a better look. At first, he hadn't known what he was looking at. He saw a gathering of pink tentacles sticking out of the hood of a cloak. She blended so well into the shadows that if there hadn't been light from the moons, he wouldn't have noticed her. There were two drunk farmers near her, rowdy and shouting. They made gestures with their hands that Jules didn't understand at first, pressing their fingers together in a point and speaking in Huttese. The next day those farmers didn't show up for work. Jules never saw them again.

The second time had been when he walked into

Dok's den and Dok and Oga were in the back room arguing. Dok had shut the doors in his face and he'd had to return to work later.

He told Izzy as much. He powered down the engines and threw a tarp over the speeder. Their escorts waited at the back door. Jules ran through the number of things that could have made Oga summon them.

"Do you think she knows about Delta?" Izzy asked.

"She has a way of knowing everything. But we're about to find out," he said, keeping his arms firm at his sides. "I should mention right now that Blutopians don't like to be stared at."

"No one likes to be stared at," Izzy countered.

"You haven't met my friend Volt." He managed to wink at her. Who was he, winking and driving a getaway speeder? He'd spent so much of his life trying to stay just adjacent to trouble so it didn't touch him. He hadn't always been successful. But he was alive. Though the day wasn't over. Neelo and Fawn's lazy, knowing grins flickered in his mind as he and Izzy were escorted down a narrow hall. *Trouble,* they'd said. Trouble had indeed come in the form of Izal Garsea, and as they stepped into the cool dark of Oga's office, he knew he'd choose her again and again. After all, that had been his wish so many years before, as a little boy asking the wishing tree to bring his best friend back.

He tried to give her a reassuring look, but her

attention had been drawn elsewhere. Though she kept her features steady, he could feel her unease.

Jules marveled at the wall hangings, square pieces of sandstone with carved designs eroded by time. They looked like they were cut from the ruins themselves. He remembered the legends his father had told him, about a queen who built that city from stone before it fell to invaders. Jules wondered if that was why Oga kept those pieces, as if she were the queen of the Outpost, like the nameless ancients from legend.

Oga Garra sat on an elaborate high-backed chair carved from Batuuan spires. Silk pillows cushioned her back, and a small stand beside her held a bowl of three-headed larvae and a glowing hookah that perfumed the air with the scent of river valley blossoms. Orbs of light hovered above her, giving her thick brown epidermis and pink face tentacles a slick sheen.

There was a carved desk in the corner, but unlike Dok's it held parcels and datapads instead of paper. Jules couldn't imagine Oga taking her own orders and filling out shipment requests, because she didn't have to request anything.

The doors slid closed, but R-3X's music session was streaming from a comm Jules couldn't see. Oga pressed a button and the sound cut out. The stiff tentacles of her mouth moved, and she spoke Huttese in a screeching voice.

Jules folded himself into a bow, and Izzy followed suit. He had no clue if people bowed to Oga, but he wanted to cover his bases and he thought it was best to let her speak first.

"Sit," Jules translated for Izzy.

They did as they were told. The stone benches seemed like they were designed to make the person opposite Oga uncomfortable. But when Jules turned to see how Izzy was doing, she looked mesmerized. Her eyes were wide, and a smile played on her lips. Jules realized that she was more used to meeting with beings like Oga than he was. He wondered—could Izzy be in love with Oga's power? Was that what she wanted? Where would that leave him? Not that it mattered at the moment. First he needed to get through the meeting without incurring Oga's wrath.

Oga spoke again, and Jules thanked the spires that he'd spent so much time in the ports listening to conversations in Huttese. When she was finished, he was stunned.

"You know my name?" he asked the Blutopian.

"I know everything that goes on in my outpost," she answered in the guttural language. "So when I hear about an off-worlder girl looking to make deals that cut me out, I have concerns."

Jules translated while Oga snatched a larva, bulbous and white, and bit off one of its three heads.

"You've got the wrong girl, then," Izzy answered in Basic.

Oga made a strange sound and Jules couldn't be sure if it was a good or bad sign, or if she was choking. She spoke more clearly.

"Who are you?" Jules translated.

"My name is Izal Garsea, and I'm here to deliver a parcel to Dok-Ondar."

Oga considered this in the time it took her to finish crunching on the larva. When she spoke again, Jules clenched his jaw and turned to Izzy.

"Garsea?" he translated. "Your mother. Green eyes like yours. I remember her. She worked for me once. One of the best. Never missed a bounty."

Izzy sucked in a short breath. "My mother was a smuggler."

Oga rattled off a string of words that made Jules flash hot. "I can't say that to her."

"Say what?" Izzy asked.

He couldn't ignore Oga. The same helpless feeling he'd had moments earlier returned. Looking Izzy deep in her eyes, he forced his mouth to form the words.

"Foolish girl. You didn't know your mother at all."

"Then tell me," Izzy said, her voice stronger than his. They waited for Oga to finish speaking. Jules hated being the one to have to deliver these words to her.

"I know she came here to get away like others do,"

Jules translated. "It worked for a while, but she grew restless. I gave her work. When she couldn't complete the last job, I spared her as long as she left that very night."

Izzy frowned but didn't reveal anything else. He'd give anything to take her away from that place. He hated that he'd done everything he could to learn to fight, to help others, but he was in front of the one person on the planet he couldn't touch. Oga had been the reason the Garseas left all those years before.

"Thank you, Oga," Izzy said slowly, as if choosing her words carefully. "This has been—enlightening. Did you kill her?"

Oga chortled, and the wet slap of her mouth made Jules suppress a shiver as he translated in a rush: "Would it matter? Would you try to hurt me? What could you do to me that I couldn't do worse?"

Then Oga stared right at Jules as if daring him to defend his friend. There was a helplessness there, like he'd felt earlier, and he hated it.

Izzy nodded in understanding, but he could feel her withdraw from him. That cloud he'd felt around her when he first saw her that day returned with a storm. He had no choice but to listen to Oga once more, each smack of her words making his teeth ache.

"I haven't seen Dok all day," he said.

"What *have* you seen, Jules?" she asked in rough, accented Basic. She continued in Huttese and said that she'd sent a runner to the shop to check up on the Ithorian since his runner was late. They had returned moments before Jules and Izzy arrived with news that Dok still wasn't there.

Jules decided it was best not to point out that he was not given a time to arrive at Oga's and that everyone would be late if she was able to choose an arbitrary time.

For Izzy's benefit, he translated, "Something is happening around here and I'm going to find out what it is. If I find out you two are involved . . ."

She let the threat hang between them, the orbs above her pulsing. He knew the meeting was over when she turned on DJ R-3X's broadcast again. He was calling out items from a lost and found.

"Dok's payment," Oga said, and pointed to a wrapped bundle on the desk. Then she added. "Take that barrel of rot back to Volt and tell him no deal. I can't make money if all my patrons keel over from poison. Now go."

As they left, Oga called Izzy back but told Jules to wait outside. He felt queasier than ever leaving her alone, but he did as he was told and leaned against the opposite wall. He knocked his head against it. A thick human male walked past him shouldering a wooden barrel of brew. He whistled at Jules, with shock in his bushy dark brows. He muttered something that sounded to Jules like, "You're still alive?"

He was very much alive, but the day was not over.

# IZZY

Izzy was almost grateful when Oga asked her to remain in her office. She couldn't face Jules after everything they'd had to listen to. She couldn't decide if it was better or worse coming from him.

"How did you find yourself here after all this time?" Oga asked in nearly perfect Basic.

After an entire conversation of forcing her features into a steely calm, Izzy finally reacted.

"You didn't need Jules to translate," she said.

"I find people like to feel useful."

"What else can I do for you, Oga Garra?"

"Ixel was one of my favorites. Such a waste of talent."

Izzy realized she never knew her mother at all. How could she have missed it? She was a fool. She couldn't be upset at Oga for telling her a truth that had died with her parents.

"Is that all?"

"Not quite." Her voice was reedy, nearly piercing Izzy's eardrums. "I was once an orphan, too. You must always know your roots if you are to know how sturdy the tree will grow. If you are going to be here, you will have to know the rules."

Izzy shook her head. Her thoughts about staying on Batuu untethered and began to drift away. "I've already stayed longer than I intended to."

Oga grunted and dismissed her with a wave. "If you want to know who put out the contract on your mother, you know where to find me."

"What's the cost?"

"You'll owe me a job. Consider it—an audition."

Her insides felt fused together. She could hardly breathe, the too-sweet smoke wafting from the burning hookah irritating her nasal passages, her eyes. She turned to leave. But before she punched the door open, Izzy exhaled. Jules was Jules. He would want to talk to her about her feelings, and she didn't want to. She wanted to fly. She wanted to fight. She wanted to use her hands. Instead of calm, she found herself worked into tighter knots.

When the door opened, there he was, leaning against the wall with worry in his eyes. He hefted the barrel onto one shoulder and offered a smile. She hated the way she reacted to the sight of him. How could she be certain that what she was feeling was real? What if it was because things with Damar had just ended? What if it was the sheer nostalgia?

None of those considerations stopped her from taking his hand and holding it tight all the way out of Oga's. She'd been wrong. He didn't want to talk, didn't even press her.

"We're walking," he announced.

"You're not worried someone might lift your speeder?"

He let go of her hand to better carry the barrel Oga had made him take. She wanted to reach for him again but shoved her hands in her pockets. "It still wouldn't be the worst thing that's happened to us."

They laughed. It was a startling relief to the longest, worst day of her life. But as she walked onto the market road side by side with Jules, she considered it was also turning into the best day.

"If our stars are lucky, Volt will be there instead of Bina and we can get back to Dok's."

"My stars are not lucky, so let's assume this Volt isn't there."

"We'll see."

The afternoon crowds were thinning. Though sheets of colorful canvas served as a patchwork ceiling, the intense suns still broke through. Izzy had no need for her jacket and tied it around her waist. When they passed a stall serving salty dried meat called nuna jerky, Izzy bought a bag for them to share. Because his hands were busy, Jules leaned over and she fed him.

She shook her head, wishing she could drink in his mirth. Perhaps if she did she could stop thinking about Oga Garra's words. How had she not known that her mother had been a killer? During the years she'd spent alone, the driving factor that got her through most days was imagining what her mother might do. Now she could truly say that she didn't know.

"Izzy," Jules said, pulling her back to the present.

The stall where they'd stopped was wide open and crowded with customers. They stepped inside, and Jules set the barrel down. The smell of hay and a distinct murky whiff of animal excrement made her nose itch. Incense smoldered in metal burners on either side of the tent entrance. Izzy wasn't sure why it was so much darker in there than in other stalls until she noticed the blinking red eyes in some of the cages. There were dozens of them stacked on top of each other and strung from metal rafters. Birds flapped inside some.

A short, broad-shouldered man dressed in a scarlet tunic with metal accents was taking payment from a mother with three children. One of the boys was poking a stick into a cage. The top was covered by a tarp, and bits of hay and what looked like a rat's tail were sticking out between the bars.

"I wouldn't do that if I were you!" the clerk shouted as he noticed the kid. As if on cue, the creature lunged forward as far as the cage would allow. Its yellow eyes glowed, and two sharp fangs that jutted from its bottom jaw lowered as it let out a yowl. "Fyrnocks have a bit of a temper, but this one is friendlier than others I've encountered. Still, you don't want to poke him."

The boy showed no fear of the creature, only opened his eyes wider and turned to his mother. "Cool. Can we get him, too? Can we please, please, please?"

He was the oldest of the three, no more than five standard years by the size of him. The other two, twins, wrapped themselves around each of their mother's legs and whimpered, "Mama, no! He will eat our new friendo!"

"He will not!" the older kid snapped, ready to wrap his tiny hands around the cage bars.

Izzy thought she saw fear in the clerk's narrow black eyes. He held credits in one hand and a small cage in the other, so he was too occupied to yank the kid back, and so was the mother.

It was Jules who swooped in and grabbed the boy as the fyrnock bit at the space where the kid's hand had been. "Easy there, bud."

The mother was slender, with brown hair braided around her head and adorned with gold thread. Her clothes were rippling silk, and delicate pearls dotted her ears and circled her wrists. Everything about her seemed soft, and as she took her child back from Jules, Izzy saw a wealth of patience in her wide brown eyes.

"Oh, thank you," the mother said, pulling her son to her.

"But I want a fry rock," the boy whined, and Izzy was ready to run and hide as his trembling lip showed signs of impending waterworks.

Jules threw up his hands as if to say, *Fry rocks are no big deal.* "I'm sure Volt wouldn't steer you wrong, kid. What do you have in there?"

The clerk brightened at the interruption. His thick, square eyebrows rose. "Puffer pig, only four months old and sweet as your own children."

Jules got down on one knee to be eye level with the kids. They turned to him like he was some great keeper of knowledge.

"Did you know that puffer pigs have an incredibly powerful sense of smell for metals?" Jules tapped the youngest kids on their noses. "I bet you and your brothers can let them loose in your yard and dig up all kinds of treasures."

"Like pirates?" the older boy asked.

Jules glances up at Izzy, and try hard as she could, she could not repress the laugh that bubbled from her lips.

"Pirates that bathe their skins and brush their teeth and drink their milk," their mother said.

The smaller kids made a face and chimed, "I hate milk."

"Thank you, Volt. Rising moons to you," their mother said.

She carried the cage as the older boy wrangled his twin brothers. Volt hurried over to embrace Jules. They clapped each other on the back like they hadn't seen each other in months.

"Wasn't expecting to see your ugly mug around here today," Volt said, letting go of Jules to look at Izzy. He rubbed a hand across the shiny skin of his bald scalp.

"Good run today?" Jules asked his friend.

Volt growled. "Until those blasted bantha brains nearly started a riot. Every time I see one—"

Jules squeezed his friend's shoulder. "Easy, now."

Volt took a second to focus, the veins on his neck throbbing as he did some kind of meditation. Izzy looked away to give him a bit of privacy. As she took careful steps between the cages and crates of chittering creatures, Izzy noticed the scarring on the left side of Volt's face, the marks pink against his otherwise light-brown skin.

"And you brought me a new client. How kind of you, Jules." Volt, recuperated from his spurt of rage, approached Izzy the way one might approach a curious bird one was trying to lure into a cage. With the smirk of a very charming feline, Volt looked like the kind of vendor who always made a sale—though Izzy was positive he'd be disappointed to learn the reason they were there.

"Izzy, and sadly I'm not a client," she said, and held out her hand in greeting. He took up her hand in both of his, and the surprise of cold metal joints against her skin made her jump. When she looked down she saw that the pinky and ring ringer of his right hand had been replaced by two mechanical digits. That kind of surgery was common, but Izzy imagined the procedure for replacements with synthskin would be harder to come by in the Outer Rim. Although, what did she know? Perhaps he preferred his hand that way.

"You're breaking my heart already," Volt said, his deep voice welcoming. "Are you sure I can't interest you in a critter? Everyone needs a pet. Perhaps a tooka cat. You're a pilot, aren't you? I'm sure my lovely Kishka here would make sure you never have another rodent problem no matter what corner of the galaxy you find yourself in, though I do hope you come back and visit."

Volt pulled back the canvas on a crate of slumbering tooka cats, their tan fur striped with black. Jules was clearly trying not to laugh. She'd had enough of tooka cats for a lifetime after the one at Salju's.

"How do you know I'm a pilot?" she asked.

Volt gave a shrug and sauntered over to a glowing tank of worrts. Their bumpy skin glowed in the fluorescent blue light. "I've met my share of flyboys—and, er, girls. I know the look. You walk like you'd rather be soaring through the atmosphere."

Izzy didn't care to be analyzed, but she didn't buy his act for one minute.

"Don't listen to him, Izzy. The first time we met, he tried to unload a barrel of scale fish because he took me as part of a group of divers that had just arrived from Mon Cala."

Volt pressed his hands to his chest, his metal fingers tapping out a quick rhythm. His black eyes turned to Izzy, then to Jules. "Do you or do you not spend an obscene number of hours in the sinkholes swimming with the catfish."

"Doesn't mean I want a tank full of them," Jules said.

"It's a yes-or-no question, my friend." The sleeves of his red tunic had what appeared to be lizards stitched on them in black thread. Izzy noticed the rough scars peeking from his collar. She'd wager he was former military, and wondered how he ended up on Batuu unloading critters on tourists. Volt gestured to Izzy. "And, my dear, are you or are you not a pilot?"

She crossed her arms and smirked. "I am. But I don't have a rodent problem."

"All of you have rodent problems."

"If you count mynocks getting spark drunk off my

wiring," she said. "Anyway, we have to be going. We have something that belongs to you."

Volt cleared his throat, amused with her. He raised a brow and said, "Is it my heart?"

"You're embarrassing me, friend," Jules said, carrying the barrel over to the clerk stand. He set it on the counter.

"You embarrassed yourself last night when you couldn't shoot a still target, but I still have nothing but love for you." Volt gaped at the barrel. It was leaking streaks of brown liquor that appeared to be eroding the metal. "What—Where—This was a gift."

A Kowakian monkey-lizard above let out a squealing laugh. It sent the other animals into a small frenzy, their own concerto of hollers and shrieks. One of them even sounded like the scream of a person. Izzy noticed the foot traffic was moving faster. Some ladies in rippling silk kept glancing back, pointing at the foremost display cage, which housed a large purple bird with a reptilian tail Izzy had never seen before.

Volt shoved past Jules to try to entice the ladies with a sale. "Loralora bird. A rare hybrid from the jungle moon of Ketz!"

The ladies didn't spare him a second glance. Jules clapped Volt on the shoulder. Izzy noticed the moment Jules did a double take down the street. She frowned, and he tilted his head to the stall's entrance. She took that to mean that they needed to leave. But what had he seen to cause that reaction?

"I'll see you at the cantina tonight, Volt," Jules said. Izzy made her way to him, but Volt showed no signs of letting them go.

"What's your hurry?" he asked.

"Dok-Ondar is waiting for us," Izzy said. "And by the way, Oga said to tell you not to send her that stuff anymore."

"'Stuff'?" Volt repeated, incredulously. "Come, I'll give you both a free sample."

Jules grabbed hold of Izzy's wrist, but as they were about to step out onto the street, Izzy realized why he was in a hurry to leave. Delta Jeet stomped against traffic, shoving people aside when they got in her way. Izzy only got a good look at her boots before, but the rest of her was just as intimidating. Cropped brown hair framed her round face, at the moment puckered into a scowl as she searched the crowd.

It was too late. Jules and Izzy had whirled around to go back into the shop when they heard a feral-sounding *"You!"* shouted in their direction.

Meaty hands grabbed Izzy by her neck and yanked her back. Delta Jeet said, "The next time you think to shoot me, you better finish the job."

# JULES

## CHAPTER 13

Jules took pleasure in watching Izzy get along with Volt. He pictured her belonging in this world, in *his* world. That all faded when he saw Delta. He hoped they could get out of there without drawing attention to themselves.

Then he felt Izzy wrenched from his hold.

"I'll mount your heads on my wall as trophies!" Delta shouted.

Izzy threw a punch, but Delta didn't seem to register it. Izzy winced and ducked as Delta swung her arm around. The woman was used to fighting in the Galma vicinity, and Jules could already see the blood that would follow.

"Hey, hey, hey!" Volt shouted, and reached for the upturned cage where the loralora bird flapped around wildly. "Take this outside! You're scaring the animals, for sky's sake."

Jules had to do something. The animals were restless, hissing and growling and snapping their teeth. Curious passersby were crowding the exit, sticking out their necks and gasping as Izzy fell into the fyrnock cage. Jules knew Volt would forgive him for what he was about to do—or rather, he hoped.

He pulled the pins keeping the cages locked and unraveled the ties that housed the orange-and-white momongs. The first one to fly out was the loralora bird, its reptilian prehensile tail swinging at Delta's head, momentarily blinding her.

"Izzy!" Jules shouted.

She stepped over Volt, who was hunched over trying to protect a petrified dokma from getting its shell trampled as the crowds began to swarm closer. Mynocks leapt onto Delta and others, their leathery wings wrapping around her head. She fell into the melee.

Jules ran ahead and barreled into bodies, trying to apologize on his way out. Behind them creatures hissed. Birds took off, finding freedom through the gaps of the canvas roof.

"This way!" he shouted, running past Jewels of Bith and Kat Saka's Kettle. For the first time in years, he'd taken a wrong turn in the alleys. The whole day felt like wrong turns. But they were so close to Dok's. They rounded a corner and he'd never been happier to see the den.

Jules slammed his fist on the door. "Tap! It's me."

He could hear Delta in the distance, and Volt, too. All right, perhaps Jules's friend would not forgive him any time soon.

The cool air of the shop hit him square in the face. Tap did not look impressed by the sweaty, dirty sight of them, but the kid stepped aside and let them pass.

"Took you long enough," Tap muttered.

Jules was almost glad. Tap needling him was the most normal part of his day. Izzy crossed the room and sank against the wall of the mezzanine to catch her breath. Tap glanced back and forth between them. Jules had never taken so long to go on a simple errand, but it was anything but a simple day.

"Dok back yet?" Jules asked.

"I closed up because I'm not authorized to price anything."

Jules patted the boy on his shoulder. "That was wise, Tap." He removed the payment Oga had given him and handed it to the boy.

Without Dok moving around the den making sure every item was polished, dusted, and meticulously arranged in an order that only seemed to make sense to him—it felt abandoned and strange.

"Has your contact said anything?" Jules asked Izzy.

She reached into her backpack and withdrew the circular holocomm. When she tried it, a blue light flickered before blurring into static. It might as well have been a coaster from the cantina.

"There's that," Izzy said, tossing it back in the pack.

"This doesn't make sense." Jules stood at the center of the den. His eyes scanned the display cases to see if anything had been moved or taken, but except for Tap's tinkering, nothing was out of place. Jules grunted his frustration. Izzy stood and walked over to him, resting her hand on his shoulder.

"Is there *anything* that feels wrong to you?" she asked.

"Nothing's been moved," he said, "and Tap can attest to that." The kid nodded in agreement.

"Could he have been kidnapped?" Izzy asked.

"Yesterday I would have told you that would be impossible, but after today? I wouldn't rule it out." Jules couldn't shake the feeling that he had missed something. When he got to the den that morning, he hadn't been worried. Dok was Dok, and he did things his own way.

He ran up the steps where Dok's desk was situated and went over everything with a sharper eye. Why hadn't he thought to look more closely before? Because he'd been ready to come and go, and because Izzy had been waiting for him. He didn't think Dok would leave the shop unattended for so long.

Dok's desk held wide-open ledgers in languages that Jules couldn't read. He wished he had Volt's knack for languages, but it was Basic, some Huttese, and enough Ithorian to communicate with Dok. Under any other circumstances, he would never disturb Dok's space. With his index finger, he closed the metal binder. Beneath that was a map of Batuu scrawled on a beige canvas scroll. Dok was old-fashioned in that he still used parchments when everyone else used holomaps.

Jules recognized the Outpost, the farms, and beyond the river gorge, the outskirts of town and cenotes near the ruins. An old tome was on the edge of the desk, something wedged between the pages. When Jules flipped it over, he found a spoon in the middle. That belonged to the cup of green spiced tea that was barely touched.

"It's like he meant to come back," he said.

"What do you mean?"

He stepped around the desk and imagined Dok sitting there. "I mean it was like he was sitting here about to drink his tea. He doesn't put anything in it, but he stirs it. I don't drink tea, so I don't know why you'd need to stir it, but maybe it's an old Ithorian thing."

"Sure," Izzy said, encouraging his train of thought. "Say more things like that. What does he do after drinking his tea?"

"He gives out assignments to his apprentices. But no one showed up today. That's why Tap came to fetch me, . . . But he didn't give us assignments. He left a scrap of paper. I thought it was strange, but Dok's a strange one. Tap, did Dok hand you the list today?"

Tap shook his head. "He was still writing it when I left. I figured I'd impress him and get started without being asked to."

Jules remembered wanting to earn Dok's trust and respect as a kid. Dok liked to test the way his apprentices handled different obstacles—rude customers, swindlers, even someone bold enough to try to rob the place. Tap was still too young to be put through those trials. But Jules couldn't shake the troubling sensation that had itched its way beneath his skin. He turned to look at the closed door to Dok's back rooms.

The metal was scuffed, but it had always been. The automatic sensors had been disabled long before because Dok paced the length of the mezzanine so much.

"What's behind there?" Izzy asked from the main level.

"Safe rooms," Tap told her.

Jules punched the door lock and it hissed open. Under normal circumstances, he wouldn't have dared. But he had a feeling. He turned to look over his shoulder at Tap and Jules. "Dok wouldn't leave this unlocked if he was stepping out."

Izzy and Tap scrambled up the steps and flanked him.

"What are you thinking, Jules?" Tap asked.

He didn't have a complete answer. He went through what he knew. Dok's walking stick was missing. His morning tea was untouched. His comlink was left behind. His radio wasn't turned on to listen to the Outpost broadcasts. Jules took a step forward.

"We're not supposed to go in there," Tap warned.

"Trust me, I know," Jules said, nerves fraying. "But

maybe there's something back here that might give us a clue."

His stomach clenched as he led the way into the dark back room that held Dok's safes, and beyond that his sleeping quarters. What if the reason why everything appeared normal in the den, at first glance, was because the real problem was back there? Dok was invaluable to the Outpost for trade, for work. He was a fixture, as much as the jagged old stone foundations and towering spires. But he had enemies.

"Can you think of anyone who might have a grudge to settle?" Izzy asked.

Tap and Jules looked at each other and chuckled. They could think of several someones.

"Yeah, but his last assassination attempt missed," Tap said.

Snooping around the dimly lit space felt wrong to Jules, but he didn't have another choice. The back room was filled with stacked crates and bins packed with items that needed to be cleaned and repaired. Dok's sleeping area was behind a curtain. Jules held his breath as he pulled one panel to the side. He huffed a breath of relief.

"What were you expecting?" Izzy asked, her green eyes amused.

"A body I'd have to explain to Oga," Jules muttered,

but wished he hadn't brought up the crime boss. He still didn't know what she'd told Izzy. Right now he had to focus.

Izzy crossed the room. She retraced their steps from the entrance and back. Her hand rested on the large safe room door.

"What are you doing?" he asked.

"I'm just trying to think—" She cut herself off and tapped her fingers on the surface. "If I wanted to get to Dok, I wouldn't do it in the den where I could leave evidence. Maybe he was moved. I still say kidnapping."

"But there's no sign of struggle back here," Jules said.

Izzy shrugged. "Maybe Dok knew them."

He laughed nervously. Should it trouble him that Izzy's mind went straight to kidnapping?

Then Jules realized. There was one thing that had been totally out of place. He'd assumed Dok knocked over the goddess figurine. But what if it had been someone else in a rush to get in or out? Who would know Dok's patterns? Who would have the nerve to even try? His gut told him what he needed to do.

"We have to try the safe room," Jules said. "It's the only room we haven't checked. If something is missing, then we'll have a direction at least. Tap, bring me Jaycee."

Tap ran back into the shop.

"You're pacing, Jules," Izzy pointed out. She, on the other hand, was leaning against the wall. Maybe she was so calm because she didn't fully understand what it meant for him to break a rule that had been ingrained in him since he was a kid.

"Whatever helps us get to Dok," he said. "Maybe after this is all over we can have a drink?"

Her eyes cut to the floor. The stone was scuffed from years of crates being dragged in and out. "Yeah, maybe."

Tap returned with an ancient astromech droid that had been retrofitted to vacuum. JC-284 powered up and began sucking up the dirt on the ground, but Tap spun it toward the safe door.

"The door, Jaycee," Tap said. "We need it open."

"Will that work?" Izzy said.

"Dok programmed it. I don't see why not."

The droid beeped wildly, clearly confused about having to do something that wasn't part of its new programming. But it complied. Jules could hardly breathe as he watched the droid spin and finally connect to the metal lock until the door sighed open.

A wooden staff swung out and jabbed Jules in the gut. He groaned and grabbed his knees, struggling to regain his breath.

"Dok!" Tap shouted, and ran in front of Jules. "It's us!"

"How did you get in there?" Jules choked out.

In deep, reverberating Ithorian, Dok muttered a string of words too quickly for Jules to understand, but he did catch a very clear "traitor." As he began to calm, Dok didn't exactly apologize to Jules for the jab to the stomach, but clearly he regretted that Jules was the one who'd been in the way. They helped him move to a sitting area behind a curtain.

The simple, plush couch was accented with a bantha-wool blanket. A small table made of wroshyr wood sat in front of it, with carvings Jules recognized from the Wooden Wookiee. Dok sat with his wooden staff gripped in his large, knobby hands.

"What's he saying?" Tap asked. He was still picking up Ithorian.

"To bring him tea," Jules said, and glanced at Izzy beside him. "And to have a good reason for being back here."

"Freeing him wasn't enough?" Izzy muttered. Fortunately, Dok was too busy taking inventory of his surroundings to hear her.

Dok motioned with his hand for them to sit. His round eyes blinked at Izzy, then turned to Jules as he spoke in his warbling voice.

"He wants to know who you are," Jules translated.

"I'm Izzy Garsea," she said, introducing herself in a strong, confident voice. "Pall Gopal sent me. I have this package for you." She tapped the side of the pack she carried.

Dok nodded, then muttered a string of curses that Jules would spare Izzy the translation of. Tap came back around with tea for Dok, but not the others.

"What happened?" Tap asked, and sat on the very edge of the couch.

Dok slammed the end of his cane on the ground, startling all of them. Dok shook his head, black eyes narrowed in anger. He set his cup down and stretched his back as he spoke. Jules had to focus to keep up. He watched the Ithorian's mouths move on either side of his neck.

"Two smugglers who owed Dok debts ran off," Jules said. "More afraid of the First Order presence than Dok. But two of his most trusted advisers went to collect."

Dok paused, picked up his cup of tea, stirred it, then drank.

"But how did you end up in the safe?" Tap asked. "You were here when I left."

Dok's voice was tinged with anger. Jules tried to imagine what it must feel like for someone like Dok to suddenly be powerless. Stuck, with nowhere to go. How many felt that way and didn't have the power and freedom the Ithorian had. When he was finished, Jules translated.

"One of his former assistants came to confront him," Jules said. "In the name of the First Order."

"For what?" Izzy asked.

"For contributing to the corruption of Batuu. He was convinced that killing Dok would somehow put an end to it. He was going to shoot him but lost his nerve. Dok fought back, but Calin caught him off guard. He shoved Dok in there and took off."

"Did you know him?" Izzy asked.

Jules shook his head. "Not well. You saw him though, when we got stuck in the street blockade. You have to get your assassin droid fixed, Dok."

Dok let out a surprising laugh and agreed with Jules.

"I took care of everything while you were gone," Tap assured his boss, holding his hand against his chest. "Didn't I, Jules?"

But Dok was rattling off more instructions. Jules paused and turned to Izzy. Her dark hair was wind-tossed around her face, her bright eyes looking expectant as she waited for him to speak. Once again, he didn't want to say the words. This time, it was because it meant their day was drawing to a close. So far, he didn't see a reason for her to want to stay longer. He hadn't given her the dazzling tour of the Outpost he'd promised.

"Dok apologizes for keeping you. It was unexpected,

and he conducts better business than this. He has your payment."

"Unexpected is one way of putting it," she said, and her smile devastated him. She took off her pack and removed the briefcase. "But at least it got to its destination."

"He says the parcel was procured for a client. That if you're in a hurry to leave you can go. You did your part."

Dok kept speaking, oblivious that Jules was trying to gather enough courage to say good-bye to Izzy once again. There were things he wanted to tell her. Maybe the reason he couldn't was because the day's events kept getting in the way, sending them running from one end of the Outpost to the other to save their skins.

Then he turned to Dok, not sure he'd heard him correctly. "You want *me* to take this?"

Dok hated repeating himself, and Jules cursed himself internally.

"Right, no," Jules said. "I'm your guy, Dok."

"Wait," Izzy said. "Respectfully, Dok-Ondar, if the job isn't finished, I will get it done. I'm not leaving until then."

Jules was too relieved to smile. "He said, suit yourself."

# IZZY

Why hadn't she taken the opportunity to leave? She had excellent reasons to go. Salju would have finished with the *Meridian* by then. The parcel was at Dok's. Delta Jeet might be looking for her still. Then there was her word to Ana Tolla that they'd stay out of each other's way. She'd just discovered a truth about her mother's past she wasn't certain how to deal with. She hadn't rested or had time to think. But she had found one reason to stay, even if it was for just a little while longer. She wasn't ready to say good-bye to Jules.

The added bonus was that she might make a good impression on Dok-Ondar in case she found herself coming back to Batuu. . . . He looked exactly as he had the one time she saw him as a girl, and she wondered what an Ithorian's life span was. For a moment, she wanted to ask him if he'd also known her mother. But she closed herself to that possibility. There was no time for the complicated feelings that would bring. What good would it do? She couldn't talk to her dead parents about it.

Back in the front of the shop, Dok retrieved a datapad. It was an old model that had been modified from other parts. Everything could be used again on Batuu. Izzy and Jules flanked him to look. Dok had also marked that place on his canvas map. He tapped coordinates on the glowing screen and warbled more information.

"The drop is here at suns-set?" Jules translated, as if he wasn't sure he'd heard right. "There's nothing there. Not even farms. There's only a bunch of rocks."

Dok scoffed a reply.

"I know rocks are not *nothing*. I mean, why can't they come to the Outpost?"

Izzy shrugged. "Maybe they don't have a transport or their speeder is stalled. You know what that's like."

He balked at her teasing, and Dok chortled but didn't speak again.

As they prepared to leave, Izzy considered where they were going. A suns-set drop-off for some hermit living in a cave somewhere on the outskirts of Batuu? Her gut told her there was more to Dok's client. There had to be. She no longer knew the typical machinations of life at Black Spire, but as she went over the day's events, there was one major difference from when she was a child, and that was the presence of the First Order. Why recruit on a planet that was only a refueling stop for most and a place to hide for others? Though clearly the assistant Calin and others had been taken in. Still, she couldn't help thinking that perhaps the real reason the First Order was on Batuu was because the Resistance was, too.

Who was she that she should even care? An orphan. The daughter of a bounty hunter, apparently. Someone trying to get by. *You don't have a name.*

She thought of Cookie's bitter anger when he'd been serving them. Of Oga's hurry to sniff out what might threaten her control over her small kingdom. Of the apprentice who had shaken with hate disguised as purpose. That thought led to another.

What was *her* purpose? Right then, it was to finish the delivery. And spend a bit more time with Jules. She watched him pull on his red canvas jacket and finger-comb his dark curls.

"You know I never ask you for favors, Dok," Jules said, "but can you put in a call to Delta and sort things out?"

Izzy crossed her arms and watched Jules try to unravel himself from that one. She'd known Dok for about an hour and could already tell what the answer would be. Dok held up one of his long fingers, his brown skin peppered with dark sunspots, gesticulating his protest.

"Yes, I know it's a problem we made," Jules said. "Yes, I know I shouldn't have set Bina's creatures loose. Yes, that is my tunic Izzy is wearing."

"I was undercover," Izzy blurted out, but she felt her

face grow hot. The Ithorian made a wheezy sound. Was that a laugh?

"I just mean that as long as Delta might be on the warpath, we can't stick around the Outpost. Unless you want us camping out here until the meet."

"You could wear masks," Tap suggested, going back to polishing metal ornaments. Dok gave a dismissive wave of his hands before making his way back up to his desk.

She was about to suggest that they could try to get back to her ship to have a conversation that wouldn't be interrupted by her seeing her old crew or riots or pets on the loose. But Jules snapped his fingers, a curious smile on his face.

"I have an idea."

She wasn't sure how, but she suspected what he would say.

"Home."

She knew exactly where he meant. Was she allowed to call it home still? She could conjure the image of her old house right away, even though she hadn't seen it in so long. If she was going to revisit it with anyone, she wanted it to be Jules. Besides, no one would look for them there.

When she stepped out the door, she almost wished she was standing in front of Delta Jeet or a furious Volt instead of the person she found standing there.

"Hello, starflower," Damar said.

# IZZY

## CHAPTER 14

There was a time when she'd thought her life would shape up differently. Perhaps if her parents hadn't been killed, or if she'd been the kind of girl who worried about her studies enough to stay enrolled in the academy. That girl wanted to explore ancient ruins like her father had before he became a farmer. But she was gone. Replaced with—well—whoever Izzy Garsea was becoming after a series of bad choices and worse luck.

She felt the doors to Dok's den shutting behind her and Jules standing beside her. Part of her wanted to be alone if she was going to have to speak to Damar. The other part—the petty, selfish part that made up too much of her being—was glad Jules was at her side. It was not to cause Damar jealousy, though the way his gray eyes took in Jules's considerable size did please her. It was because with Jules there, she had a reason to keep walking away.

Damar anticipated her direction and stepped in front of her.

"What?" she asked.

"Don't be like that, Iz," Damar said, extending his arms dramatically. He liked to think that there were always eyes on him, and hadn't she been one of his many admirers only a day before? "If you're mad about Actlyon City, I know you're a good shot. I wouldn't have left if I thought you couldn't take care of yourself."

She felt Jules move beside her, but she caught his eye. This was her problem to deal with.

"You must be the farm boy I've heard so much about," Damar said, extending a hand, which Jules did not accept. She bit down hard, her mouth dry at the thought of Damar repeating the words she had said to Ana Tolla. The only reason she'd said those things about Jules was because she'd wanted to discourage Ana Tolla's interest in him.

"Julen," he said, not giving his nickname to Damar.

Her fingers twitched like they had a consciousness of their own, wanting to reach for her weapon. When she'd been a girl, her mother had always slept with her blaster beneath her pillow, and when Izzy had asked why, she'd said, "The same reason you sleep with your stuffed bantha, darling." Those words held new meaning.

"Ana Tolla and I had an agreement," she said. "Stay out of each other's way."

"About that . . ." His smile was twisted, beautiful—cruel. "I convinced the others that we acted too rashly."

She laughed. "Did you?"

"I did. Ana Tolla sent me to ask you to come back."

Izzy crossed her arms over her chest. She recalled her conversation with Ana Tolla that morning. Then she'd seen the woman skulking in Smuggler's Alley before Oga's men had picked them up. What had changed since they'd spoken?

"I'm surprised Ana would take a job she couldn't see through," she said, lowering her gaze. She bit her lip and chanced a look at Damar.

He seemed delighted. "You see? It was all Safwan's fault. Went and got himself trampled by the riots earlier." Damar smoothed the front of his fine shirt, picking off a green leaf that had the misfortune of landing on his shoulder. "I told Ana you'd be perfect. You too, Jupen."

"Julen." His voice was dark, almost hurt when he turned to her. "You're not considering this, are you?"

Of course she wasn't. But she wanted to know what they were planning. Oga Garra had believed Izzy was looking to make deals with the locals. Had she confused her with Ana Tolla? Maybe not—there were plenty of young women new to the Outpost. But Izzy also knew Ana well enough to know that her jobs usually required a local or two.

"I'm going to have to pass," Izzy said, and shrugged. She enjoyed the way Damar had swallowed his pride. No doubt he hadn't wanted to be the one to come get her. But Ana Tolla's word was their personal law.

Perhaps Izzy did have lucky stars on her side, because the only person she had to answer to was herself. And, well, Dok-Ondar at the moment.

Damar held his hands up, a thread of panic lacing his voice. "I don't think you understand what kind of payout we're talking about. It's more than whatever drop-off you've got going on. You've been here all morning, and all you've managed to do is run around with the fa—" He considered Jules. Damar was tall but slender, and she knew quite well how useless he was in a fight that didn't involve blasters. "Julen."

"If it's so much money, why couldn't you find someone in Smuggler's Alley earlier?" she asked, and looked at her nails. There was dirt under them, just like there used to be under her father's. Even when they'd left the planet, he couldn't get them clean for weeks. But not her mother. *Her* hands were always clean. "Let me guess. No one in town will take a job that might mean upsetting the Outpost boss."

Damar scowled but recovered quickly. He scratched his temple, the glittering gem on that finger nearly blinding her when it caught the light. "You know, Izzy. I'm a little bit hurt that you're over me so soon."

That was low, even for him. "What did you think I was going to do? Cry over you for six moons and send you holos if I got lonely in the middle of the night?"

He grinned, exposing a sharp canine. "I thought our time together would take you longer to get over than a single night of sleep. But I always knew you were a little bit ruthless."

She leaned forward, her mouth forming a smile she did not feel in her heart. "You think too highly of yourself, Damar. The answer is no."

"Perhaps now," he said, resting a hand on her shoulder. She was surprised to find that it made her sad . . . until he finished: "But eventually you'll change your mind."

"I won't."

"I'm certain of one thing when it comes to you, and it is that you loathe being alone."

She wrapped her hand around her blaster. *"Leave."*

Damar waved and started to walk away. "Oh, and, Julen," he said, training a finger at Jules's head like the barrel of a blaster. "Make sure you take her somewhere nice to celebrate."

A spike of anger drove through her, and she drew her pistol. The shot burned a spot on the ground at Damar's feet. His electric gray eyes were all that much brighter with rage. He muttered a curse they couldn't quite hear as he *ran*. Though a few vendors had looked up at the sound of the blast, they lost interest in a blink.

Jules turned on Izzy. "I have more than a couple of

questions, Izzy, but maybe we can talk about why you keep shooting at people."

She holstered her blaster and shrugged. Her mother wouldn't have missed on purpose. Would she? "Jules, I'm sorry—"

"You don't have to explain anything to me."

But they stayed there in the shadow of the tree behind Dok's den for a moment longer.

"I wish you hadn't seen that," she said finally.

"Between the snakeskin boots and the flashy jewelry, he's hard to miss." Jules tried to laugh it off, but there was an awkwardness that hadn't been there before. "What did he mean about celebrating?"

She shook her head. "It's nothing."

He leaned in close, smiling playfully like he was trying to draw her out of a shell of her own creation. His voice was a whisper surrounded by the cacophony of vendors calling out to them. "I thought we were done with lies, Izzy."

She leveled her eyes at him and was surprised when she recalled her mother's words. "Lying is a skill."

# JULES

They made quick work of getting back to the cantina, where Jules's speeder was parked. Though Izzy's infuriating former boyfriend had gone in a different direction, Jules couldn't help feeling like they were being followed. He checked the favored hiding places for pickpockets, but they were clear. The entire Outpost seemed quiet as the day stretched into late afternoon.

The silence between them gave Jules space to think about Damar, with his hair a shade of blue Jules had only seen on the tongues of underwater animals. Everything about him was polished. His snakeskin boots were new, his pants were wrinkle-free like the clothes of the high-class dignitaries who liked to spend their time gambling at Oga's. But Jules couldn't give a Kowakian monkey-lizard's ass about what he was wearing. It was the smirk on his face as he spoke to Izzy that drove an ugly, hot sensation through his core. At least she'd gotten the last word—or the last shot, rather.

"Thank the ancients," Jules said, and peeled back the tarp he'd used to cover his speeder.

Izzy pointed at him. "Do *not* say it was luck."

"I won't *say* it, but I'm definitely thinking it." He powered up the engines and they took off, leaving the Outpost behind for the empty road that bordered the Surabat River Valley. He inhaled the first moment of true quiet and relief they'd had since their collision that morning. He tore his gaze away from her, trying not to think about how much he loved the sight of her in his tunic.

She rested her elbow on the side of the speeder and leaned out, watching the landscape roll by. Her hair was pulled back, but the loose strands whipped around her face. If he wasn't careful, he would drive straight into the next spire, because Izzy Garsea was the most beautiful girl he'd ever seen.

The more he tried to understand her, the more tenuous his grasp seemed. She was like the singular occasion when the three Batuuan suns shone at the same time a thunderstorm was rolling in. His mother had had a saying about that—something about sun gods fighting with rain gods, from when she was a little girl and her parents spun tales to go with the ruins they zoomed past. Izzy was two impossible things at once: his childhood best friend and a stranger who'd swept him up into her troubles. She was both fiercely independent, wanting to get off-world, and a girl who'd chosen to stay with him. She was laughing one minute and shooting at someone's foot the next—though that someone had deserved it. She was a wonder, and she might be his ruin.

But he wouldn't have it another way yet.

The broadcast from DJ R-3X crackled as they got farther from the Outpost. "Here's Sentient 7 and the Clankers with their smashing hit 'Droid World.'" When the signal was too scrambled, Jules shut off the radio.

"When today is over I think I might take a holiday," he said.

"Where to?"

"I don't know yet."

"I'm sure you've earned it, no matter where you end up."

He wanted to revisit their conversation from breakfast. But each time he began, he cut himself off. Why was he afraid to tell her what he'd done when he met Trix Sternus at Hondo's?

After he'd told the spice trader his entire life story, she'd asked him one question: "Do you want to see her again?"

Naturally, the answer was yes. But he'd listed his concerns aloud to Trix. He didn't know where Izzy was going. It seemed crazy to search the galaxy for a girl he hadn't seen in years. Plus, he didn't have a ship.

"Well, kid," Trix had said, "it so happens I'm here to sell my ship and stay awhile. I'll give you a good price."

He'd signed so quickly, he didn't even have time to process what he'd done. Then he'd stepped off the ramp and seen Izzy. Regret was the furthest thing from his mind. Even if they went their separate ways for a time, he'd done something he always wanted to. But he probably should mention it to Belen. . . .

They arrived at the abandoned settlement where they had once lived as neighbors. The cloudless sky blanketed them and a feeling of infinity came with it, like they were the only ones on the planet. That far out from Black Spire Outpost, the homes were smaller, simpler. The sandstone on the domed roofs was sun-bleached.

They got out and approached the crumbling structures. Smoke stained the outsides of the houses along the edge where the fire had started. Izzy put her hand close to handprints where someone might have used the wall to support their weight.

"You know, Izzy," Jules said, "you think louder than Neelo's caterwauling on live music nights at Oga's."

"And you drive slower than a ship running on fumes." Her words teased a smile from him. She rested her hands on her hips and stared at the small houses. "I can't tell them apart," she said sadly.

"Your homestead is further down," he said. "Next to ours."

She followed him along. It was like stepping through

a door into the past. When he was little, Belen told him that the cenotes near the ruins were portals. They were pocked caverns filled with pools of pale blue water. He swam to the bottom but only found pebbles and catfish.

"The things I remember from our time here are like flashes," she told him.

"If it's any consolation, I don't remember meeting you," he said. "You were always there."

"Until I wasn't." Their boots crunched pebbles. "And now I know why."

When he'd been waiting for her to return, he'd wondered why she left. Knowing, truly knowing, that it was Oga Garra, he felt even worse.

The small house the Garsea family had called home for five years was nearly overrun with vines and new, bright green trees. The entire settlement had been left behind, and the community had moved farther away from the farms and spread out. What remained looked much like the rest of the Outpost, an ongoing battle between the land and those who would build on it.

Izzy placed her hand on the entryway and peered inside. Faint light broke through holes in the roof. Jules lingered at the threshold. He marveled at her just as he had done since they were children.

There was nothing left after the fire, but still she searched the place that had once been her home.

"This is where my parents had their bed. I had

my own, but I used to crawl out of mine and curl up between them. Sometimes I'd wake up and my mother was gone, but my dad was still there. It was like sleeping next to a hearth because he ran so warm."

"I'm sorry, Izzy," he said, closing the distance to where she stood.

She found a drawer that had only been half-consumed by the fire and hadn't been ransacked by scavengers. "For what?"

"My intention wasn't to make you upset by coming here."

"I'm not upset, Jules," she said. There was something in the drawer—a doll that had seen better days, stitched around the sides. He recognized the work because he'd had the same one as a kid. "You know, I never retrace my steps? When I was small, after Batuu, we never stayed in one place longer than six months to a year. The shortest was on Corellia for two weeks, and the longest was here. I never allowed myself to miss anything or to make friends because I didn't want to ever feel what I felt on the night when I woke up and we were leaving the planet. I wish I had thanked your mother for this."

Izzy set the doll on the table. He couldn't stand the way she looked then and there. Lost. Like she had nowhere to go. Jules was not in a position to make promises to her or offer her anything but his presence.

"My mother asked for you before she passed," Jules said.

"Really?"

"The virus made her forget a lot. She also thought my da was still alive. I think she called you the frilly girl next door."

"My father called you my shadow."

He supposed he had been, once. But he said, "I still say you were the one following me."

Her face bloomed into a smile, her green eyes flecked with gold brighter under the ray of light where she stood. Her hand moved up his forearm and rested over his heart. Could she feel how fast it was beating?

"Izzy, earlier today I did something—"

Then they both heard a noise and turned toward the doorway. It was a shrill wailing sound. The spell of the past was broken as they went back out into the harsh light of day. There were no new footprints on the ground besides theirs.

"Are there animals out here?" she asked.

"Batuuan rats and nightsnakes, but nothing that makes that kind of noise."

"You were saying before?"

The moment was gone. But now that they were alone, he could ask her the things he'd wanted to know all day. They went back into the shade of the house and sat on the floor. He pulled out the bag of chocolate-covered caf beans and her eyes went wide.

"Thief!" She snatched it from him.

"Don't tell Tap."

"Tap? These were in *my* pack. I've been dreaming about these all day." She poured some into his hand.

"You've certainly gotten more generous since we were children," he said.

"I shared everything with you."

"Izzy," he said, "after your parents—why did you leave the academy?"

She crisscrossed her legs, fidgeting with the necklace under her shirt again. "At first it was an accident."

"Leaving or going in the first place?"

"I went to appease my father," she said. "He said when he was in school it was the best time of his life until he met my mother and then we became his world. We'd finally stopped moving around and Eroudac would do. A lot of good it did him to have followed her."

"You don't mean that," he said softly. "And you wouldn't be here if he hadn't."

She took a deep breath and looked away. "I wish—"

Izzy cut herself off. She rubbed her lips together and frowned. Was she afraid of what she was going to say? She rested her hands on her knees, and he reached out to hold the tips of her fingers. It was the only way he could let her know that she could talk to him. He'd wait if he had to.

"I wish I could talk to them both," she said. "Even for just a minute. Though I know if I could, I wouldn't have the courage to confront my mother and tell her that you shouldn't have a family if what you do is going to get you killed. All you do is leave people behind."

He licked chocolate from his tooth and considered that. It upset him in a way he couldn't explain until he voiced it. "That's not fair. My parents were average people, as far as I know. My father worked every day of his life doing what he was supposed to, and at the end of the day he still ran back in that fire to pull people out. He still left me behind. That doesn't mean that he shouldn't have ever had a family."

"But your father saved people," she said.

"Doesn't change the fact that sometimes I'm angry with him, too, Izzy." He took her hand in his and squeezed. "Keep going."

She let her fingers trace his. "The reason I dropped out and the day I took my first job were connected. My genetic science professor was always frazzled but had figured out a way to make a very potent tea from the haneli flower. But a drought on Haneli had made them nearly impossible to buy on her salary."

"She hired you," Jules said.

"I offered my services," she corrected. "I was running out of credits. I'd watched my mother, and I was so sure that smuggling was the reason we never stayed put. I thought I could do that. Besides, without my parents, I would have to start making my own way.

"I was friendly with some of the guards at the spaceport because I spent most days burning fuel by taking the *Meridian* for solo runs to nowhere. I'd watched my mother smooth-talk her way out of violation citations and get police officials to grant her landing permits to planets she had no business getting onto. Unfortunately, charm is not hereditary."

"I disagree," he said.

She nudged his leg with hers, then said. "Well, I got caught."

"What did you do?"

"The only thing I could think of. I panicked and dropped the cargo. I couldn't exactly show my face to my professor after that. I'd already spent the credits. Besides, I knew I belonged in the sky, not in a classroom relearning things my father had taught me long ago."

Jules wanted to point out that the haneli flower was not just used for teas, and her professor might have conned her. But he didn't want to spoil her memory.

"And after that you just kept going?" he asked.

Instead of answering she asked, "Do you still want to fly?"

"I've been saving for years. I woke up this morning not sure of what I wanted to do or where I wanted to go. I always find something that keeps me here."

She squinted at him—this girl he'd never thought he would ever see again, who had consumed him in the hours they'd been together. "What's keeping you here now?"

He licked his lips. "I haven't found an adventure worth chasing."

Izzy's gaze flicked to his mouth again. He wanted to lean closer to her, to see if she would meet him halfway. But there was too much sadness tugging at her smile, and he didn't feel right about it.

"The worlds out there aren't all we dreamed they would be," she said.

"Maybe they are and you've been with the wrong people."

"I wasn't always with Ana Tolla's crew."

"You're better off. If they make the mistake of crossing Oga—"

"I never liked that about them, you know. She'd never give details about the score. But her crew does everything she says, when she says it. People know Ana Tolla's name."

Jules scoffed. "I've never heard of her. Smugglers are as common as the rats in the landport. No offense."

"Those who send for her aren't moving shipments of rare pelts from Batuu to the Core. Ana Tolla drains your bank account to ruin, she holds people hostage, she gets sent in to unravel corporations and crush them."

Jules grimaced and crossed his arms over his chest. "My point stands. They'd be crazy to try. Ana Tolla, whoever she is, is small-time on Batuu."

"Then that makes me a nanosecond."

Jules watched the frustration that brought a pout to her sweet mouth. He shouldn't be noticing her mouth like that, but there he was. "Is that what you want? To be infamous in the galaxy?"

"I won't be much of anything in the galaxy if I can't get a simple delivery done."

Then the sound they'd heard before—a terrible squawking—returned, this time followed by the flapping of wings. The creature flew through the open door. It ruffled its purple-and-blue wings as it waddled to Izzy and settled in her lap, wrapping its prehensile tail around her arm.

"What's happening?" she asked, holding up her other arm.

Jules had to compose himself. Had the bird been

following them ever since the chaos at the market stall? "Volt told me about these. They sort of latch on to people with a strong bond."

"No bond," Izzy said, and tried to lift the creature off her lap, but that only made the loralora bird nestle deeper. "*You're* the one who freed her!"

"What's her name?" Jules asked.

"I can't name her," Izzy said. "We have to set her loose. Or return her to Volt."

He snapped his fingers. "I know."

"We are not naming the bird, Jules."

But as he said the word, the loralora bird flapped her wings and squawked in agreement. "Lucky."

# IZZY

## CHAPTER 15

The last thing Izzy needed was a stowaway. She wanted the loralora bird to bond with someone else. Though the bird *liked* Jules, she seemed particularly attached to Izzy. Izzy had never been good with pets, mainly because she had never been allowed to have any. In a last-ditch effort, Izzy grabbed the doll she'd found earlier and waved it in front of the purple-and-blue creature. It squawked and pecked at the figurine's head, but stayed put. A strangled laugh escaped her when the beheaded doll began falling apart at the seams. She remembered Mother Rakab had made it for her after she'd seen Izzy crying with jealousy over Jules's toy.

If Julen Rakab had shown up weeping on the Garsea doorstep, Ixel Garsea would have let him cry until he got it out of his system, then set him to cleaning spare parts that would be used for fixing the ship.

Among the skills her mother had taught her, wrangling a domesticated animal was not one of them. The loralora bird, aptly named because of the sound it made, went in the speeder with them.

"Do you think we can feed Lucky caf beans?" Jules asked as he drove. He was clearly relieved not to have to worry about Delta Jeet or Damar for the moment. They had a couple of more hours until the suns set, and he wanted to show her more of the surrounding area. She was happy to, but her mind lingered on the past. "Izzy?"

"Sorry, I was thinking about how kind your mother was compared to mine."

Jules smiled in that unbearably charming way of his. "Your mother was kind to me, Izzy."

"When?" Why did she question that so readily?

"There was one time when you were sick. All the kids had caught a strain of valley fever, but for some reason I was fine. She told me to go back home, but I said I could help take care of you."

She couldn't believe him. "I'm surprised she didn't tell you that you were being an idiot and would get sick, too."

"She gave me a piece of candy from her pocket and said that the best way I could help you was to let you rest. When I saw you earlier today, I thought you looked just like her in that jacket, you know."

Izzy looked down at the bird in her lap, using her jacket as a nest. When she looked in the mirror she liked to think that she resembled her father more, but everyone saw what they wanted to see when it came to their parents.

"It doesn't sound like her," Izzy said. "I never got any candy. Unless I stole it."

"Do you think that we're supposed to understand our parents?" he asked, taking his eyes off the road to look at her.

"I think we're supposed to at least know who they are." She hated that Oga had deepened that. She hated that it bothered her so much, because all she kept thinking was that if her mother had made different decisions, they could have had a normal life instead of jumping around more than a gorg in the middle of summer. Maybe she needed sleep to untangle her thoughts.

They crested a small green hill, and a quick memory came surging back to her. Running through golden fields of wheat. Laughing at the top of her lungs. She'd been there with her dad once. He didn't take her to work often, but on that particular day, her mother had been—away.

"I remember this," she said as Jules powered down the speeder. Up ahead were rows of crops, silos, and a water tower. "This is a grain farm. Is it bigger than before?"

"Kat's very proud of her operation. Business is booming lately. I mean, I've never tried the corn or grains from anywhere else, but I don't have to."

"She could make a fortune if she sold it to big farms."

Jules widened his eyes. "Don't mention big farms around here. She's gotten offers from all sorts of corporations. She's too proud."

"I mean, you can be proud and also rich."

Jules shook his head, but he was grinning at her as they got closer to the farm. Izzy could see where they'd recently expanded, adding more white storage barns. Two water towers flanked the fields in the distance. There was a small lot for speeders, but there weren't many parked there despite the number of bodies congregated at long community tables. Jules left his speeder at an angle and shouldered Dok's parcel.

"Time for you to go," Izzy said to the loralora bird.

"I don't think Lucky's going anywhere," Jules reminded her.

But the bird took off on great wings. She swooped around in a large arc before landing on Izzy's shoulder, wrapping that thick reptilian tail around Izzy's arm again. Jules looked ready to speak, but she held up a finger to silence him.

As they approached, Izzy noticed that the farmers were all kinds of species, some Izzy had never encountered before. Izzy had once thought of herself as cultured enough to have seen it all. Over the past day she had realized that she'd been pretentious. She had a lot to learn. She was only eighteen, after all.

A group of Twi'lek males with pale green skin and dark brown eyes were playing a game of cards. As they got closer, Izzy could see they weren't gambling with credits or spira but with everyday items—buttons, a couple of metal bolts, screws, pins, anything that seemed unusable until you needed to find one in a pinch. That seemed to keep everything friendly, though as one of the smaller Twi'lek males showed his cards, the others slammed the surface of the table and everything rattled. Izzy jumped at the noise, but in the next moment they were all laughing uproariously.

The next couple of tables were occupied by some younger humans and Sullustans, and a being with a long neck and wide eyes that Izzy had no name for. They were clustered together, watching a stream on the holonet. When one of the girls looked up and saw Jules, she perked up like a flower for the sun. Her skin was a shade darker than Izzy's, and her two braids made her look young.

"Jules!" she called out, then flicked her gaze down to the table. The rind of a fruit was coiled in front of her.

"Hey, Shari," he said warmly. "How's the day?"

Shari sat up straighter, running her fingers down the bottom of a braid. Her face was round and there was a tiny scar on her cheek. That kind of clean cut had to have been made with a very sharp blade. It looked like it was done on purpose. She wondered how the girl wound up there.

*One rock is as good as the next.* Her mother's words rebounded in her thoughts. But was that true? If one was as good as the next, why were some planets the kind where you could make a home and others were the kind where her parents didn't even allow her to step off the ship? Jules had said he always found a reason to stay on Batuu. She should ask him what those reasons were. Maybe then she'd have a better sense of where she could belong.

"It goes," Shari answered. "Surprised to see you here today. Did you change your mind about quitting?"

Shari, as well as the other farm kids, kept turning their eyes to Izzy. They looked at everything from the cuffs of her leggings to her windblown mess of a ponytail. She wasn't used to so many people staring at her, and she felt self-conscious. She let her hair down, allowing her scalp to breathe as the strands tumbled loose.

"Who are you?" someone with a squeaky voice asked her. "Is that a monkey-lizard? My gran won't let me get one."

"This is Lucky," Jules said, rubbing the bird between her eyes. "She's a loralora."

Izzy looked at the small Nautolan child who'd asked

the question. She had large brown eyes and tentacles for hair. Her skin was green with gold freckles, and her plain beige dress was adorned with fabric wildflowers.

"I'm Izzy. Who are you?" she replied.

"Ksana!" she yelled, and reached up to try to grab the bird's tail. The loralora flapped her wings and flew to the taller, safer perch of Jules's shoulder.

Jules laughed and said, "Hey, kid. I haven't seen you since you drank all my milk this morning."

The little girl giggled, and it reminded Izzy of a running brook. "Are you Julen's *girlfriend*?"

The other kids snickered, and Izzy wondered why her first reaction was to look at Jules's face. All she had to do was say that they were working together, that she was a girl and also his friend. But over the course of the day, her eyes had kept straying to his lips and his hair. The whole thing felt so complicated that she decided not to answer at all.

"Julen has a girlfriend?" someone said behind them. "Since when?"

"I'm not—" Izzy stopped when she turned and saw a face that was so much like Jules's she almost froze.

"Belen," Jules said nervously. "Overtime?"

"Did I hear right? Is this Izal Garsea?" she asked. Belen Rakab was almost as tall as her brother. The woman's age—nearly thirteen standard years older than Jules—and the hard work she put in showed in the crinkles around her eyes. Izzy had always associated those wrinkles with people who enjoyed life and smiled a lot. Her father had lines around his eyes, but her mother? She'd looked young, almost petrified in time.

Izzy went to shake Belen's hand, but the older Rakab sibling pulled her into a warm embrace.

"Please, please don't tell me that my brother has roped you into one of his wild schemes."

"I'm offended, Sister," Jules said. "Izzy's visiting and we're only catching up."

Julen Rakab was a terrible liar. Izzy almost wanted to laugh at all his tells. His eyes shifted from side to side, and his normally deep voice escalated in pitch when he said her name. He was too pure for this world, for any world probably. He scratched the back of his head to boot.

Belen's gaze cut to the bird, then Izzy, who simply shrugged. The look they shared held an understanding that there was something more, but the woman would not pry—yet.

"Right," Belen said, her tone underscoring that she knew her baby brother better than he knew himself. "Well, I'm working overtime today. A couple of the new hires took off this morning."

"That seems to be going around," Izzy said.

"Are you staying?" Shari asked Jules. "There's plenty of topato stew left over."

Jules rubbed a hand over the muscles of his abdomen. "If that's all right."

They had until the suns set, so Izzy saw no reason why not.

"I'll be right back," Jules said, leaving her at a table where the farm kids were congregated. Lucky flew down beside her, pecking at the small insects that crawled between wooden slats.

Izzy listened in, and found out that Shari was thirteen, as were the others, except for the Twi'lek boy who was sixteen and in charge of their little group. They were entrusted with harvesting the rows of the purple Surabat grain, which would be sweeter than the average one.

"I have the record for speed," a Sullustan girl said. The half-circle jowls of her face split wider as she beamed with pride.

"What do you do, Izzy?" a young Gungan asked. His accent was the same as the other kids'.

She leaned forward and drummed her fingers on the table. "I'm in between jobs."

"Then how did you get here?" the Sullustan girl asked.

"My ship. It's called the *Meridian*."

They all gasped. "You have your own ship?"

"You could work here," the Gungan said. "Kat's always making room for people and her farm is small, but Da says it's going to be the biggest season yet."

"Yes, Izzy!" Shari said. "Stay."

There was something starry in their eyes. They were so—innocent and hopeful. It dug deep into Izzy like a bruise. When was the last time she'd felt that way? *I always knew you were a little bit ruthless.*

"Are you daft?" the Twi'lek boy said. "Why stay here when she could go literally anywhere in the galaxy?"

"This is our home," Shari said, confused.

"Maybe for you," the Twi'lek said. "Your grandparents needed somewhere to hide after the Clone Wars."

That made Shari turn red. "Says you—"

Lucky squawked and flapped her wings. Izzy saw the argument was ready to turn ugly. Unlike in a cantina, though, she didn't need to worry about a bunch of kids shooting the place up. She was the only one there with a blaster, after all.

"I already used to live here," Izzy told them. Their shock was enough to settle them for the time being. "My ship has been my home for so long. It's the only thing I have left of my parents. But it's good to know that if I did stay, I'd have a friend. Thank you, Shari."

That seemed to make the younger girl smile again, just in time for the Rakab siblings to return with food. Lucky took off chasing after field mice. They ate, and Izzy told them a story about the *Meridian* running out of fuel and being dead in space. If it hadn't been for the

Frinn Mak Traveling Circus heading to Cuyacan, she might have floated until she ran out of supplies. Belen was mortified, but the younger kids (and Jules) were amused.

As the day grew cooler, Izzy volunteered to fill some canteens for those working overtime. She walked to the well near the water tower with the Twi'lek boy named Jac Lodain.

"I don't think you're between jobs at all," Jac told her as they trudged in the sun. He had the smirk of a kid who thought he knew it all. It reminded her of Damar for a moment.

"Yeah?"

"I've heard the whispers. There's Resistance here."

"You've got me all wrong, kid," she said, laughing. "But you're right about one thing. I'm not here between jobs. Or rather, a smuggler is always between jobs."

"How's that?"

"Well," she said coolly, "even when you're doing one job, you're trying to figure out how to find the next one. So, you see, technically, you're always between jobs."

He seemed to like that. She'd been around enough Twi'leks to know their lekku were an extension of their emotions, and according to his, he was pleased as a Hutt counting credits. That kind of smugness was dangerous. As they filled the canteens, she realized he wanted someone to listen to him, to see him.

"Well, my mom said she heard about them." The boy looked over his shoulder. He was trying to impress her, and she was going to let him. "She said she's seen a couple out in the old ruins. But my da warned her to be quiet. Especially if these bucketheads are still here."

"Your dad's right," she told him.

They made their way back to the long break tables. Only a handful of people remained.

Jac shook his head. "My dad and my aunt fought against the Empire. But she died. Da lost his arm. My parents brought us here. I want to be brave like that."

"Like what?"

"Brave enough to leave. To fight for something."

She looked at him. He had energy to burn. She thought that the galaxy was so big, there would be someone out there to give him what he was looking for—a cause. Just like the people they'd seen in the Outpost before the stormtroopers put on their display.

"Fight for your family," she said. She could not tell him what to believe in, but that was one thing she was sure of. "The ones who are blood and the ones who choose you."

He nodded in agreement.

"Wait," he said, "what family did *you* choose?"

"I still haven't," she said.

An alarm sounded. Izzy was about to stand and react out of worry, but the Twi'lek said, "That's the end of the day for me and the overtime bell for the others. See you around, Izzy."

She slapped the hand he held out as he flashed that smirk again. She decided it was less like Damar's—kinder. "You could always choose us, you know?"

Izzy sat alone at a table and told herself that she shouldn't get comfortable. This sort of camaraderie wasn't real. It was liked platonic infatuation. Sometimes people like each other in the beginning, but then something went wrong. *You loathe being alone.* She hated to admit it, but Damar had been right.

"You seem to have made quite the impression on them," Belen said, coming up beside Izzy. She took a seat, and they both watched the boy they had in common.

Jules was chasing the little Nautolan girl around, looking like a two-meter-tall toddler as he ran across the grass.

"Thanks," Izzy said. Why did she feel like she wanted Belen to *like* her? To approve of her?

"I didn't say it was a good thing."

Izzy's stomach clenched. Heat spread across her entire body. "Oh?"

"That came out wrong." Belen sighed. "I'm sorry. But you don't know my brother."

Izzy wanted to argue. It was on the tip of her tongue. She knew that he was beautiful and honest and strong. She knew that he'd stuck by her even though he had no reason to. She knew that she cared about him more than she was willing to admit. But she surrendered those thoughts, because what could she truly offer Jules?

"You're right," Izzy said.

"I know you aren't just taking in the sights. I know what your mother did."

"You and everyone else," Izzy said in a whisper that was nearly drowned out by the shrill cries of the kid. "I'm not like her."

"You're close enough. I've seen enough strangers to know someone looking for trouble."

"I don't want trouble."

"It's part of your line of work, whether you want it or not."

She shrugged. "I have a ship. People need things delivered. It's not much different from what Jules does for Dok."

"Maybe. But Jules isn't going to do that forever. Things follow you home," Belen said, as if her harshness was out of protection and not malice. "People follow you home. Why do you think most smugglers and pirates don't live to be old and gray?"

"Some do. I've seen—"

"That's not the life I want for my brother."

Izzy was breathing quickly. Why did it matter what Belen thought of her and her life choices?

*You could always choose us,* Jac had said.

"We're doing a job for Dok," Izzy said. She felt her skin tighten and imagined she was being shielded by the toughest, most indestructible armor. That was the way she survived. "That's all. I'm leaving tonight as soon as it's done."

"I blame you, Izal Garsea," Belen said.

"For *what*, exactly?"

"I wanted better for Jules. He got recruited for the New Republic Academy and he wouldn't go. He wouldn't leave. Even as he got older there was something keeping him here. I used to think it was our mother, but then she passed. Seeing the way he looks at you breaks my heart. I know, I just know that you're the reason he threw away opportunities."

Izzy shook her head. She didn't want to hear that. How could that be true? Belen was wrong, trying to blame Izzy for something that wasn't her fault. "Jules stayed here because he *loved* this outpost."

Belen's eyes, so much like Jules's, were difficult for Izzy to meet. "Answer me this, Izal. In all that time you spent flying from planet to planet, did you even think about coming back?"

Izzy's throat felt swollen. She *had* thought about it,

but she'd never done it. How was she supposed to know Jules was waiting for her?

"You finish what you came here to do, but if you leave, you had better not come back."

Izzy stood abruptly. She glanced up at the loralora bird flying in circles above her. She hadn't wanted the creature attached to her. Bonded, as Jules had said. But as Lucky began to fly away from the farm, something inside Izzy went cold. Hadn't she attached herself to Jules all day? He made her laugh. She'd never been able to talk to anyone the way she did with him. He was patient and had a good, strong heart. She couldn't break it.

"I won't come back. That's a promise."

Belen nodded once, then said, "I need to get back to work."

That was when Izzy realized Belen was keeping two hands on her stomach in a protective way. She was showing the barest signs of pregnancy. She imagined Jules caring for his future niece or nephew. He was good with children. He was good with *people* in a way she had never even attempted. Jules belonged on Batuu with his family.

"It was good to see you, Garsea. Good journey— well—back to wherever home is."

Though that bothered Izzy more than she wanted to admit, she did her best not to flinch as Belen embraced her before returning to the farmlands.

Jules chose that moment to return to Izzy's side. His hair was messy and his skin looked warm. She wanted to shake him. She wanted him to hold her.

"Sorry I left you alone with my sister," Jules said. "She's intense. She's a surrogate mother to every kid here who doesn't have one. Where's Lucky?"

Izzy didn't need a surrogate mother, but she needed someone to remind her where she belonged. Wherever home was? That was the *Meridian*. It was old and chugged fuel, but it was the only place where she felt safe. Being on Batuu was messing with her mind. She had to stop vacillating between nostalgia and dreams and do the job.

"Izzy?"

"She flew away," she said, then walked past him, down a path where the labyrinth of weeds grew unruly and tall, hiding her from sight. She breathed in the sweet smell of grain, of fertilized soil, of grass. Jules.

She let out a pained laugh at the thought of having made promises to both Rakab siblings. To Jules she'd promised to come back. To Belen she'd promised to stay away. She could keep both of those promises, even if the first one had been thirteen years too late.

# JULES

## CHAPTER 16

There had been a good rainy season, and it showed in the wildness of the trees, in the lands that lay on the periphery of the farm that gave way to jagged spires. Just as they had when they were kids, they hiked over the crags, keeping balance with their hands. They stopped on a small grass mount enclosed by narrow rock walls, far enough from the farm that no one would notice them.

Something had upset Izzy, and Jules had a good idea what it could be. "Did Belen say anything to you?"

"No," she said, her voice tight.

"Lie. I think I've earned some goodwill from you today."

She whirled on him then. The green of her eyes was just as wild as the weeds that towered over them. She ran a hand through her hair and shook her head.

"You want to talk about lies? Let's start with you."

His heart beat wildly against his ribs. "What *about* me?"

"You told me that you didn't know what was keeping you here," she said. "That you haven't found an adventure worth chasing."

238

"What's wrong with that?"

She waved her hands in the air, her voice tense. "Everything. I'm not your adventure, Jules."

"I never said you were." He took a step back. What had Belen said to her?

"Then why are you still here on Batuu when you could be anywhere else?"

He'd had enough people in his life asking him the same question. Belen. Haal. Other farmers. Lee. Even Dok. He'd never been able to give a real answer. He understood why Belen believed that Izzy was the sole reason he'd never left the planet.

One year, when he was around eight years old, there was a bad harvest. There wasn't a lot of work to go around, and some families were taking off on transports to nearby worlds in search of jobs. All Belen had done was suggest it to her parents. Jules wouldn't go. He remembered it had been one of the few times he'd thrown a fit. What if Izzy came back? What if he wasn't there when she did? The Rakab family had stayed put, but it hadn't been to appease Jules. It was because his parents had found temporary work instead. His father would have put up with Jules's cries no matter what. He knew that.

Another time, after he'd gotten the opportunity to enroll in the academy after most of his friends had left the planet, Belen had taken him out to celebrate. It was the first time he'd been drunk. He'd confessed that he'd declined and thrown out his application. He'd never seen her so upset. He remembered saying something about Izzy when Belen asked why. But he couldn't recall exactly. Maybe it was just her name. That memory was cloudy, blurred by his first time being intoxicated.

Maybe when he was a boy he'd been heartsick and waiting for a girl to return. But he had been a child then. Children were allowed to have ridiculous dreams. He couldn't lie to himself though. Even after he'd given up the notion that he'd ever see her again, a tiny part of him still wished. Had that wish embedded in his mind so deeply that even earlier that morning he couldn't figure out what to do with his life until she'd shown up?

The answer wasn't simple. Even if what Belen had said was true, he was his own person. He'd had a good life on Batuu. It didn't matter why he'd stayed.

"Why wasn't it enough that this is my home?" he asked. "I can imagine what my sister said. But, Izzy, everything has changed. Now I have—"

"Oga offered me a job," she said quickly. "An audition, really. I'm going to take it."

The wind blew around them, cooling as the suns began their descent. He'd been hit by a lot that day, but nothing compared with those words.

"Why would you do that?"

"Because it's the only thing I have." Her eyes were glossy. "I was just beginning to think I belonged here, but now I'm not so sure. But I do know one place that has always been constant for me, and that's my ship. It's the sky."

He wanted to hold her, to tell her that she could have him. She didn't have to feel she was alone in the galaxy anymore. But he didn't think she wanted to hear that. "An hour ago you were furious at your mother for leaving you behind. What now? You're just ready to follow her into the grave?"

"Do you even know what's out there, Jules?"

He scoffed. "You know that I don't. But please, enlighten your farm boy on the great wide galaxy."

"I *asked* you to come with me," she said.

"That wasn't a real offer and you know it. That was you wanting to be certain that you can't trust or count on anyone. You set me up to take that fall."

"You don't know me." She shook her head. "We can do this little tour of the Outpost, but at the end of the day we are virtual strangers."

"Lie," he said again. She was so close to him that if she tilted her head up they would be close enough to kiss. Why did he want her more than it was reasonable to? Why did she have to come back only to keep reminding him that she was leaving again? "I know the galaxy will never be big enough to fill that emptiness in your heart, Izzy, because you don't want it to. You want to keep running because you wouldn't know what to do if you had to stop."

"And you want to stay here because the *second* you left atmosphere you'd lose the only safety that you know."

He reached for her, to hold her, to tell her that there was nothing wrong with safety. He wished he could make the galaxy safe for all of them, but he was only one person. So he closed his fists around air and put more distance between them until he was leaning against a rock wall.

"You're right," he told her, weary and spent. "It's best you leave. Chase the memory of your mother or Ana Tolla. Skies, even Oga's a better option for you than I am. But while you're chasing that, don't forget that you had a father, too, and from what you've said he wouldn't have wanted this for you."

She walked over to him and pressed a finger into his shoulder, hard. "That doesn't change that I can't give you what you want."

He was so angry with her. But when her jab softened into a touch, some of that anger melted. She pressed the palm of her hand on his shoulder. "What have I asked of you that you can't give, Izzy? Because I think we're fighting for the same thing."

"Me," she said. "You were willing to change the course of your life on a whim. That's too much pressure to put on one person. I don't know how to be that much to someone."

He felt his anger simmering, melting, and reshaping itself the way he'd seen the vendors in the glass market stall do with bags of sand. Breakable. Fragile. He could not afford to be that. Neither of them could.

Izzy and Jules had a long past and seemingly no future, but as she brought her lips to his, the singular thing in their lives that hadn't changed was that they had each other.

# IZZY

## CHAPTER 17

She should have kissed him hours before, but it was as difficult to be honest with herself as it was to be with others. Jules gripped her softly by the shoulders and pulled her against his chest. Her anchor, solid as the boulders around them.

When she'd woken up that morning, angry and heartbroken after being left behind, she couldn't have predicted where she would end up—surrounded by jagged rocks and trees so crooked they looked like they were hitchhiking their way up the cliffside. She pressed herself against him, wished they could take back all the terrible things they'd said to each other. But wasn't that where they'd gone wrong? Her lying. Him holding back.

She thought of the little girl she used to be, chasing spiran fireflies across the plain behind their homes, her hair in the two braids her father would make every morning before dropping her off to play with Jules. They skinned their knees when they climbed rock spires. Equipped with rusty screwdrivers, they carved their names into the rock. She wouldn't be able to find the spire where they'd done that, or the cliff where they'd spent their last day together, but she bet Jules would.

It was Jules who broke their kiss first. Somehow they'd ended up on the ground. He propped himself on one elbow and they stared at each other. He met her hands with his, farm boy hands. Now that she knew what it was like to kiss him, how was she going to keep her promise to Belen and leave?

Jules let out a deep chuckle. "Say something, Izzy, because my brain is fried."

"I wish I'd come back sooner."

He took off his canvas jacket and offered it to her as a pillow. She watched the sky. They had to leave soon to go to the coordinates Dok had given them, and then the strange day would be over. Izzy felt a kind of excitement she hadn't in so long. The tight knot of anxiety that seemed to always be lodged in her chest had unraveled sometime between leaving Dok's den early that morning and reaching the farm. Perhaps it was a side effect of being with Julen Rakab.

"It might not have been the same." He touched the cluster of freckles along her jaw. "I shaved my head last year on a dare from Volt."

"You're right. I would have just kept walking." She scrunched her nose.

He shook his head, grinning. "I mean maybe I was too busy working or running around with my friends and you were with your crew. We're not done figuring ourselves out. But maybe you came back at the right time."

He was right about that, too, she supposed.

"Thank you for bringing me here," Izzy said. "I'd almost forgotten that my dad brought me to work a couple of times."

He bit his bottom lip. "I'm sorry I said that about your father."

"You weren't wrong. My mother might have taught me how to fly and shoot," she said, "but I always felt like I was chasing after her love. My father just gave it."

There were other things her father had taught her: How to be kind when you didn't always feel it in your heart. How to read star charts, because there was always a way to fly yourself out of anything but a black hole. He'd taught her other things she couldn't put to use, not if she wanted to pursue a career as a smuggler—like you could love someone even if you didn't always understand them. It was never an official lesson, but she'd watched and gathered that love was the only reason her father had stayed with a woman who'd been practically married to the stars.

It was stupid to think of her parents at a time like this, but she couldn't help it.

In truth, Izzy felt out of her depth, though she loathed to admit it. "I made a promise to Belen."

Jules frowned. "Please tell me it did not involve me."

She met his eyes, even though she wanted to look away. It was easier to be honest when she didn't have to look at him. "She told me that if I was going to leave, not to come back."

He groaned. "She shouldn't have said that to you."

"No, she shouldn't have. But she did, and I agreed."

"Then—don't leave."

"What do you mean?"

"You asked me to leave with you, and I said no because I thought the only reason you were asking was because you were afraid."

She had been. A part of her still was.

"But I'm not afraid," Jules said. "I'm not asking you to stay forever. Stay for a couple of days. I bet it's been hours since you last slept. "

She turned his offer over in her mind. What would she do in the Outpost? She felt like she'd seen it half a dozen times over that day.

*Be with Jules.* The answer came instantly.

"For a professional liar, you take your promises seriously," he teased her.

"Do you *want* me to stay?"

The Jules she'd been with all day was back. His laughter was contagious as he fell against her. Jules pressed a soft kiss on her jaw.

"I do want you to stay," he said. "I'm not done getting to know you.

Izzy had been so consumed with him that she hadn't realized the sky was beginning to show the first signs of color, so bare it was like a drop of ink in a glass of clear water. She sat up and handed him his jacket back.

"What's wrong?"

"Suns are setting," she said.

They raced back to the speeder.

# JULES

Jules Rakab had kissed girls across Black Spire Outpost, but he had never felt a fraction as elated as he did the moment Izal Garsea pushed up on her toes and reached for him. The wind around them was cold and the ground even colder, but their lips weren't. The moment felt like it went on forever and was cut too short.

Whatever they had begun that day, it could continue. She was staying. He was already thinking about how they should celebrate after getting rid of the blasted parcel that had rained chaos on their day.

"How far are the coordinates?" she asked.

"We'll make it," Jules assured her.

The worry mark on her forehead was back. "Are you sure?"

He put everything he had into his speeder engines, and the force of the velocity kept them from being able to speak. He wished he could tell her that he was unsure of so many things—what he wanted to do with his life and where he might be in the next year. He was unsure if he'd ever turn into the man his father wanted him to be. He should have been unsure about his feelings for

Izzy, too, because they were irrational. At first it was brought on by her beauty and nostalgia for their youth, but throughout the day he had wanted more of her. Her anger, her fears. He *was* certain about her.

When they reached the drop-off location, Jules thought about the day he'd fallen into a cave. He'd been out with his friends searching for the cenotes and came upon a cave covered in roots and crumbling ruins. He'd slipped on the wet rocks and gone through a hole in the ground he hadn't noticed. Naturally, his friends ran because they were afraid of getting in trouble. Belen had found him on her own. He loathed being so small. But he hadn't been as terrified as he should have been, because he knew Belen would come for him. She'd been trying to look out for him when she asked Izzy to stay away from him. But he was his own person. He hoped to make her see that.

"If anything could get me to believe in magic," Izzy said. "It would be this place."

He squeezed her hand. That part of the land was covered in pale gray rock formations and rich green grass fed by the water in the cenotes. Trees grew low, their wispy leaves brushing the ground as if they were bending forward in prayer. There was a stillness there. It was a place of secrets from the time of the ancient ones who once roamed those lands. There was nothing new on Batuu, and nothing about it ever went wasted by new settlers, no matter how long they stayed.

The suns were bleeding toward the horizon, giving way to two silver moons. He could have stood there watching her until the light went out, but then they heard a clicking noise behind them.

They whirled around, staying close to each other.

"Bright suns, travelers," Jules said.

The two strangers who approached were dressed in plain trousers and long-sleeved shirts that had seen better days, and they carried blasters at their hips. One was a young Mon Calamari man, and the other was a woman a little older than Jules. She had dark brown skin and tight curly hair kept short. Her eyes narrowed with suspicion.

"And rising moons," the Mon Calamari said. "I'm Lejo."

"Dok-Ondar sends his regards," Jules said.

"May the spires keep him," Lejo said. His voice carried a heavy weight.

"Thank you for coming all this way," the woman said. She didn't introduce herself, and neither did Izzy and Jules.

Izzy shook off her pack and knelt to take out the parcel. After everything they had been through that day, she somehow managed to say, "Just doing my job."

The other woman flashed a knowing smile. She turned to Jules and watched him carefully. "In that case, thank you *both* for doing your jobs."

It hit him all at once. No one lived in the ruins, not even new settlers. But he realized, if the First Order was a loud display parade in the Outpost, then wouldn't the side that opposed it be hidden whispers waiting for the right time? Something within him shifted for a second time that day. The first was when Izzy had kissed him. That was possibility. This shift—he couldn't name yet. But it was bright.

"I'd heard rumors that the Resistance was on planet, but I didn't think it was true," he said.

Lejo quirked his head to the left. "Why's that?"

Jules smiled and lifted a shoulder. "You never know what's true around these parts."

"Dok wouldn't have sent just anyone out here," the woman said.

"How do you know Dok?" Izzy asked.

"My mother was a botanist on Raysho. She used to procure bulbs for Dok's gardens."

*Dok's gardens?* was Jules's first thought, followed by the realization that Raysho was in the Hosnian system. Before he could say anything, she spoke again.

"I've heard that everyone on Batuu is always either looking for a new life or running from one. Which one are you?"

Jules thought about that for a moment. Why did she want to know? He had nothing to run from. People always seemed to want more—more credits, more things, more space. But that didn't mean a new life. And he had never wanted to run from his. When he looked at Izzy, the emotions she kept behind her steel walls, he reconsidered what it would mean for her to have a fresh start. What it would mean for him, if she would have him.

"Neither," he said. "I know who I am."

The woman smiled. She turned to Izzy and asked the same question. He was expecting her not to answer, but then she said, "Both."

Before the strangers turned to go, Izzy hesitated.

"Wait," she blurted out. There was something bright in her eyes. "I know I wasn't supposed to ask. But can you tell us what we've been carrying all day?"

The two strangers looked at each other. Lejo nodded at the woman, who squared her shoulders and said, "You didn't care before. What's changed?"

Izzy glanced at Jules, then back at the strangers. "Maybe my curiosity is getting the best of me."

"Imagine being pushed so far to the brink of something that you think you might fall," Lejo said. "You're alone in the galaxy. You're cut off from the most basic necessities and medicine. But sometimes there is hope and allies surprise you. Does that clear your conscience?"

Izzy gave the barest nod. "Good luck."

"If you want to keep doing some good," the woman said, "you know where to find us."

A strange feeling sparked within Jules. He thought of the helplessness he'd felt throughout the day. Could he change that?

"We have to go," Lejo said.

"Rising moons," the young woman said, "and may the Force be with you."

Jules stared as the two figures disappeared into the dark caves that snaked beneath the cenotes.

"What's down there?" Izzy asked when they were out of sight.

"I've only been down there once, and I thought it was a pit," he said, remembering waiting in the dark for someone to find him. "I suppose I was wrong."

They stood there for a moment, listening to the sound of the breeze over water. He considered what might have happened if Calin had never abandoned his job. Would he have been sent instead of Jules? Dok never got involved in politics, as far as Jules knew. How long had Dok known about the "hermits" in the ruins? He *was* over two hundred years old and had seen his share of political upheaval and wars. If he wanted to stay out of it, he would have. Then again, the sooner the First Order got what it came for, the sooner the Resistance would leave. And then what? Black Spire would return to normal, or what passed for normal? Just when he thought he knew everything about the Outpost, he'd been surprised.

"We did it, Jules," Izzy said. "We should celebrate. I'll wire you half the credits I get for the job."

He took her hand in his. "Dok can pay me. I'm not taking your money."

She smirked and glanced down. "You'd make a terrible smuggler."

"I wouldn't say no to a celebratory drink at Oga's. But I should wash first. I wouldn't be the first person to show up there covered in dirt, sweat, and blood, but it's really frowned upon."

He started walking away from her.

"Wait, where are you going?"

Jules turned and kept walking backward, daring Izzy to follow. "The cenotes. The waters are the perfect temperature."

"We shouldn't go there. That's where—"

"You scared, Garsea?"

Izzy and Jules shared a look. The entire reason she had returned to Batuu was gone, but he'd offered her a reason to stay. Part of him wished he could draw out the suns-set so he could always look at her bathed in those colors.

He kept walking, and he thanked the stars that she followed.

# IZZY

## CHAPTER 18

That was either the best idea he'd had all day or the worst. They might have delivered the parcel as they were supposed to, but when they returned to the Outpost, they'd have another problem: Delta, and perhaps even Volt. Salju would be finished with the repairs, and Izzy would need to find a place to dock for a few days.

But as Jules walked backward with that crooked smirk on his face, she knew she wasn't going anywhere but with him. The path deeper into the ruins were was lined with crooked trees. Patches of grass grew taller amid boulders, and vines clung to jutting rock walls. At the center of it was the cenote, its blue surface dotted with leaves blown in by the wind. It felt like entering the past, and not just because of the deteriorating structures around them.

When she stood at the edge of the water and took in the crumbling stones and rock formations, she was overcome with a sense of familiarity. She had been there before. Not with Jules or her father. But with her mother. She squinted at the willowy trees that looked like they were bowing to the pool. She concentrated on the memory, tugging it closer. Her mother had loved to swim. When Izzy thought about swimming, she always remembered her father teaching her how to float, how to cut through the water. But before that, there had been her mother and these ruins. Izzy could see herself as she was then, scared of the black fish swimming. Her mother had laughed, but let her sit and play with the critters in the grass.

She smiled to herself and thought that Jules *was* the best tour guide in the Outpost. He'd helped her retrace her steps. She wouldn't have done that on her own.

The cenote was illuminated in the colors of the suns-set. Tiny black fish swam at the bottom of the stone basin. If not for the ripples on the surface, she would have thought the creatures were floating through air. The water was that pristine.

Now that they were alone again, Izzy was faced with everything she'd agreed to. She was staying, for a few days at least. But it wasn't worry or anxiety that made her buzz. It was Jules.

He stripped down to his underthings. She felt a blush creep up her face and turned toward the outcrop of trees. Thank goodness it was dark enough that he wouldn't see how red her face was.

Jules bunched up his dirty clothes in his hands. She allowed herself to look at the rest of him. She told herself it was just skin and muscle and there was nothing extraordinary about it. But as she had done many times throughout the day, Izzy was lying to herself. The crystalline light danced across his taut muscles.

"My eyes are up here, Garsea," he told her with a wink.

"I wasn't—" She was getting flustered. Honestly, there were dokmas with more poise than she was displaying.

He jumped into the clear water, which was emanating a soft blue glow. Bioluminescent creatures cast a soft light that replaced the setting suns.

He splashed her, but she would not devolve to his level. He brushed water out of his eyes and treaded water a few paces from her. The fish directly below him scattered into the pockets beneath the ground.

"My mother brought me here once," she told him. "She preferred quiet places like this. I hadn't remembered until now."

"Did she tell you how this was created?" he asked.

"I don't think she knew. She wasn't much into local history. My dad might have known." She took off her jacket, boots, and socks, but did not get in the water yet. "Tell me."

"My dad said that thousands of years ago, when the original people of Batuu lived here, there was a small meteorite that hit right in this spot. It created these basins, and they filled with water. It was sacred. They're ruins now, but they could have been temples before, homes."

"Why don't more people come here now?"

"It's too far from the Outpost. Besides, not many people like to swim unless it's terribly hot."

"But you do."

"Of course I do. I was about seven when my friends and I thought we discovered this. I had no choice but to learn because this kid, Lu something—I don't even remember him, really—he shoved me in. I had to either learn to swim or sink to the bottom."

"I have this vivid memory of learning to swim when we lived on Glee Anselm. Back then it felt like my father and I were always waiting for my mother to come home from her trips." She glanced at the stone, light reflecting off it. "After we left Batuu, we didn't talk about our life here. It was like this unspoken agreement. Every time I thought of this place I thought about how we left. I didn't want to feel that way again."

"You won't," he said. He sounded so optimistic that she believed him.

Jules swam away, and everything inside her told her to jump in, to chase him. Why were the doubts louder than her heart, where there had been none when they kissed? She considered that it had to do with Damar. But as angry as she was with him for leaving her, she didn't feel hurt to lose him. One day with Jules had been better than the past year with Damar.

*What are you afraid of, Garsea?* Those words tumbled in

her head, and she weighed them. Fear was a fuel that usually set her into action. The fear of starving and winding up dead in space made her keep searching for jobs. The fear of becoming her mother had troubled her for a long time. Now that she knew more about her mother, she wanted to hold on to her memories of her. Her mother had still chosen Izzy, for as long as she was able. The fear of being alone had kept her at the academy, with Damar, and then with Ana Tolla's crew. She feared losing Jules again, but this time she was in control of the outcome.

So while Jules was chasing the fish at the bottom of the cenote, she finished removing her clothes, adding to the dirty pile on the ground.

She dove headfirst into the water. Julen Rakab had lied to her. It was cold—so cold that she couldn't breathe as her arms flailed. She kicked to the surface.

"Liar," she said, her teeth chattering. When she licked her lips, she was surprised to find they were salty.

"Swim to me," he said. "You'll warm up as your body moves."

She did just that, relishing in the movement of her arms and legs. It had been months, maybe even years since she'd done this.

"See?" he asked, when she surfaced in front of him. "Are you cold now?"

She wrapped her arms around his torso, her knees

on either side of his waist. "Now that you're swimming for both of us? Definitely."

He licked his lips. She dragged her fingers around the base of his neck. Droplets of water clung to his dark lashes. She found that she didn't want to look away from him. She wanted to tell him all the things she'd been holding back.

"I've thought about you all the time. Sometimes I'll fly to a new world and think about how you would love the mountains or frozen lakes or the lights. I wanted to come back to you after my parents were killed."

"Why didn't you?" His arms were moving faster, propelling them to the other side of the cenote, where it was shallower. When had the night grown so dark?

"I was afraid," she said. "We were friends when we were children. What if you didn't remember me? What if too much time had passed? I couldn't take the chance."

"All you do is take chances, Izzy. Why would this have been any different?"

She considered this. He wasn't wrong. If Damar was right about anything, it was that she didn't like being alone. She thought about who she'd been during that time in her life. Scared, reckless, impulsive. Lonely. At times she'd thought of Jules, of charting a course to him. And then she'd convinced herself not to. "Because I'd lost my mother and father already. It was better to dream of what could have been instead of facing a truth I wasn't ready for. What if you looked right through me? What if you hated me? I didn't want to find out."

"Believe me when I say that I have missed you every day for as long as I can remember."

She couldn't believe him. "That's a bold statement."

"It's true. You're the one who said I was a terrible liar. Tell me, Izzy—am I lying?"

She knew he wasn't. But that familiar panic took hold of her. If he hadn't been carrying her, it would have pulled her under. "What happens tomorrow and the day after? What happens if a week from now you decide that I'm too terrible, I'm not the girl you remember. What if you decide that I'm not what you wanted?"

"I want you," he whispered.

"Why?"

"Because you're everything. You are the reason I can find bravery when I don't want to be brave. You were right. I did follow you around when we were kids. I wanted to keep up with you."

"I'm not brave, Jules." Without wanting to, she was thinking of Damar again. Unlike all her moments with Jules, she couldn't remember a single moment with Damar being so emotionally intimate. "If I was, I would have gone on my own sooner. I wouldn't have followed Ana Tolla even though I knew she did terrible things. I went along with more than I ever want to tell you."

He kissed her jawline. "You don't have to. I think you're stuck with me, Izzy."

"I wish I'd spent yesterday with you."

Jules rested his hands on her waist to hold her tighter. The water was around their shoulders. "Is this about what Damar said?"

She nodded. "When I was a little girl, my dad used to get these candles for my birthday. They had them on Coruscant or someplace he'd been to before. They lit up like fireworks. After he died, I didn't celebrate my birthday."

"Why?"

"Because it was only me for a while. This might surprise you, but I don't have as many friends as you do."

"I'm your friend, Izzy. What does that have to do with Damar?"

"I was with Damar for almost a year. I knew things weren't right, but when I tried to end it he told me that I needed to give him another chance. That he had something special planned for me. He said that on my birthday he was going to light up the sky the way I deserved. Instead, he left."

Jules watched her with dark eyes. The light of the cenote around them gave their skin an incandescent blue glow. She hated that she had taken the smile from his face.

"I told you, it shouldn't matter. I know how to be on my own. I should've known better—"

"You said that he left you yesterday," he said.

She traced the outline of his shoulder, and somehow it felt like she had always been doing it. "It was the best thing that happened to me because it led me here. Oh, skies. I sound like you, don't I?"

Jules frowned, but it only lasted a moment. "We have two things to celebrate now. Tell me what you want."

They floated toward the center of the water, and everything around them fell away. If she would only look up, she'd see the canopy of stars above them, the shine of the moons. But her eyes were fixed on Julen Rakab, and for a moment, she was certain she was where she needed to be.

"I want you to kiss me."

# JULES

## CHAPTER 19

Julen Rakab had been imagining what it would be like to kiss Izal Garsea since the moment she'd punched him in the face. Then she'd kissed him outside the farm. He wanted nothing more than to do it again. So when she said the words, he should have jumped at the opportunity.

If he were a different kind of person—a scoundrel, a scourge, a pirate who stole hearts for the sake of doing it—he would have kissed her in an instant. Perhaps he wasn't the good guy everyone thought, because he so badly wanted to. But Izzy had just been through one of the worst experiences of her life since losing her parents. Being abandoned by someone who had professed to care for her had to have done something to her. Would kissing her be taking advantage? Before she'd confessed to him, he would have done it. Everything inside him ached to do it.

"Are you sure that's what you want?" he asked, needing permission.

"Yes."

Jules pulled her against him and kissed her.

She tasted faintly of salt from the cenote and sugar

from the fruit they'd eaten at the farm. He felt her wet eyelashes against his cheekbones. He was forgetting to breathe, to kick and tread water. All he could do was hold her as they sank below the surface. She broke the kiss first. In the light of the water they could see each other clearly. The tips of their noses were touching. She bit his bottom lip and then swam away from him.

As they resurfaced, his chest burning and aching to inhale, he saw the flash of her smile and followed her. Whatever Izzy was running from, he would follow her as long as she'd allow him.

They swam to the edge of the cenote, and she pulled herself up and over the ledge where there was a patch of grass. Water sloshed from his body as he climbed up beside her.

She rested her head on his shoulder and intertwined her fingers with his. They looked up at the sky and watched streaks of light and distant ships arriving and leaving the planet. The thought of anyone hurting her burned through him. Then that thought was gone when she leaned in to kiss him again.

Her kiss had a different effect this time. They were getting to know each other in a way he'd only dreamed of before that evening. He pulled her on top of him and held her tight. She gasped at the strength of his hold. For a moment he was unsure where to put his hands. He could hardly breathe from the warmth radiating off her, despite the cenote water dripping from their skin, despite the cold breeze that enveloped them.

"Jules," she whispered, pressing a kiss on each of his close eyelids, on the side of his neck, on his mouth.

He couldn't speak at first, afraid that if he did he would say something that would ruin the moment. He cleared his throat and took a long, heady breath.

"Izzy?"

"I have something that I want to give back to you," she said.

"Is it the kiss? Was it that bad, really?"

Her laugh was low. She brought her lips back to his, and every other thought fell away. They ended up lying on the grass. Rather, she pressed her hands on his chest and the force of it pushed him back. He traced the soft skin of her lower back, where her top was riding up.

When they couldn't breathe, they broke apart. She sat on his lower abdomen, and he was struck by three things: One, there was nothing and no one in the galaxy as beautiful as Izal Garsea. Two, he was certain that the mechanisms of the world, the stars, luck, the Force itself, had brought her back to him somehow. And he loved her.

He looked up at her as droplets of water from her hair landed on his bare chest. Her thin black top clung to her skin. She tugged on the leather cord around her neck. At the bottom there was a small black pendant flecked in gold. She dangled it from her finger. It was too dark to see at first.

Then he realized what it was.

"You kept it all this time?"

"Of course," she said.

It was his family ring, the one he'd given her as a thank-you for saving his life. Perhaps even as a child he'd known how much Izzy would mean to him, despite how long it would be until they saw each other again.

"Why?"

"At first it was to remember you and the life we had once. For a little while I thought I was giving it back to you."

He touched her chin and guided her gaze back to his. "I've been here all day, Izzy. I don't think you want to return it after all."

"Maybe I'm a hopeless romantic deep, deep, deep down."

"Deep down."

"You want it?" she asked, a challenge in her voice.

He reached for it, but she held it over her head. Then she jumped back into the pool of water. He watched her swim away, her body graceful as she made for the other side. He was a fast swimmer, and he knew he could catch up to her. But it wasn't the ring he wanted back; it was Izzy.

As he stood to dive in, something grabbed him and

yanked him into the shadows. The skin of a calloused palm slapped over his mouth and cut off his warning to Izzy. He felt the barrel of a blaster against his temple. A man with blue hair stepped in front of him and his attacker.

"We weren't finished," said Damar.

# IZZY

## CHAPTER 20

Perhaps Jules hadn't lied after all. The water, once she returned to it, was perfect. It welcomed her like an embrace. She could feel how old everything around her was, the natural archways below where fish gathered. The night was darker, but there was light in the water. She didn't believe in magic, but as she swam to the other side of the cenote, she knew that at least she believed in herself. She had to trust her gut just as her parents had taught her. The galaxy would still be in flux, but she could be a better version of herself. All those impulses she'd had to help others, she could do that, and her day on Batuu proved it. Her mind felt clearer than it had in so long.

When she swam to the surface, she was still smiling. She looked up at the stars and felt something like hope.

"Jules?" she asked. He wasn't in the water, and he wasn't where they had been sitting before. The tree-lined path they'd taken to get there was clear. She suddenly knew something was wrong; she could feel it.

"You really shouldn't leave this thing lying around," Damar said, stepping from the shadows of a boulder holding her blaster.

Her body flashed hot and she struggled to stay afloat at the sight of him. It was only rage that fueled her enough to swim to the edge and pull herself out. She felt bare, her clothes gone. Everything was gone.

"Where is Jules?" she snarled.

"I always liked this weapon," Damar said. "Your mother modified it, didn't she? It always shot true. Or it was supposed to."

"Damar," she said again. "What are you doing?"

He stepped toward her, something wild in his gray eyes. He was stripped down to his open-necked tunic and dark pants, his blue hair in disarray. She'd never seen it that way before. He never even *woke* with it that way. The family ring he always wore was gone. Izzy had never seen him so desperate, either, not even when they were cornered once in a hangar during a job he'd bungled by setting off an alarm. Then, she'd been afraid of the panicked look in his eyes. She'd been afraid that he was going to leave her behind to take the fall. If she hadn't shot their attackers fast enough, he might have.

His strange gray eyes seemed to catch the moonlight. "You should have listened, Izzy."

"I did listen!" she shouted. "Ana Tolla and I had a deal."

She looked around her. She could make for the caves, but then she'd be leaving Jules alone with Ana Tolla's crew. There were rocks strewn around, but the ones big enough to do any damage were just out of her reach. He would shoot her before she had a chance. Though she was sure he needed her enough not to hurt her, it didn't change the fact that they had Jules.

"Go," Damar said. When she didn't move, he shouted, "If you want your farm boy alive, you're going to move!"

Izzy put her hands up. Humiliation rippled through her as she walked barefoot in her underwear across the dewy grass. She cursed herself for letting her guard down. She cursed Damar for ever coming into her life. If they hurt Jules—what? What could she possibly do? All her thoughts of helping and selflessness went out the window. All she wanted was to fight. But she kept walking, retracing the steps she'd just taken, when he shoved the blaster into her wet spine.

"Believe me, nothing would have made me happier than to find someone else for this job. But the locals here are a lot harder to bribe than we thought they'd be. It's a good thing we found your friend."

*Friend?* The salt on her tongue tasted sour. There was a speeder stationed directly beside Jules's. The sky was cloudless, and both moons illuminated them in silver light: Delta Jeet and Jules.

A dark smirk tugged at Delta's lips. She didn't know what a fool she was being played for. She had a blaster aimed at Jules. He was bound and gagged, but he lunged forward when he saw Izzy with Damar.

A red blast shot at Jules's feet, and Delta screamed.

"That was a warning, Jules," Damar said. "Don't be a hero."

"You almost *hit* me," Delta hissed.

"I can aim," Damar snapped, shoving Izzy forward.

"I want to talk to Ana Tolla," Izzy said. "Make a deal."

Damar shook his head. His usually perfect coif was damp. What had happened throughout the day to make him so desperate? People did terrible things when they felt there was no way out, no choice. She could almost hear what Jules would say to that. He'd say that everyone had a choice. That was the sort of person he was.

She wanted to assure Jules that everything would be fine, but she worried her eyes only contained an unshakable fear.

"You had your chance, Izzy. We need the farm boy for the job. You're just insurance."

Damar pointed, directing her to stand face to face with Jules. Delta clipped her wrists with magnetic cuffs. "But first, Ana sends a thank-you gift."

He pulled out a holodisk and held it on his palm.

"Stop," Izzy said, a strangled sob erupting from the back of her throat.

"Why do you care about what happens to him?"

Damar asked. "You told me you hated this place. That you had nothing but bad memories."

Jules glanced up then, hurt in his eyes. Even Delta, who was still pointing a blaster at Jules, grimaced. Izzy shook her head. She had said that to Damar once. But she had been referring to her mother's frequent absences and the terrible, vivid memory of the day they left.

"You were only half listening, Damar."

"I know you well enough," he said. "Like how you're stalling. I'm starting to think this simple farm boy doesn't know you at all. The real you that you don't want anyone else to see. But he's about to find out."

Her heart sped up. She knew even before Damar hit play what would be on that disk. Izzy watched Jules's features harden as he stared at the holo image of her. It was from when she had been with Ana Tolla outside of Cookie's. Why hadn't she considered that she'd been baited?

*"That farm boy you were with. What's his story?"* Ana asked.

Izzy watched the expression of disgust she'd made. *"He's just a stupid farm boy who's never going to get off this rock. He's no one."*

There was a moment when the image flickered and no one moved. Wind moved the willowy leaves. She could feel how hard and frantic her pulse was.

"Jules—" she started.

But he was not looking at her. The tension drained

from his shoulders, and he stared at the ground. He was giving up on her. How could he do that so quickly?

She turned her attention back to Damar. "Why are you doing this?"

"I told you. We need your boy. I can't have him wanting to do anything noble for you. But maybe he's changed his mind now that he knows how you truly feel. What do you have to say for yourself, farm boy?" Damar asked, still holding the blaster—her blaster—at her back. Delta pulled the gag down from his mouth.

Izzy stepped forward, hands bound. She had nothing with her but the necklace, a relic. The happiness had ebbed away, replaced with helpless anger. There were no stars, no light, no hope. She wanted to say his name, but her words wouldn't form.

"You *know* I didn't mean it," she finally said. "I wanted her to stay away from you."

Jules chuckled and shook his head. Why couldn't he just look at her and see that she was telling the truth? Only he could tell when she was lying. When he finally turned to her, she saw the same intensity as when they fought near the farm right before she'd kissed him.

"Lying is a skill," he said. "Go home, Izzy. Take your things and go."

He'd quoted her. She wasn't sure if that meant he believed her or if he was just calling her a liar.

She shut her eyes and cursed Ana Tolla, herself,

everything and everyone. If she lost Jules she—She didn't let herself finish the thought.

"Unfortunately for you," Damar said, "Ana likes her toys a little broken before she uses them. Delta, if I don't arrive safely, you have permission to shoot her."

She couldn't see Jules's face as he climbed into his speeder. Delta shoved Izzy into the second speeder, and they took off side by side.

# JULES

## CHAPTER 21

"That's not going to work," Damar told Jules.

As they'd darted down the moonlit road, farther away from the Outpost, Jules had kept trying, and failing, to break free of his bindings. They were magnetized. At least he'd been able to push down the foul-tasting strip of cloth they'd used to gag him.

"You're new here, pal," Jules said. "Maybe you should save yourself the trouble because you're not going to get away with this."

"I think we already have," Damar said.

Jules wanted to bash the creep's face with his metal cuffs. Then he could drive back to the Outpost to get help. But he thought of what Damar had threatened them with. Delta would be angry enough with Izzy to hurt her; of that he was certain.

He wished he'd been paying more attention back at the cenote. They'd been so close to getting through the day.

"What's that?" Damar asked, moving the wheel from side to side as he tried to regain control of the speeder.

Despite being half naked, freezing from the salt-water drying on his skin, and bound, Jules laughed as his baby, his speeder, came crawling to a stop.

"Don't worry," Jules said. "It does this. You have to hit the dash a bit."

Delta's speeder slowed to a stop beside them. "What's happening?"

The blue-haired creep was trying to hit the dash, but he'd clearly never hit anything before. The lights flickered on and his smile brightened before it went dead again.

"Go ahead of us," Damar ordered. "Tell Ana that we're on our way."

Jules took that moment to catch Izzy's eye. She was clearly terrified. Worst of all, she seemed to have believed his act. They were fools if they thought that was going to be enough to scare him away from her. Didn't she know that he could tell? Whatever reason she had for saying those things, he believed her. He believed she had to do everything in her power to get help or get away.

But as she wrenched her eyes from his, he wondered if it was enough or if they were both doomed.

# IZZY

Pulsing pain shredded her temples from the tension. Regret was bitter on her tongue. She groaned into a night that did not acknowledge her struggle.

"Quiet!" Delta shouted, clapping a hand on Izzy's shoulder to keep her in the passenger seat.

"Delta, why are you doing this?" Izzy asked.

"Ana Tolka, or whatever her name is," she said, "offered me a boon. I get a thousand credits to track you two down and I get to kill you for what you did to me."

"Really though?"

"Which part?"

"I get that at this point you'd kill me for free," Izzy said, though she hated that her life was worth so little. "I'm sorry that I stunned you. But I had to get that parcel. People needed it for survival."

Delta shrugged. "Everyone needs something."

"I know," Izzy said, bringing her bound hands to her chest. "But how are you going to spend your thousand credits when you're being fed to Dok's dianoga? Or worse, Oga might eat you herself."

Delta shook her head. "No. This job is sanctioned by Oga—"

"Oh yeah? What's the job?"

Delta frowned.

Izzy could already see how it had played out. "Let me guess. Ana approached you. Paid you half. Asked you to find Jules and me. Then gave you just enough detail to make you feel like you were part of the crew. I bet Lita even shared her sweets with you."

"You're trying to trick me," Delta growled, but she gripped the wheel tighter.

Izzy nearly beamed when she saw Jules's retrofitted speeder powered down up ahead. He wasn't looking at her, but he seemed to be enjoying Damar's lackluster attempts to get the speeder started again.

When Damar waved them forward, Izzy seized the opportunity to reason with Delta. Self-preservation was the best motivator she'd ever encountered.

"You're telling me that Oga doesn't know Ana is working a job here?" Delta asked.

"Have you ever been *summoned* to Oga's office?" Izzy paused to let the woman consider this. "Because I have. I know for a fact that Oga is trying to find the woman sniffing around *her* outpost trying to cut Oga out of a deal."

Delta didn't need to know that Oga didn't know what Ana Tolla looked like. Izzy just needed to make her see that Ana was using her.

"They said it was an easy score over at Kat Saka's," Delta said.

It was too dark to see exactly where they were, but they had to be approaching the farm soon. She needed Delta to keep driving.

"Why would Oga hurt her own pocket?" Izzy said, desperate. Reasoning with Delta now was the only way she wouldn't be outnumbered later. "I've been where you are. Ana got me for weeks, and part of me fell for it. But they abandoned me. They're not going to want to cut into their profits for *you*."

Izzy stopped to breathe. She was leaning so close to Delta that she shoved Izzy back to her side of the cockpit. "The only way we live is if we get help, right now."

"You know what? Fine. I'd rather Ana kill us, because if she doesn't Oga Garra will," Delta said. "Who's going to help us?"

"Oga," Izzy said.

Delta shook her head. "We wouldn't get past her guards."

Izzy thought that perhaps she might. But it didn't matter; she needed someone who would prioritize saving Jules first.

Izzy got an idea. "Where would Volt be this time of night?"

"Hold on tight," Delta said, and Izzy's entire body slammed against the seat as they zoomed toward Black Spire Outpost.

# JULES

All Jules's humor vanished when the speeder powered up again. He was really going to have to rip it apart to figure out what was wrong. But first he had to get through the next few hours alive.

They drove with the live broadcast from Oga's Cantina blasting from the speakers. Jules's gut turned with every swerve.

"Where did you learn to drive?" Jules asked.

Damar made a face. "My chauffeur taught me."

"Great," he muttered.

"Why do I get under your skin, farm boy?" Damar asked. A punchable grin split his angular face. "Is it because Izzy was with me for awhile?"

What had his father said? The overconfident farmer doesn't yield enough harvest for a drought? He couldn't remember the exact words, and Damar was not a farmer, by the look of his delicate hands, but he *was* overconfident. Jules was bigger and stronger, and he could get the jump on him. He could save Izzy and set things right.

Jules raised his elbow and slammed it into Damar's eye. He grabbed Izzy's blaster from Damar's lap, leaning into the swerve of the speeder. Damar winced and cried out, but kept one hand on the wheel.

"Get out of my ride," Jules said.

Damar had the nerve to laugh. "You didn't think we'd do this without extra insurance, did you?"

Jules's body flashed hot. He tentatively lowered the blaster.

Damar retrieved the holodisk again and pressed a button. Jules recognized the unconscious farmer immediately. Belen. He'd never seen his sister slumped like that before. Her wrists and ankles were bound. What would she do when she woke? She would fight and get herself hurt. He couldn't allow that.

"Now," Damar said, "I'll take the blaster. Sit."

Jules clenched his fists all the way to Kat Saka's farm.

# IZZY

"You don't happen to have my clothes, do you?" Izzy asked. "Not to mention the key to these?"

"You're already asking for too many things when you should be happy I spared your life." Reluctantly, Delta removed a cube and pressed it to the top of the magnetic cuffs. They fell to Izzy's lap, and she swept them aside. Her clothes had been shoved into the foot of the cockpit. They were damp and smelled of hangar grease, but at least she wasn't half naked anymore.

She closed her eyes against the wind and thought of those perfect moments kissing Jules in the cenote. There were times when she was on a job and the only things guiding her were food and fuel. She was aimless in a galaxy she'd never live enough years to explore, but that was not going to stop her from trying to find her way. Now she had something guiding her. Whether he forgave her or not, she had to save Jules. If nothing else went her way, she would hold on to those moments with him.

The headlights illuminated the path she and Jules had traveled—their cliff and the farm. The entire planet was peppered with her history.

*Go home, Izzy.*

That hurt even worse coming from him because he knew she didn't have one. He wasn't wrong to be angry with her. But all she had was a pilot who wanted to kill her and a creatures vendor who probably also wanted to kill her. At least she wasn't alone?

She concentrated on the patch of light where Black Spire Outpost was nestled in dark lands. Her mind cycled back and forth from the elation of kissing Jules to the moment Damar had held her up with her own blaster.

Things would have been different if she had listened to Belen—Belen, who didn't like her and believed she would only bring Jules trouble. Belen's maternal intuition had been right, hadn't it?

No, she couldn't think that way. If she'd left, Ana Tolla might have taken Jules regardless, and then where would he be? Dead.

"That was cold before," Delta said after a stretch of uncomfortable silence. "With your boyfriend."

"I know." Izzy glanced at her. They both simmered with impotent rage. "I thought I was helping him. The worst part is not knowing if he bought it or not."

Delta made a choking sound. Was that a laugh? "I'd say getting kidnapped is worse than your *feelings.*"

She was right. She had to remain focused.

"That's why I took the deal," Delta said, shouting

over the wind and the hum of the speeder. "To help my family. I should have known it was too good to be true. But I only came to Batuu a month ago."

"Where were you before?"

"Chibbier. A forest planet. Everyone was laid off two months ago."

"Why?"

"No trees left means nothing to cut down. I was lucky to get out. My cousins wanted to get work in the Core, but I'd heard of Hondo needing pilots and I thought, I can fly well enough."

Izzy thought of the two seeming Resistance fighters she'd met before they were captured. What had the woman said? *Everyone on Batuu is always either looking for a new life or running from one.* She'd had no idea that Delta was both, too.

"I really am sorry about what happened," she said.

"You mean stunning me and leaving me on the floor in an office?" Delta said dryly.

Izzy repeated her apology and made sure it sounded real, because she meant it.

"I'll be fine," Delta said. "Since I can't kill you, I *would* like something to hit."

Izzy stared ahead and nodded slowly. Black Spire was not like the glittering cities she'd been in, but there was something about seeing it at night that stole her wonder. Lights in homes blinked on, and the market remained open for the after-hours crowd. Shuttles carried people from either end of the Outpost, and ships were still landing, bringing mysterious cargo from every corner of the galaxy.

Izzy had never had many friends. She'd never stayed anywhere long enough. She was too quiet. Too strange. Too angry. Too scared. Too *much*. There were dozens of excuses she could have used. But that night she didn't try to think of any. Delta was as close to a friend as she was going to get, and Izzy was going to need her to get Jules back.

They came to a halt in the spaceport and hopped out. There was one person directing traffic for Ohnaka Transport Solutions. GI-MD wandered around barking orders. Izzy didn't see the Karkarodon, which was a relief. The Avent100 light freighter was still docked.

"I don't see him," Izzy said.

"He'll be at the game," Delta replied.

Izzy ran behind Delta, their heavy boots beating a rhythm on the launchpad. Delta punched a code into an office door and it hissed open. She heard Volt's voice before she saw him.

In the smoky room, there was a game of sabacc going, but unlike the card game she'd seen on the farm earlier, this one used credits of all shapes and sizes. She even spotted a turquoise ring in the pile.

"Delta! We thought you weren't coming. How goes—"
Volt's eyes widened, and the veins in his neck bulged,
resembling nightsnakes moving across the ground. He
jumped up from the table as he said, *"You!"*

# JULES

He recognized Ana Tolla from the holovid recording they'd played for him. Even though he was nearly certain Izzy had said what she had for his benefit, it still burned. He'd been so beaten up that day that he felt like the loser droid in the death matches run in the Galma vicinity. If Izzy had waltzed into the storage barn at that moment to say she'd been playing him the whole time, he might have believed her in his current condition.

As Damar led him deeper into the back of the barn, he tried to get a sense of what they were planning. Izzy said that Ana Tolla didn't give her crew all the details. He knew others, like the Botsini crew, who operated in a similar way. The captain gave everyone a specific job; that way if one person screwed up, he would know who. Jules always thought that could only be productive if there were backups.

Why was he thinking about their crew? He needed to find a way to get Belen out. They weren't keeping her in the storage barn.

He took in the sight of Ana Tolla, dressed in head-to-toe black with a blaster rifle slung across her chest.

There was a nervous-looking Ketzalian flying back and forth on thick purple wings. She had a humanoid head with lizard features and waxy feathers for hair. The only other time he'd seen the species was when some were on-world trading loralora birds for golden lichen. Against the door was the muscle, a Zygerrian with a gray feline face and yellow eyes. He made a guttural sound when he looked at Jules. Last was a Twi'lek with pale coral lekku that faded into multiple colors. One arm, heavily modified with tattoos, was in a sling, and the left side of his face was covered in blue bruises.

"They should have been here by now," the husky Zygerrian said. When he crossed his arms over his broad chest, his muscles looked like boulders.

"They were right behind us!" Damar shouted.

Ana Tolla stepped close to Jules. Bile rose in his throat. He wasn't used to steeping in anger this way. He hated it.

"I can see why she spent all day with you," Ana Tolla said, looking him up and down. "Someone get him clothes."

Jules scoffed. "I'm guessing you didn't bring me all the way out here to dress me up. Where's Belen?"

"I would worry more about where Izal Garsea is," Ana Tolla said.

"You heard your *sleemo* over there," Jules said. "They left before us."

The Ketzalian flitted over with a pair of loose green pants. Jules held up his cuffed wrists. "Do you mind?"

The Zygerrian growled his disapproval.

"Don't worry, Oksan," Ana Tolla said. "He'll do as we say or his darling sister won't make it out of where we're keeping her. Izal, on the other hand. She's a survivor. I imagine she's half way to abandoning you."

Jules forced himself to stand his ground. Ana was wrong about Izzy. The certainty of that helped him focus on his sister. He could almost feel the freedom of his hands when Ana Tolla waved the key in front of his eyes.

"Try something," Ana Tolla said. "I like a challenge."

"You came to the wrong planet," Jules told her.

Ana Tolla looked down her nose at him and smiled with red-painted lips. "Tell me why that is."

"No one has crossed Oga Garra and lived."

"Not yet." Ana Tolla's smile was arrogant. "Are you ready to get to work?"

He shrugged and summoned everything he'd learned from Izzy that day. Lying was a skill. "I'm just a simple farm boy. What am I supposed to do?"

She traced a finger along his jaw. Her eyes were an eerie pale blue. "I need you to do exactly as I say."

# IZZY

## CHAPTER 22

"You!" Volt abandoned the game table and marched out to the open area of the landing pad like a rancor ready for dinner. "How dare you show your face here. After what you and Rakab did to me! I'll feed you to my tooka when I'm done with you."

"Please, just hear me out!" Izzy shouted. She held her hands up to show she was unarmed.

He slowed when he noticed Delta beside her. His eyes cut from the speeder and back to them. Though Volt's answer simmered, he was visibly thrown off by the sight of the young women together. Delta examined her short, oddly clean nails. Izzy knew that just because they had a temporary truce didn't mean that Delta would protect her from Volt.

"I'm sorry about what we did," Izzy said.

"Do you even know what you did?" Volt's expression was crazed, his eyes wide as he ran his palms across his veiny skull. "I almost lost another finger! Bina is furious with me. I had to buy a one-month supply of the milk dokmas drink. Do you know how many batches of Volt's Special Juice I'm going to have to sell on the side to pay for that?"

As Volt's pitch rose and his yelling increased, her resolve began to wither. Less than a day in the Outpost and she had caused such a mess.

She thought of Jules in shackles. The moment he'd told her to leave. It would be the easy thing to do. Hadn't she run every time before? Floating around space was often an easier option than facing reality. After her parents had died, she'd run. The thing about running was that sooner or later there was nowhere left to go.

"How many batches of your rusty venom would you have to sell?" she asked. "I'll cover it."

He looked from Izzy to Delta. "Wait. What's the catch?"

"How many?" she repeated.

"Ten at one hundred spira each."

"A thousand spira?"

"Never underestimate how much milk a dokma will drink," he said with a smirk. "Plus there were the other messes—"

Her laugh was near hysterical. She was down to the dregs of her money. "I have half of that. The rest I can get from Dok once this is over. But first I need to buy a fyrnock from you."

Volt put his hands on his hips and regarded her with suspicion. "Again, why are you doing this, *off-worlder*?"

"Because Jules is in trouble and I don't have any weapons."

Volt's expression went blank. He turned around and went back into the card game room.

"Wait!" Izzy looked back at Delta, who simply shrugged. "I thought we had a deal!"

Before she could despair, Volt marched back out to the landing pad, and this time he carried a rifle blaster. It was New Republic issue, probably dropped off the back of a freighter. She raised her hands.

"Wait a minute, let's talk about this—"

But he wasn't aiming at her. He was waiting for her to give instructions.

"What about the fyrnock?"

Volt harrumphed. "You think I'm going to bring it *out* of its cage? It took me one hour and six rats to get it back in there in the first place. Besides, who's going to drink after work with me if some lunatics kill Rakab? Nope. I'm coming with you."

For the first time since being held up with her own gun by her own ex, Izzy smiled. "Let's go get our boy."

# JULES

Ana Tolla released him from his cuffs. They fell to the floor with a sharp *plink*.

"That's not a good idea," the Twi'lek said. "What if he attacks you?"

Ana Tolla raised an eyebrow. Jules couldn't tell if she was skeptical of Jules's strength or annoyed that someone had spoken out of turn. "Then his sister dies, Safwan."

He followed the crew captain out of the storage barn, where they passed an open crate full of what looked like white bricks. The floodlights had been turned off so as not to set off any sensors. He could see the Ketzalian flying high up on the outside wall, where anyone without wings would need a ladder or lift to reach. The rest of the lights across the field went off. Dread pooled in his gut when he saw the silver cargo freighter with an open ramp in front of the silo. Ana climbed aboard.

The lights in the ceiling made her red hair look like a flash of fire. He wasn't afraid of fire, but something about the situation, about her, made him remember that night. Jules and Belen running away from their collapsing home. He'd stood there waiting for his father to come out of the neighbors' house. He'd never been that afraid in his whole life. But then his da had walked through the flames with Tap in his arms, and for a brief moment, everything was as it always had been.

"I'm glad you've seen who Izal truly is," Ana Tolla said, pulling him out of his memory. "She's abandoned you. Can't bring you anything but pain. It's best that she's gone. But me? I can give you an opportunity."

He didn't believe that Izzy was gone. He had to believe in her. He had to hope. "There is no opportunity you could give me. If I cross Kat, I cross Oga, and crossing Oga means being as good as dead. The only good thing is you'll be right alongside me."

Ana Tolla glanced over her shoulder. "I'm not offering you a job, farm boy. I'm offering you the opportunity to be a hero and save lives."

She held out her hand to the lounge area. When Belen saw him, her eyes went round as orbs. She had been tightly gagged, and her wrists and ankles were bound by magnetic cuffs.

Jules was breathing hard, his hands balled at his sides. He could try to overpower Ana Tolla. And then what? Face four others with blasters? Even with the Twi'lek injured, Jules was still severely outnumbered and outgunned. He'd never get Belen to safety.

"Now, what do you say, farm boy? Are you ready to do exactly what I tell you?"

He thought of Izzy. Her bright eyes. Her lips. The lies that spilled from her mouth. He focused on Belen. Ana Tolla was not going to get away with this. He could only hope to stall whatever it was. Izzy had told him about some of Ana Tolla's jobs, and he expected the worst.

*Hurry*, he thought at Izzy.

"I'm ready," he said. "What do I have to do?"

"We're going to burn this farm to the ground."

# IZZY

## CHAPTER 23

"Excuse me!" shouted the green-and-white protocol droid G1-MD. "Excuse me. What are you doing here? There are no shipments authorized at this time. Delta! What is the meaning of this?"

Delta walked around the shipping container and waved her arms. "Calm down, Gee-One."

"We aren't stealing anything," Izzy said, but she made her way to the red-striped Avent100 light freighter that had been stationed there all day. "Except this ship."

"This vessel is not authorized for transport!" G1-MD shouted. Her already round eyes appeared even more startled as her head moved side to side.

"You can come along," Izzy told her slyly. "You *are* supervisor of this operation, aren't you? The ship will be in safe hands."

The droid registered her words, then considered. "When you put it that way, the probabilities of success *will* increase if I'm there."

Volt and Delta ran up with their weapons. G1-MD marched forward, spouting off regulation infractions and rules of Ohnaka Transport Solutions. They froze when they heard the zooming sound of a swoop bike.

The bike appeared too big for the boy who rode it. Tap cruised to a stop in front of them.

"What are you doing here, boy?" Volt shouted.

Tap shook his head. "I saw Izzy and Delta without Jules and knew something was wrong, so I followed you here."

Volt let out a heavy sigh. "It's too dangerous, kid."

"I'm useful! Aren't I, Izzy?"

"I'm sorry, Tap," she said. "But Jules has been taken. We can't risk you, too."

"I can pick any lock. Can any of you say that?"

Izzy looked to Volt and Delta for help, but they offered none.

There was a fierce look in the boy's eyes. Izzy was about his age when her mother began teaching her everything she would need to know. How to fly. How to shoot. But Tap wasn't hers to make that decision for.

"If I say no what are you going to do?" Izzy asked.

Tap smiled. "Follow you anyway."

"Fine. Everyone get on the ship *now*. I don't know how much time we have." Izzy led her crew aboard. "Who has a channel to the cantina?"

Everyone turned to Volt. He shrugged. "My girl's a bartender there. But she doesn't know about the game—"

"Do it now," Izzy told him, "or I will feed you your own gut rot."

Volt stalked off to the ship's cargo bay, muttering a string of curses.

Izzy settled into the cockpit and strapped in. Delta took the copilot seat. Everything felt so new to Izzy. She couldn't read a single word of the unfamiliar alphabet on the control labels. She was about to press a button that on her ship would shut the access ramp.

"No!" Delta shouted. "That's the forward cannon. This is Teklada, a mathematical language."

"You can read it?"

"No, but I remember it from one of the labels in Hondo's storage. Gee-One, get over here and translate this, will you?"

Izzy took a deep breath. She was so nervous she'd forgotten about GI-MD. The droid strapped in behind them, craning her head over Izzy's shoulder and rattling off her interpretation of the symbols.

"This ought to be fun," Izzy muttered. "Hang on tight, everybody, we're going to Kat Saka's farm. Buckle in, it's going to be a short ride!"

The ship took off. It was the smoothest ship she'd ever piloted, though she'd only flown the *Meridian* and a single-pilot flier at academy before that.

"Okay, Delta, now's the time to tell me what you do know about Ana's plan."

GI-MD recited as if she was reading off all the information on their destination: "The grain from

Kat Saka is the finest on the planet, some might say in the Outer Rim. The unique minerals in the soil of Batuu—"

"We get it, droid," Delta said, then turned to Izzy. "What Ana did tell me was that she needed someone who would know the silo override access codes. That would be Jules."

Volt was back in the cockpit. "Sent a warning to Oga's. I heard last season Kat refused to sell to StarFlora Corp even though they offered enough credits to buy a yacht. Or fill a yacht."

Izzy thought about the jobs they'd done together. Ana Tolla didn't just steal things. She destroyed them.

Izzy felt hope bleeding out of her with every passing moment. She struggled to breathe. Jules, she thought. She wouldn't be fast enough to get to Jules.

"Whose ship is this anyway?" Delta asked.

Izzy remembered the stylish spice trader Jules had made friends with. "Trix Sternus's, I think."

"According to the Ohnaka Transport Solutions sale logs, the ship now belongs to—"

A series of beeps went off. Izzy grabbed the yoke and said, "Be ready to fight on landing."

# JULES

## CHAPTER 24

The first time Jules had worked on Kat's farm, he'd been shorter than the wild grass. Sometimes he still felt like the scrawny little kid who'd run through those fields—frail but free. It didn't matter how tall he'd gotten, how big he was; he still felt helpless. He loathed that he was going to help Ana Tolla and her pirates destroy a part of his homeworld. He thought of Belen in Ana Tolla's ship, who was waiting for him to rescue her. He thought of Izzy.

Just Izzy.

So he stood at the main building and punched in the code to the stores where Kat kept the seeds she and her family had been cultivating for four generations. After everything he'd said about protecting his world, his home, he had to save the person he couldn't lose. He wondered if that was why Izzy was so guarded. Love was a vulnerability.

He felt the butt of a blaster pistol jab into his back.

"Hurry it up," Damar said.

"I said I'd help you get in here. I didn't say I'd help you carry anything. I'm not crew."

The blaster moved to his forehead. He could feel

the cold metal of the barrel on his skin. Helpless. He gritted his teeth. He wasn't faster than a blaster, but he could take this bantha's ass by surprise. He could—not do anything. Belen. He thought her name like a prayer to the spires, to the Force, like a promise that this was not going to be the end.

"You do as we say," Damar said.

"You kidnapped my sister and are holding me at blaster point." He was defeated in his anger. "You know I will."

Ana and Oksan were off preparing what she'd called phase two—the actual destruction of the crops. They'd taken the crate of white bricks with them. He'd heard her say something like "sodium mines"? No matter what they were, he had to get to them somehow. He eyed the door.

"Keep staring, farm boy," Safwan said. With his arm in a sling and the Ketzalian's short arms, it took two of them to load one crate. At least they moved quietly.

Jules begrudgingly grabbed a crate and began loading with the others.

Damar smirked. How could Izzy have been with someone like him? She didn't deserve that. Jules slammed the crate on top of another.

"How come you talk so much more than your friends?" Jules asked.

Damar held Izzy's blaster up, making sure Jules kept

his part of the bargain. "They don't have anything to say."

Jules laughed, and the Twi'lek and Ketzalian frowned but kept working. "Must be nice to stand there while your crew does the heavy lifting. I bet you and Ana Tolla will celebrate together while they do the dirty work?"

"Shut your hole, farm boy, or I'll blast you an extra one," Damar growled, but the threat lacked any guts. Jules had already been threatened by Oga that day, and compared with that everything else lost its bluster.

"Did you learn to speak like that in the Core? Does Safwan get less because he's injured and doing half the work?"

"Don't listen to him, Safwan. We all get an equal share," Damar said. "I can't believe you were Iz's rebound. Slim pickings on Batuu, right?"

He tried to joke with his comrades, but Jules hoped that the doubt he'd planted was the reason they didn't laugh.

"You didn't deserve her," Jules told Damar.

"Even after all the things she said about you?" He used the blaster to scratch the side of his head. "I'm going to need a week to get the dirt of this planet off me. I'm thinking a nice spa retreat on the Risso hot springs moon. I hear the thermal waters are amazing."

Jules wouldn't be goaded into a fight that would end in his death, not when he needed to get Belen to safety.

"Perhaps I'll find Iz after this," Damar said. He was getting comfortable. He lowered the blaster and leaned against the wall. "How much do you want to bet I can get her to forgive me?"

Jules had a crate in his hands. It wasn't heavy, but if he threw it, it would at least hurt.

"Cut it out, will you?" the Ketzalian squeaked, her plum head feathers ruffling. "You're getting in the way, Damar. Go prep the ship so we're ready to go."

Jules averted his eyes from the alien. He wanted to hate her. He wanted to hate all of them. Just because they weren't taunting him like Damar didn't mean they were *good*. It just meant they were in a hurry.

Then he thought—how many times had he done a favor for pirates in the Outpost. What made Ana's crew different from the others? Well, for starters, the others weren't stupid enough to steal from the people who kept the blood of Batuu flowing, and they certainly didn't mess with his family. Ana Tolla was bold, if not mad.

"You're not my boss, Lita," Damar told her.

Safwan slammed the crate down, and Lita went off balance in the air. "No, but I've been Ana Tolla's second for five years. I outrank you. Go and prep the ship so we're ready after she's done with the fields."

Damar turned red. He curled his lip and left.

Jules must have stared at the exit for too long, because Safwan tapped the blaster holstered on his good side. "Don't think about it, Jules."

"I think I'd much prefer it if your lot called me farm boy. It makes it less personal."

"Makes what less personal?" the Twi'lek asked. He wrapped his hand around the blaster in warning, eyes steady.

"This—" Jules shoved the large crate at Safwan's bad shoulder. The Twi'lek slammed into the wall, busy cradling his own head and screaming in pain.

Jules grabbed the pirate's blaster and set it to stun before firing at Lita, who was mid-flight to get help. But as he made for the exit, it felt like a storm was rolling in. Blinding light flashed, and wind blew dust in his eyes.

He didn't believe the sight in front of him. A ship had landed next to the silo. But not just any ship—the one he'd impulsively bought from Trix Sternus that day. When the ramp lowered, he had never been so relieved his friends had stolen his ship.

# IZZY

## CHAPTER 25

When Izzy saw Jules Rakab, she wanted nothing more than to run to him and make sure he was unharmed. But as Volt, Delta, GI-MD, and Tap stormed down the ramp ahead of her, there was no time for that.

"Help is on the way," she said.

Jules nodded, more tense than she'd seen him all day, and that included their session with Oga. He went right to Tap, rested a hand on the boy's hat, and said, "Belen is in their ship's lounge. She's got magnetic cuffs and anklets. Can you do it?"

Tap nodded. "What kind of question is that?"

Despite everything he'd been through, Jules grinned. He glanced up at Delta. "Go with him. Damar is prepping for takeoff."

"The reunion's great and all," Volt said, raising his rifle. "But we're about to have company."

They all drew weapons and took cover behind the legs of the Avent100 freighter.

"Gee-One, ready the ship!" Izzy shouted. "As soon as Tap and Delta return with Belen, take them back to Hondo's."

"I am not programmed to take orders from you," the droid said.

"Are you programmed to survive?" Volt shouted.

"Right away, beast master," GI-MD said, then turned, muttering, "Master Hondo *will* hear about this."

"You two lovebirds," Volt said, and fired a warning shot at the entrance of the grain storage unit. "I know this is about to get a world of awkward, but can you save it until after we stop these pirates from destroying our crops? What's the sitrep, kid?"

"Two in the grain storage," Jules reported. "The Ketzalian is stunned, but Safwan is on his way out. He's got a broken arm."

"I like those odds." Volt slapped Jules's shoulder. "I sounded the alarm. Kat's private security should be here any moment."

"Not yet," Jules and Izzy said at the same time.

Izzy's stomach felt like exposed wiring. She let Jules speak.

"Do you know what sodium mines are?" Jules asked. "They look like white bricks."

"No. I've only seen her use a fire torch."

Volt's dark eyes practically glimmered. "I want a fire torch. But I have heard of *sodilium* detonators. Highly toxic and flammable. They will make sure nothing ever grows in that soil if they're activated."

"How'd a crew like hers get ahold of something like that?" Jules asked.

"From whoever hired her," Izzy said. "She'll keep the control detonator on her. And she'll have the Zygerrian with her. Volt, I think you should go with me. I can handle Ana."

"Izzy—" Jules started.

"No time," she said. "Take care of Lita and Safwan."

Izzy ran with Volt toward the fields. For a man who hadn't seen action in years, he was fast on his feet. The sensor lights had been disabled, leaving them to run in darkness. She wished she had more than the old blaster model Volt had let her borrow, but it was going to have to do. She was the one who controlled the shot, not the weapon, lucky or not.

"Talk to me, Izzy," Volt said. "How are we supposed to get that control detonator to deactivate it?"

"You said that stuff is toxic, right?" Her heart was a fist punching her chest. "She won't do it if she's within the explosives area, so the best bet is to box her in. And I'll—Lucky?"

As she spoke, the loralora bird soared above her. She wasn't prepared for how relieved she was upon seeing the creature again. Volt glanced up, and she didn't miss the moment of anger that flashed across his face. She would have to deal with him later.

They kept running. Ahead Izzy could see that Ana Tolla and Oksan were halfway up the water tower, attaching the white bricks as they went.

"Lucky!" Izzy shouted, ready to put their bond to the test. She pointed at Oksan. The loralora let out a brilliant shriek, then swooped down and pecked at him until he let go of the water tower. He fell three meters, but landed on his feet.

"No, you fool!" Ana Tolla shouted. She clung to the metal rungs.

Oksan drew a blaster and shot as he tried to run. Volt pushed Izzy to the ground, and she rolled on her side. Everything was upside down, the sky dark and the moons spinning around her. She could hear the red laser fire Volt and Oksan were trading. The flap of wings. Her blood pumping in her ears. Amid all that, there was a loud grunt, and then a ceasefire.

When she sat up, Volt was back at her side and Oksan was limping to his feet. Ana Tolla flung herself off the lower rungs of the tower. She caught up with the Zygerrian and held up the detonator.

# JULES

Watching Izzy run into the fields with Volt was almost physically painful. Jules should be the one beside her. He should be the one helping her stop Ana. But she'd made the right call. Volt could disarm the detonator. They all had their roles in saving Kat's farm.

But Jules had a role in helping destroy it. There were times when he couldn't understand why people made the choice to hurt others. In the moment when Ana Tolla made Jules choose between the farm and his sister, he hadn't hesitated. Guilt weighed heavily on him. The only way he could make up for what he'd done was to stop Ana and her crew.

Jules returned to the storage silo, his blaster trained before him. Someone had turned the lights off. He kept his back along the surface of the walls and slunk from crate stack to crate stack. He listened for footsteps, heavy breathing, anything that would give away Safwan and Lita's location.

He thought of where he'd been the night before, almost to the minute: out in the empty fields using hollow droid heads and helmets for target practice, wishing the answers to his future would unravel. He'd spent years waiting for his life to change, and in the course of a day, it had changed over and over again. Izzy was to thank for that. He should have said something more to her before they split up, reassured her that everything was going to be fine.

He heard it then: wings beating directly above him. He reached up to grab Lita's tail, but his hand closed around air.

"Now!" the Ketzalian shouted.

Jules turned around in time to see the towering crates falling toward him. He jumped out of the way, but each column slammed into the next. Metal warped and hundreds of thousands of individual grains spilled from the containers. He crawled through the avalanche covering the ground. As he neared the door, he struggled to his feet and ran outside. Safwan and Lita had a head start, but not by much. He could catch up.

Aided by the light of the moons, he ran toward Ana's ship. He knew something was wrong because his Avent100 was still docked there. What had happened to Tap and Belen? Jules dug deep down and found his strength to run raster. He thought of the people who depended on him. He thought of Izzy. He hadn't heard anything from the fields. Did that mean they were safe or not?

When he reached the ramp of Ana's ship, he was

thrown back by a sucker punch to the face. He tumbled off the ramp and onto the grass. For the second time that day, his nose was bleeding. He wiped it with the back of his hand.

"Come on!" Lita shouted, her already nervous voice shrill.

Damar whirled around. "Not without Ana!"

"She'd leave you in a heartbeat," Jules told him.

"No, she wouldn't." Damar sounded so earnest, so adamant, that Jules almost felt sorry for him. It wasn't enough though. Not after everything he'd put Izzy through. Not after their attack on his home.

The sound of blaster fire rang out, followed by screams, then silence.

Jules wanted to turn to the fields, even though it was too dark to see. What if that had been Izzy or Volt? What if something terrible had happened? Damar had the same thoughts. Jules hated to think that he had anything in common with the blue-haired slug, but he recognized the frantic worry that had overtaken Damar as he stared off into the distance. It might be the only distraction Jules was going to get, and he took it.

He fired at Damar, the pulse of the blaster as blue as his hair, and dragged him away from the ships. Jules took back Izzy's blaster with the intention of returning it to her.

There was a low rumble in the distance as speeders made their way to the farm. Jules threw his head back and laughed.

"No celebrating yet," came Delta's voice. She was out of breath, jogging back to him.

"Why are you still *here*?"

"Take it up with the others!" Her sweat glistened in the moons' shine. "Your sister and Tap won't leave without you."

"Where are they?"

"Tap said he could turn the lights back on, and Belen is trying to take Gee-One apart." Delta looked down at Damar, then back at Jules. "Aren't there two more?"

"In the ship," Jules said, and handed her the blaster he'd lifted from Safwan. "I'll go help Izzy."

# IZZY

## CHAPTER 26

"There are bombs everywhere," Ana warned. "In the fields. On the tower. You'll never find them all."

Izzy took aim. "Hand the remote over, Ana, and we'll let you go."

"Liar."

Izzy shrugged. "I had to try."

"So selfless all of a sudden?" Ana asked. "Don't forget, Izal. If I hadn't left you, you would have been following my orders like the rest of them."

Izzy saw Oksan's head jerk up. He didn't seem to like that comment.

"Maybe," Izzy said. "But you should have honored our agreement."

She wanted to think that once she'd known about the plans to cause so much destruction, she would have walked away. Izzy remembered standing on the cantina patio on Actlyon. The foul smell in the air. The confusion of the fight. As awful as those moments had been, Izzy knew that it needed to happen that way. She'd been shaken out of a stupor. Knowing she was helping the people she'd met on the farm was a feeling she could get used to.

"And here I didn't think you were capable of surprising me," Ana said. Her red braid swung at her back. "Maybe there's room for you on this crew after all. It's not too late, Izzy."

Izzy took a deep breath and looked at Volt. She saw three landspeeders approaching in the distance.

"I work better alone," Izzy said.

Every light that had previously been off came back on, from the barn to the fields.

"You're surrounded," Volt added.

Ana Tolla held out the detonator and grinned at Izzy. Her smile was wide and cruel. "A captain goes down with the ship."

Izzy's body went rigid with fear. Beside her, Volt was raising his blaster, but Ana held the control too closely to her body for him to get a clean shot.

"But I don't," Oksan said, and in a flash he reached out and grabbed the woman's wrist so tightly all she could do was scream and let go.

Izzy raced to catch the detonator, but before it fell to the grass, Lucky swooped down and caught it with her prehensile tail. Izzy couldn't stop her forward momentum and fell to the grass. She groaned as she rose onto her knees and back onto her feet. Lucky flapped to a rest on her shoulder, tail up in the air. Izzy carefully retrieved the detonator and choked a sigh of relief.

"You owe me for that bird," Volt said, but his lips quirked when he said it.

In moments, Oga Garra's thugs descended on them. Izzy recognized at least one of the rough-looking humans from when she and Jules were surrounded in Smuggler's Alley. But under the bright lights of the farm, their faces were a welcome sight.

Oksan knelt with his hands behind his head and went with them peacefully, but Ana fought the entire way as a large woman carried her off in a vise-like grip.

"Oga wants them all alive," a blue-skinned Balosar said in warning.

"I'll find you one day, Izal Garsea!" Ana Tolla screamed. "I will remember this!"

"Don't worry, kid," Volt told her as he took the detonator from her open palm and carefully deactivated it.

"What about the bombs in the field?" she asked.

"They'll have the bomb sniffer droids in tomorrow I'm sure."

They were crossing the dark green grass back to where the two ships were docked when the silver cargo freighter belonging to Ana Tolla flashed its lights. With the ramp still down, it began taking off. Izzy wasn't sure who was flying the ship, because it swooped up in a strange arc, then slammed back to the ground, but not before clipping the side of Izzy's stolen ship.

Izzy groaned. Volt turned to her and cackled. "May the spires save you, Izal Garsea!"

- ⊂⊃ -

All around her there were pockets of celebration. Izzy kept to the shadows along the side of a barn and watched the chaos begin to settle. Ana Tolla and her crew were loaded onto the speeders. She watched Damar as he was taken away, shouting her name the entire time.

Wasn't that what she'd wanted? To watch him hurt after what he did to her? The feeling of satisfaction never came, even after the speeder was out of sight.

Volt was running around, trying to maintain his adrenaline spike while Delta laid in the grass nursing an arm injury. Fortunately, Belen and Tap weren't hurt, even though they hadn't been able to get the ship back to the hangar. She didn't know what had happened to change their plan, but she didn't see Gee-One among the others. She tried to work up the courage to walk over to them, but her old fears returned and she stayed put.

Izzy felt herself slipping away. She was part of the moment but at a distance from it, as well. She had done what she wanted to do—save Jules and the farm. He was embracing his sister, and they were joined by another man, who Izzy guessed was Belen's husband.

Izzy climbed into one of the landspeeders and

powered it up. It wasn't stealing if she was going to give it back. She would have left then if someone wasn't standing in front of her, blocking her way.

Tap, of all people, had found her. "I turned on the lights. I told you I'd be helpful."

"Good job, kid." She couldn't help smiling. "Where's Gee-One?"

"Belen powered her down, but she's up and running again."

She didn't feel *too* bad about leaving the stolen ship behind. If Gee-One didn't fly it back out of sheer will, then someone responsible like Jules would.

"You were going to leave without saying good-bye?" he asked.

"Not everyone gets good-byes," she said. "Go back to the others, okay?"

"I don't understand," he said. "We won. You don't have to go."

"I made a promise to someone." She was thinking of Belen. Everything Belen had feared for her brother had happened, and she'd been put in danger, too.

Izzy held out her hand, and Tap slapped it despite his protest. "I'll leave the speeder at Salju's, okay? Let Delta know."

"*That'll* go well." Tap shook his head.

Then she left, and it took all her strength not to look back.

# JULES

CHAPTER 27

He kept trying to slip away, but everyone wanted to thank him personally. What had he done? Yes, he'd fought, but he had not been alone. *That's how you survive— together.* That's what his father had always said. He was convinced it was how they had all been able to get out alive.

Jules found himself searching the crowd for Izzy. They had to talk. He needed to tell her that nothing had changed the plans they had made. He believed her. He loved her. He needed her.

The night was so clear, the moons shone in beams. Oga's people carried Ana Tolla's crew away. His eardrums were almost pierced by Damar's screams of Izzy's name.

Then there was another matter entirely: his ship. His new ship, which he'd never flown, was already damaged from being hit during Safwan and Lita's attempted takeoff. If not for Delta, they would have vanished into hyperspace. When she'd run back into the crew's ship, her aim put a hole through the Ketzalian's wing and grazed Safwan's good shoulder. It was enough to impede their take off.

Volt walked up to him. His two mechanical fingers twitched as he scratched the side of his face.

"Heya, kid," he said, rubbing the shiny plane of his scalp. He looked awake in a way that only fighting made him. He clapped Jules on the back, which was the last thing Jules expected after the creature stall incident.

"I'm sorry about earlier," Jules said. "I'll pay for the damages."

"The girl already took care of it."

Jules wasn't sure why he was surprised. Something stirred in his chest. "She did?"

"She came to me for help. Naturally, I couldn't let anything happen to you. Who would buy any of my hooch if you were gone?"

Jules laughed, and pain bloomed across his ribs. He was pretty sure he'd bruised a few when he'd rolled off the ramp after Damar's punch.

"Tap was brave," Volt added. More and more it felt as if his friend was trying to distract him. "I know since your father saved him from the fire you feel protective of the child."

Jules looked at the boy as he helped Delta up from the grass and they slowly made their way to his ship. *His* ship. "And Izzy?"

"She's a good girl." Volt gripped his shoulder. "She did the right thing."

"What are you distracting me from?"

Volt sighed. "I don't want to see you upset. She's gone. Took a speeder and left. And I like her—I do—but you shouldn't chase after her."

Jules walked away before Volt was done speaking. He stood in the shadow of the barn. When he had woken up that morning, he'd thought he would never see Izal Garsea again. There was only one time he'd wished for her, a solid, tangible wish with a piece of yarn. It had been a month after her family left, and there were no signs that they'd ever return. He'd dreamed of her, and the reality had turned out more complicated than imaginable. But he wanted her despite it all.

Now he could divide his life into two segments: before Izzy and after. How could he love someone who was dead set on running from him? He watched the smattering of stars and imagined counting the freckles on her jaw, along her arm. He could connect the dots all the way to her heart.

As he rejoined his friends and family, he had never felt so far from a future he'd almost been able to grasp—there and then gone.

# IZZY

## CHAPTER 28

Izzy pulled up to Salju's.

The woman was still working, tinkering with a small green waiter droid under the filling station's lights. She took off her goggles when she heard Izzy approach.

"Glad you survived a full day on the Outpost," Salju said, too cheery for how late it was. As she took in Izzy's damp clothes, flushed skin, and disheveled hair, she added, "Just barely, I see. And you brought a friend!"

Lucky had caught up to her, but when Izzy stopped so did she.

"It's been a long day," Izzy said, and plopped down beside the girl.

"I see you've been to Volt's," Salju said, and pointed the screwdriver at Izzy. "I tell you, he tried to sell me back my own tooka after Kuma went on a personal holiday once. Come to think of it, I can't find Kuma anywhere, so maybe Volt's about to try it again."

She wasn't sure why, but that made Izzy double over with laugher. Salju laughed along, nervous at first. Surely, she'd seen an off-worlder or two break after spending a day on Batuu. When her abdomen hurt and her cheeks even worse, Izzy stared at the sky.

"I haven't laughed like that in a long time," she said. "I want to do it more."

"Another happy customer. Did you get everything you needed?"

Izzy wanted to say that she had. She'd delivered her parcel and retraced the steps her parents had once taken. She'd learned about her mother, about herself. She'd kissed the boy of her dreams. She'd saved him. And then she'd let him go. She was filled with so much *want*, it scared her.

"Mostly," she answered.

"Did you go to the obelisk when you got here?"

Izzy frowned. "I think I passed it this morning. Why?"

"Well, people rub the obelisk for good luck. We love our good luck around these parts. Can't get enough of it, really."

Izzy chuckled. "Thanks for everything, Salju."

"Don't mention it. Be sure to send your friends my way if they need any work done."

Friends. She needed to make some of those. Good ones, without guerrilla warfare tactics.

Izzy paid the spira she owed Salju, instructing her to give Volt what she owed him. After all the damage she'd left behind at the farm, she wanted to run. Dok could give her share to Jules. She didn't feel right taking it.

"Oh, and Delta will be back for that speeder," she said just before the ramp of the *Meridian* closed.

Though it had been hours, it felt like days since she'd walked the halls of her ship. She ran her palm along the smooth panels. Her mother had chosen turquoise for the cushions in the lounge because it was her favorite color—the color of Izzy's father's eyes. It was something her mother had confessed later in life, when they lived in Eroudac Citadel and were trying to be a normal family. Izzy had thought it ridiculous then, but now it was a memory she held dear. As much as she felt she didn't know her mother, every moment she understood her a little more. Ixel Garsea hadn't been perfect. No one was. Izzy had seen her share of lonely kids across the galaxy. At least her mother had wanted her, taught her how to survive without her. Jules had said that people could choose which parts of their parents to keep. She started the launch sequence and thought that she would take the good and bad over and over again if it meant keeping them forever.

She sat in the cockpit and toyed with the black and gold ring resting on her chest. She had wanted to give it back to Jules and she had failed. She strung it up above the console and ran her thumb across it. For luck.

"What do you say, Lucky?" Izzy said to her loralora. "Are you ready to get off this rock?"

But the loralora was nowhere in sight. She turned around and called out to her. She knew she'd shut the ramp after the bird flew in. She checked her quarters and the small shower. When she reached the cargo hold, Izzy's heart froze and her stomach roiled.

Lucky and Kuma were there, feasting on half a dozen dead Batuuan rats. Hadn't Volt warned her? *Every* ship had a vermin problem. At least she hadn't taken off with Salju's pet. Izzy went into one of the closets and dug for some cleaner. It was then that she came across a loose flap, like the one where she'd hidden the briefcase early that morning. It was smaller, and at first glance, it was empty. But then she noticed a datacard.

She wondered if it was left behind from one of her mother's missions. But that didn't seem like something Ixel Garsea would do. Izzy's stomach was in knots as she carried it back to the helm of the ship. She transported it on her palm with the same care she had held the sodilium detonator. Izzy stared at it for too long, wondering what its contents would be. She wasn't ready for any more revelations.

What would Jules say to her if he was there? Something encouraging followed by a nudge or a smirk. She mustered her courage and keyed up the datacard.

The soft blue recording showed Izzy a face she

hadn't seen in years. It was her mother. At first, the message was rippled like a bad holo stream. There was no sound. Only Ixel Garsea's face. Her mother looked as nervous as Izzy felt. Then her mother spoke and looked straight at her.

"If you're watching this, then you're without me. I wish we had more time. But if I'm wishing for things, I would have liked to give you the home you always wanted. Your father did all the things I could not, but I'm afraid I did not do enough. I'm not good with words or sharing them. But I have so many hopes for you. I hope you live a life without regret and that you have a stronger heart than I." She looked over her shoulder, then back. "You and your father are the one thing I did right in my life. I love you, my darling Izzy."

Izzy replayed the message over and over again.

# JULES

## CHAPTER 29

Oga's Cantina was full of warm bodies. Jules was sure every species was in attendance, even a group of Wookiees, each of whom carried two drinks.

After a long shower and clean clothes, he felt like a new man—a little battered, but still new. Well, new-ish. DJ R-3X was at his station, dancing to the music he played. Next up was Joh Yowza, formerly of the Max Rebo Band, who would be on Batuu for a solo concert in a few rotations.

It was as if everyone in the Outpost had heard of Jules's adventures throughout the day because even strangers patted him on the back and offered to buy him drinks. Both bartenders, who had never looked twice at him before, ran fingers down his arms.

"Enjoy your fleeting moment of fame, kid," Volt said, slapping him on the back.

They wove through the crowd to get to the bar. A great thick hand clapped on Jules's shoulder. Cookie offered his congratulations and told him to come back to the docking bay in the morning for a free breakfast.

Jules was at a loss for words. He didn't want to be under a spotlight, not ever. Julen Rakab loved people.

He was a rare breed who always wanted to help, even when he was powerless. Now that everyone was trying to help him, all he wanted was to crawl in bed and nurse the bruises on his body. But he had to put on a brave face because he'd made a promise earlier that day.

Neelo and Fawn were at the bar having the free drink musicians got before their set. The Togruta was fingerpicking the air, and Fawn was chugging his drink so carelessly that he was very close to poking himself in the eye with the garnish pick.

"Jules!" they shouted when they saw him approaching. "Oh, hey, Volt."

"I helped, too," Volt said, affronted. "Majorly helped. I disarmed—"

The bartender on their end, a three-meter-tall Gigoran covered in white fur, stomped back over. Volt ordered two Fuzzy Tauntauns.

"Where's your girl?" Neelo asked. He'd splashed up his look with metal cuffs around his lekku. "I liked her. We gave her a lift earlier."

Fortunately, the drinks landed in front of them just then. The Fuzzy Tauntaun was one of the most expensive available, dusted with the golden lichen that shimmered like the night sky. Jules had never been able to order it before, but since everyone was offering . . .

On the other side of the room, Oga was in a private booth with Dok-Ondar. Everyone was whispering about Oga coming out that night. Oga and Dok raised a glass to Jules, and it felt infinitely wrong. He'd done nothing but get captured. All Jules had done was stun Damar.

It was Izzy who had come back for him. She'd gathered his friends. She'd found him. And then she'd left him without so much as a good-bye. It burned him up so much that he drained his drink in seconds. Neelo and Volt exchanged looks that said they should not ask any further questions about the girl.

"I'm fine," Jules said. "I'm totally fine. I want to hear my friends play. I'm going to sleep for an entire day, and I swear if anyone wakes me up I'm going to—"

"Whoa," Volt said, and raised a glass, looking away as he said, "I've never heard you lie before. This is fascinating."

Jules scowled and was ready to tell his so-called friend what to do with his accusation when DJ R-3X paused the music and leaned into the mic.

"Volt Vescuso, there's a Kowakian monkey-lizard in the storage room that belongs to you. Please go and retrieve it."

Volt whirled around to look at Oga, whose tentacled lips puckered into a snarl.

"Guess I missed one," he said, and scurried away to take care of the problem.

Neelo and Fawn went off for their sound check. Some of the farmers surrounded Jules. They hadn't had so much excitement in years, even vicariously, though they were glad nothing would be amiss when Kat returned.

Jules sipped his drink and realized that as much as he loved his people and as much as he loved his home, he didn't want to wake up in five years and say that he couldn't remember the last time he'd had an adventure *or even heard of one*.

"What was the name of the girl?" Ksana's dad asked.

"Izal Garsea. Brave one," said a Quarren who must be new. The tentacles of his lips were covered in beer foam. "Is she around? I'd like to buy her a drink, too. I rode past Salju's and her ship was still there."

"She's long gone by now," Jules said, and he blamed the bitterness in his mouth on the drink.

The Quarren shook his head. "I just got here, kid. I promise. It's still there."

They all turned to him. He blinked fast. Her ship was still there.

"I have to go." Jules stood up. His body felt possessed. They called after him, then there was a volley of hollers as everyone realized where he was going.

As he stepped out of the cantina, the scent of cloves and flowery smoke clung to him. There was a flash of white in the dark. He recognized the stormtrooper first and then the man the stormtrooper was raising a fist to.

"Hey!" Jules shouted.

The trooper whirled around. Staring into those unseeing black eyes made Jules take a step back.

"Nate, everyone's waiting for you," Jules said, fear making him breathe fast. The same boy he'd helped on the road earlier that day was pressed against the wall. "Oga said drinks are on her. She was asking about you."

Jules's eye gave an involuntary twitch. He didn't like to lie, but he wasn't above it to save someone's life. He smirked and thought, *Lying is a skill.*

Jules considered it a test on the state of the Outpost. If the First Order knew to respect Oga's name enough to walk away, then perhaps things weren't so bad. Though he wondered, how long would that last? Knowing what he knew now, Jules sensed that things wouldn't be the same around Batuu for much longer.

Without another word, the trooper turned and walked away. Jules helped Nate dust himself off.

"That's twice I am indebted to you," Nate said, straightening his clothes. He grabbed hold of the rough-cut clear crystal. It was one of many necklace charms that twinkled against each other and caught the dim light of the holoboards. Something in that action of toying with his necklace reminded Jules why he'd stepped out. Izzy.

"Don't mention it."

"The Force does move us together and apart as it needs to," Nate said.

After that day, Jules was certain it was true. When he looked at the sky, he saw a cluster of ships taking off, soaring across the sky to the stratosphere. Among them was a ship he'd not soon forget—a triangular freighter called the *Meridian*.

"Yeah," said Jules, waving good-bye to Nate and turning back to Oga's. "It sure does."

# IZZY

## CHAPTER 30

She wasn't used to dressing up, but after cleaning up vermin innards in the hold, Izal Garsea needed a shower. The only clean clothes she had were a simple black dress and a capelet her mother had once bought on Cloud City.

She walked through the market. Despite the lateness of the hour, there were still stalls open, and vendors who sold street food had customers gathered around small grills. A contortionist on a colorful rug was doing tricks for a horde of children, bending himself into a position that didn't look physically possible. He looked the way her mind felt.

What was she going to say to Jules when she saw him? What if he wasn't even there? What if he didn't want to talk to her? Once she'd replayed her mother's message enough times to memorize it, she could only think of one person she wanted to tell about it.

When she rounded a corner, she saw the obelisk. After her trip from the Outpost to the ruins and back again, she wondered if what she was about to do made her look like a tourist. She hopped up on the circular stone shelf carved with symbols similar to those she'd seen in Oga's office. Then she reached out and rubbed the obelisk for good luck. She needed it.

Izzy didn't stop again until she stood at the door to Oga's.

The bouncer out front, a lizard-faced Trandoshan, took one look at her and opened the door. Entering through the front was a much nicer experience than being escorted through the back. It was dim, but far nicer than any cantina she had ever been to. Yes, there was wear and blaster marks on one wall, but the exposed metal around the bar and the colorful lights around the stage and tables gave it a romantic ambiance. No one noticed her as she walked in, but she didn't expect them to.

The droid DJ she'd only heard on the radio earlier stopped the music. "Would the owner of an XP-38 speeder move it from the parking lot? You're going to be towed in ten seconds."

A skinny white creature with a long neck shot up from the gambling table and ran out the door.

That was when she saw him sitting at the bar.

Jules Rakab had cleaned up. Even in the dark she could see the bruise on his cheekbone, the cut on his lower lip. He was listening to some of the farmers she'd met earlier. She wondered what Oga had done with Damar and the others. She wondered if Ana Tolla would come seeking revenge—if she wasn't dead.

Perhaps that revenge would hurt Jules all over again.

That old fear of losing people raked its claws across her back, and she turned around. She couldn't breathe. The smoke was too much. He would reject her. He would—

"Would Izal Garsea please come to the bar for a celebratory drink?" DJ R-3X said over the mic. Feedback and distortion made everyone cringe. "That's it! No more special requests for the night."

She could feel all eyes on her even before she turned around.

When she finally did, she told herself to be brave. She'd raced across Batuu to deliver a package to the Resistance. She'd stopped a chemical attack. She'd kissed a boy under three suns and two moons. She'd heard her mother speak again. She'd lived a thousand lives since her parents died, but she had never chosen to stay instead of run.

As she walked through the throng of bodies, they parted to make her way a little easier. Every step felt like wading across a wide sea. But she would do it because on the other side waited Julen Rakab.

They stood facing each other.

"This would be a lot easier without an audience," she said.

"Nothing with you is easy, Garsea," Jules said, the corner of his lip quirking as the giant, hairy bartender slid two drinks in front of them. They glittered with gold specks.

He handed her one glass and raised the other. Everyone in the bar was turned toward them.

"To Izal Garsea," Jules said. His voice was confident and carried across the entire cantina. "Who saved a lot of lives tonight."

There was a round of cheers and people chanted her name.

*No one in the galaxy knows your name.*

Except that had never been true. Jules had always known her name. He'd remembered her before she remembered him. He'd trusted her before she trusted him. Oga Garra, knew her name, too. Now Ana Tolla and her crew would never forget it.

She took in the congratulations and thank-yous. She did not feel deserving of them—not when the galaxy felt so much greater.

"I saw your ship fly away," Jules said. "Not moments ago."

She relaxed a bit. Both of them leaned on the bar. "I told Salju she could take it for a spin. She added some new thrusters. Plus, don't tell Volt, but I had a terrible vermin problem and Lucky ate six of them."

Jules nearly spit out his drink. They laughed and reached for each other at the same time.

"I thought you left again," he said.

"I was about to."

"What made you change your mind?"

"A couple of things." She held the ring between them. "Starting with this. I told you I was going to give this back to you."

That had been the moment when everything went wrong. Part of her was holding her breath in case something else crashed in and interrupted their happiness again. But the music flowed, and the noise of conversations grew louder still.

He leaned closer to her ear. "I never caught you. I guess you'll have to keep it a little longer."

She restrung the necklace. It felt like it was where it belonged. She was where she belonged as long as Jules was with her.

"I'm sorry," she said. "I didn't mean those things—"

Jules shook his head. He reached for her hand, and their fingers intertwined. "I told you. I know when you're lying. But you don't have to protect me."

"I want to." She stared at his face. Had someone broken his nose again? "I even stole a ship for you."

He laughed and kissed the inside of her wrist. "That was my ship. Izzy, you stole *my* ship."

She clapped her free hand over her mouth but could not stifle the scream. "No. Oh, no."

"Oh, yes. I'd just bought it when we saw each other again. That's what I'd been trying to tell you."

"What are you going to do with it?"

He shrugged. "First I have to wait until it's *fixed*. Then, see the galaxy with you if you'll have me."

She ran her fingers through his hair. "Meet me on Eroudac."

"Isn't that where you dropped out of the academy?"

"It's also the last place I lived with my parents. It had ancient ruins and a pink moon."

"It's a date," he said, and drank from his glass.

"You have a little something on your lips."

He touched his chin. "Here?"

The gold lichen that stained his fingers spread. She chuckled and tapped the corner of her mouth. "You missed it."

"Here?" he said, like he enjoyed making a mess of himself. He was covered in gold dust, like a child who'd devoured a bar of melted gold chocolate. "You have to help me, Garsea, because there aren't any mirrors in this place."

She pressed her thumb to the corner of his mouth and then moved in for a kiss. Gold lichen tasted like burnt honey. She leaned into him, the anchor, the tether, the balance she needed. This time it was Jules who broke the kiss. He stared into her eyes, and she had a strange sensation. It was the opposite of vertigo—a steady, unshakable certainty that she couldn't properly name.

Another set of drinks slid in front of them. This time they were round fish bowls with a real fish garnish. Volt returned from wherever he'd been, his cheeks and scalp covered in scratches.

Neelo and Fawn got onstage and kicked off the lineup of bands with the Frozen Wampas. Jules twirled Izzy in place. She felt limber and free of *some* of the regret she carried with her. Sometimes heading in the right direction required taking a few steps backward.

The music played long into the night. Her exhaustion evaporated, replaced by the electric sensation of kissing Jules Rakab until the suns rose again and stalls that had been closed for the night began to reopen. Life in Black Spire Outpost went on as if nothing had changed. It was a place that was rebuilt day in and day out. New strangers, forgotten faces—they all intermingled.

They said everyone on Batuu was always either looking for a new life or running from one. For that moment, Izal Garsea found a third option. She could come home.

# EPILOGUE

The girl flew higher and higher out of the spaceport and leveled out over the Surabat River Valley. Swells of green land opened up beneath her ship. For a moment, she took in the rows of jutting spires ahead and the river that cut a path through ancient rock. In the cockpit of the *Meridian*, she turned to the empty copilot seat. When the boy's voice crackled over the open comm channel, she flashed a grin he could not see.

"You're not stalling again, are you, Izzy?" Jules asked. He flew beside her in his own ship, and she imagined the playful look in his eyes, always daring her.

She adjusted the comm around her ear and asked, "Why would I be stalling?"

"Because you don't want to admit I beat you last time."

"Did you ever consider I was being a good teacher?"

Jules barked a laugh. Sometimes she thought she could listen to him laugh for hours. With the exception of when he won their races. During the weeks it took for his ship to get repaired, Izzy had let him aboard the *Meridian* and taught him to fly. He'd grown up on simulators and single-pilot vessels, so he needed to get used to piloting a freighter for their pending adventure. The Batuu landscape provided the perfect obstacle course of rock columns and wide plains.

"On your go, Garsea," he said. "*If* you can keep up."

She couldn't keep herself from rising up to meet any dare or challenge he put in her way, even one that kept her in a place she'd never thought she would see again. She hadn't regretted a moment of it.

"Don't worry about me. I'm trying to pick out my celebratory drink."

They took off in a blur, weaving through the gaps between giant black spires and diving along the jagged rock that flanked the river gorge. Her heart leapt as a hunk of stone cracked off and dinged the left wing of his ship.

"Blast!" he shouted, sounding hurt.

"Jules?"

"I will never not be repairing this ship!"

"Bad luck, Rakab," she said, and punched up the speed, imagining the *Meridian* as one of the needles Belen used so precisely in her sewing. She slid between two narrow columns and held her breath, hoping he'd follow.

He always did.

When she reached the end of their course, Izzy let out a whoop. Jules was a breath behind her.

"We tied," he said. "That was most definitely a tie!"

"Tell yourself that. I'll meet you at Oga's for my celebratory Bespin Fizz."

When they docked in the spaceport, Jules found Izzy waiting in the moving crowd. Families huddled together onto transport vessels. They carried large bundles, and Jules knew that they were leaving Batuu. A feeling he couldn't place wedged between his ribs and made him wince. He wanted to make things better in the Outpost, but he was only one person and he didn't know where to start. He promised himself that after he and Izzy went on their journey, he'd come back.

Izzy tugged on the sleeve of his tunic. "Base to Jules."

Looking at her made him feel better somehow. It was one of the many things about being around her that he couldn't explain—like the way his breath caught when he spotted her in the clusters of people that descended on Cookie's during lunch, or the way he found any excuse to hold her, or how he could love someone as much as he loved her.

He lowered himself to steal a kiss. She threaded her fingers through his and they went off to continue what they'd been doing for weeks—making plans. Sitting at the counter at Oga's, they mapped their route and the myriad possibilities. They listed planets Izzy had loved and others they had only heard of in stories, like Endor and Mandalore.

"We've gone over this," Jules said, drinking his Carbon Freeze. Smoke billowed from the glass. "I'm ready, Izzy. You're hesitating. What's stopping you?"

"Credits?" she offered. When she'd decided to stay, Jules had forced her to take her share for the delivery. She'd made it stretch, but it was time to start moving again. When he took her hand in his, she couldn't avoid the thoughts that kept her up at night. "I'm afraid."

He rested his hands on her knees. "*You* are afraid? Of what?"

She gave him a gentle shove. "Where do I even start? What if we end up dead in space? What if we get halfway across the galaxy and we want to kill each other?"

"But think of all the fun we'll have making up after." He gave her a look that made her blush.

"I'm serious."

Jules set down his drink and cupped her face. "You're the only thing I'm sure of in this galaxy, Izzy. The rest, we can figure out."

They paid their tab and left the cantina, then headed toward Ohnaka Transport Solutions. Along the way, Izzy and Jules took in the vendors waving customers to step forward, the kids chasing one another through the market streets. The air was thick with humidity, and as billowing clouds drifted low, Jules kept his eyes on the sky. He saw flashes of ships coming into orbit.

"Have you ever met this Hondo Ohnaka?" Izzy asked as they joined the queue. At the very end of it was Delta, clutching a datapad.

"I haven't," Jules said. "He comes in and out of the Outpost, mostly to pay his debt to Oga. But lucky for us, he's always looking for flight crews."

They were certain that working for Hondo would help them travel the galaxy together while getting steady work. Jules wasn't in a rush. The first time they'd left the Outpost it was to go to the other side of the planet. The land there was rugged, wild in a way he'd never seen before. Then they'd traveled to a nearby small ice moon called Ielo. It had been his first time seeing snow. It fell in fat, soft drifts. He jumped in it. He ate it. He did that for nearly an hour before he was done with snow forever. After that they'd never made it to Eroudac, but they would one day.

It was then that everyone around them turned to the sky. Pinpricks of fire blasts illuminated the clouds. Ships swarmed from the direction of docking bay nine and into space. The traffic tower blared an alarm, and chaos descended on them as everyone ran, picking up what they could. There was screaming, fears of the cyclical tragedies of war. But Jules and Izzy remained on the landing pad, suspended at the center of a storm.

"Looks like the Resistance is coming out of hiding," Jules said.

Izzy watched him while he watched the fight happening thousands of meters above them—too far and too close. He often felt the helplessness he had that day in the market when the crowds had been ready to descend into riots. When black and red and white flags had begun to unfurl across the Outpost and hadn't stopped. Dreaming about his future and the girl he loved pushed away that encroaching dark. But how long could he keep dreaming? What could he do? He was only one person. And that would have to be enough.

Was that what each and every one of those fighter pilots thought before they flew? *I'm only one person, but together we are more.*

Izzy and Jules were not the only ones who watched laser fire punch a hole in the sky. Delta didn't leave their side, and Volt, who had seen such things before, forced himself not to look away.

People shoved across the landing pad to get indoors and away from the landing platforms. Screams melted into the wail of sirens the way the buildings blended into the spires. A part of Izzy still wanted to take off. It was safer to leave. It was harder to stay. She thought of her mother's holomessage. She'd watched it again and again. At first on her own, then later with Jules. Ixel Garsea had wanted her daughter to live without regret and a stronger heart. Those things weren't earned so easily.

Izzy realized it did not matter where she'd been in the past. She was rooted, not to a place but to everything. She was born on a ship flying through space. She'd left pieces of herself scattered across the galaxy like stars. The world out there was Izal Garsea's home as much as Batuu, as much as Jules, and she would do anything to protect it.

"I have to do something," Jules said.

"We will." She took his hand, ready to rise up for the battle that was coming.

# ACKNOWLEDGMENTS

My first real memories of *Star Wars* are the days spent with my brother Danny in our old Queens apartment reenacting fight scenes from *Return of the Jedi*. Now we are adults, or adult-ish, binge-watching the next generation of heroes in our favorite galaxy. *Star Wars* and family are so intertwined in my life, which is why I am always grateful to my Ecuadorian tribe for their constant support and for letting me work in a corner during every party and holiday celebration. Finally, you can point to the finished product.

Huge thanks to my agent, Victoria Marini. This book would not be possible without the phenomenal team at Disney Lucasfilm Press, especially my editor, Jennifer Heddle, and Michael Siglain. Thank you to the ultimate keepers of *Star Wars* knowledge, Story Group executives Matt Martin and Pablo Hidalgo, and copyeditor Megan Granger. Leigh Zieske for designing such a beautiful book, and Matt Griffin for the incredible jacket cover art. Margaret Kerrison for guiding me through the landscape and characters of Batuu; you've helped build something incredible and I can't wait for everyone to explore this planet.

Every writer needs a deadline squad: Victoria and Dhonielle, you constantly inspire me to just keep writing. Brick by brick. Chapter by chapter. To the friends who took care of me while I was a Hot Deadline Mess: Sarah Younger, Natalie Horbachevsky, Tessa Gratton, and Natalie Parker.

Finally, to the *Star Wars* community. We are all just kids who still dream of adventuring among the stars, and that is a beautiful thing.

Que la Fuerza te acompañe. May the Force be with you.